ALS

The Billionaire Banker Series

Owned
42 Days
Besotted
Seduce Me
Love's Sacrifice

Masquerade

Pretty Wicked (novella)

Disfigured Love

Hypnotized

Crystal Jake

Sexy Beast

Wounded Beast

Click on the link below to receive news of my latest releases, fabulous giveaways, and exclusive content.
http://bit.ly/1Oe9WdE

Cover Designer: http://www.kevindoesart.com/
Editor: Caryl Milton & IS Creations
Proofreader: http:// http://nicolarheadediting.com/

Beautiful Beast

Published by Georgia Le Carre
Copyright © 2015 by Georgia Le Carre

You can discover more information about Georgia Le
Carre and future releases here.

https://www.facebook.com/georgia.lecarre
https://twitter.com/georgiaLeCarre
http://www.goodreads.com/GeorgiaLeCarre

BEAUTIFUL BEAST

Georgia Le Carre

Dedication

To my darling husband,
I couldn't do without you.

Contents

One

SHANE

'My milkshake brings all the girls to the yard.'

I stand at the bar, my hand loosely curled around a bottle of ice-cold beer, and try to imagine a hundred years passing inside these glittering walls. And in a flash I am connected to every sad, twisted fucker inside that cavernous former theater. In a century we're all going to be nothing but a fistful of dust. But today ... Hot blood throbs in my cock and I am still king of my empire of dirt.

I cast my eyes around—and everything is exactly as it should be.

Cool air filters out of vents in the ceiling, loud music beats on my skin like morning rain in the tropics, and roving spotlights pick up waitresses in fluffy white tutus. With their tight little butts on show, they glide around as perky as fucking swans.

Sometimes the spotlights stop to lick one of the scantily clad, insanely glamorous dancers sprinkled around the place like magic dust. They are the candy in my sweet shop. Because … Hidden in the cool shadows of the booths where the spotlights never go, soulless men in dark suits and bulging wallets wait with buckets of champagne and an insatiable taste for pussy. Not that they can actually have any while they're in here, obviously, but hey, they can jerk off to the memory until their dicks drop off.

Yup, all is well in Eden.

I pick up my beer, bring it to my lips, and notice something that *isn't* exactly as it should be.

Martin, my manager, is escorting one of the dancers out of one of the VIP rooms. His lips are compressed into a thin line of fury, and she looks shit-scared as she struggles to keep up in her seven-inch-high transparent, plastic shoes. They have red lights inside the wedges that flash every time she takes a tottering step. Fuck, my four-year-old niece wears trainers that flash. I have never seen her before, so she must be new.

A row of beautiful girls preening by the bar exchanges knowing looks. One or two giggle heartlessly when a discreet, black exit door draped with thick, red velvet curtains swallows the pair. Beyond is Martin's office where the hiring and firing is done.

I take a sip of cold beer, my eyes swinging back in the direction of the VIP room they have

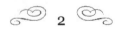

just vacated. In an impressive show of clockwork precision, the housemother, Brianna, is already slipping into it. You can tell by her purposeful air and the veiled expression on her carefully made-up face that she is on a clean-up mission.

She emerges a few minutes later, smiling serenely, and nods to one of the girls loitering by the bar. The girl immediately starts walking toward her. They meet by the mirrored pillars, exchange a few words before the girl makes for the VIP room, and Brianna continues, unruffled, on her journey.

Problem solved.

The music changes and AronChupa's quirky track 'I'm an Albatraoz' fills the charmed air. One of the club's favorite dancers, Melanie, a sleek black girl in a skin-tight catsuit with geometric patterns, struts energetically onto the stage. The effect of her appearance is instantaneous: the atmosphere in the club becomes electric. The stage lights are switched off, and Melanie disappears. All that remains is the collection of fluorescent patterns on her costume working their way strongly up a pole. It is a marvelous sight and the audience erupts in a collective roar of approval.

I place my drink down and turn back to watch the curtained door. I don't tend to interfere in the day-to-day running of my club. Why would

I? Any fool can see that between Martin and Brianna they run a very tight ship. And yet something about flashing shoes has my interest piqued.

Perhaps it is because I can always tell an innocent with one look, and she is as green as they come. I wouldn't be surprised if this is her first attempt at strip dancing. But mostly because I can never let an injustice pass. It used to get me into all kinds of trouble when I was a kid, but it's in my DNA; I just can't look the other way.

Less than five minutes later she tumbles back into the club. Her ridiculous wedges are still flashing, but tears are streaming down her face. Martin has cracked the whip. She has been fired. She lurches toward a side door that leads to the changing rooms. I walk quickly to the door nearest to me and enter my pass code. The door opens into the passage she has entered.

'Oh!' she exclaims when she sees me. In the bright lights of the corridor, her face, under its thick make-up, has a washed out hue, and her eyes are glassy and distraught.

'Come with me,' I say, and she silently follows me upstairs to my office. I hold the door open and let her precede me. Closing the door, I then walk toward my liquor cabinet.

'Would you like a drink?' I throw over my shoulder.

'No thank you, Mr. Eden,' she replies meekly.

I turn my head and meet her eyes. She is actually a stunner. 'Call me Shane,' I tell her softly.

She frowns with confusion.

'Have a seat,' I invite and pour two stiff measures of brandy.

Walking over to her, I hold out a glass. She accepts it with a murmur of thanks and I notice the sudden change in her body language. She thinks I am coming on to her. Unsure about my intentions, she has reverted to her usual routine. Sweet, really.

I have occasionally dated girls from the club if they're totally irresistible and they get my 'have cock will travel' rules, but generally I prefer not to. It's bad business all round. I move to my desk and, leaning my butt against the edge, cross my arms over my chest and smile at her.

She smiles back tremulously, her eyes moist with invitation. In a practiced gesture of seduction, she looks down and bats her waterlogged eyelashes coquettishly.

'What's your name?' I ask her.

'Bubbles.'

I hide a smile. 'Right, Bubbles. Want to tell me what happened?'

She turns bright red. 'Martin fired me,' she confesses painfully.

'Why?'

'I ... I ... let a customer ... uh ... touch me,' she reveals.

'You must have known you're not allowed to. Why did you do it?'

She looks up at me, her eyes large and begging. 'I swear I didn't want to. I told him no, but he said if I didn't allow him to he would call for another girl. I've only been here for a week and I've hardly made enough to cover my house fees. He was the first man who asked me for a private dance. I didn't want to break the rules, honestly I didn't, but at the same time I didn't want to lose my best chance to make some money, especially after he told me that everyone did it.'

She opens her left palm in an appealing gesture. 'So I told him I needed to go to the toilet and I went out into the club and asked Nikki for advice, since she's the best earner in the club.'

Her face becomes bitter. 'She told me I'd be stupid to let such a high flyer escape. And that any of the other girls would have touched him without a second thought. "It's totally harmless. Just touch him from the outside of his clothes and no one will be the wiser," she said.'

I frown. 'Were you not told there are cameras inside every booth?'

'Yes,' she admits sadly. 'And Martin has just taken me to his office and made me watch myself act like a fool. But Nikki convinced me that the cameras are just there for show. That there is no film in them and no one actually monitors them. I know I did wrong, but I truly believed her. She is the star of this club. Nobody makes more money than her. I'm a nobody; I've just started working in this club and I'm no competition to anybody, so I never thought that she would play such a dirty trick on me. How wrong I was.' Her voice is filled with regret.

She leans forward suddenly, her face intense. 'I felt I had no choice. She told me that if I don't start earning money soon I will be thrown out because I was taking the place of a girl who could be earning big money for the club. I really didn't know what else to do.' Her face fills with sadness. 'I have commitments. My mother, my babies. I have twins in Brazil. My mother is taking care of them. I need to send money back. They need me to survive.'

She is so young, it never occurred to me that she is a mother. 'How old are you?'

'Nineteen.'

I nod and gaze at her. She lacks confidence, but Brianna did not make a mistake taking her on, and Nikki had good reason to try to eliminate her. She has something very special, and one day she

will be a valuable asset to this club and great competition to Nikki.

I put my brandy down. 'I'll give you another chance, but if you ever break any of my club's rules again, you're out and, as per industry practice, your name will be circulated to all the other clubs.'

She clasps her hands together, her eyes shining with gratitude. 'Thank you. Thank you so much, Shane. I promise on my two children's lives I'll never let you down.'

'Good.'

As if unable to contain her excitement she bounces out of her chair like a puppy.

'Go home, Bubbles. I'll have a word with Martin later.'

She comes close enough for me to feel the heat coming off her body and, tipping forward in her flashing wedges, plants a feather-light kiss on my cheek. I cock an eyebrow and she lets her heels drop back to the ground and, slowly, licks her thickly glossed lips. Yes, Bubbles definitely has something.

A ripe, tight, eager pussy. Very predictably, my cock is interested, but my cock is always full of bad fucking ideas. Girls like Bubbles, they look like they're figuring on a cheap thrill with a hot, hard dick for the night, but that's like watching a snake slither up to you and thinking, Awww ...

look, it wants a little cuddle. Take it from me, they don't even give you a chance to take the condom off before they're making wedding plans in their heads. Me, I like a little bit of Angela, Pamela, Sandra and Rita.

I pull a fifty from my shirt pocket and hold it between my index and forefinger. 'Take a taxi home tonight,' I tell her.

Disappointment flashes in her chocolate eyes, but she takes the hint and deftly plucks the note from my fingers. The same action has been performed ever since man first invented currency, and its primal nature tugs at something in me. Have I really done Bubbles a favor today? She's naïve and innocent now, but one day she will learn all the things that strippers learn about men, and their greed, and their lust, and their ugliness. She will learn to exploit those qualities and she will make lots of money, but will that really be a good thing?

'Don't do anything the little voice inside you tells you not to,' I tell her.

She nods slowly. 'You are a very beautiful man. Not just your face and body, but your heart too,' she whispers. She pauses for a moment. 'I promise you will never regret this decision.'

Then she walks out of my office and closes the door quietly behind her.

Two

SHANE

The early bird gets the worm, but the second mouse
gets the cheese.

—Steven Wright

I hear her shoes clatter down the wooden stairs as I light a cigarette and take a deep drag. Walking over to the large one-way mirror, I look down at my club. My eyes look for and immediately find Nikki. She is sparkling like a diamond. Sitting next to a man, her pose provocative, she raises perfectly manicured fingers and over the thin material of her gown, sensuously rubs her nipple. Her mark—I can tell straight away he's got a cock full of bad fucking ideas too—stares, transfixed.

You have to hand it to her, she's good, she's real good.

She even had me fooled once.

With girls like Bubbles you see them coming. But when Nikki approaches you, you don't even

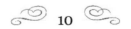

see the snake, you just see the grass moving. Nikki is poisonous even when her legs are splayed wide open and she is moaning, in that crazy Russian accent of hers, 'It's so deep, baby. Oh yes, fuck me, baby. Fuck me hard. Show this nasty pussy who its owner is.'

She crashed a vase into a mirror when I ended it. Good thing I'm an old hand at ducking. Sometimes, I still catch her watching me with a strange mixture of frustrated lust and venom, but she refuses to leave. Why, I don't know. Any club would welcome her with open arms. I could have fired her, but why spoil a good thing? She's the club's highest earner.

I am suddenly distracted by a flash of white that appears in my peripheral vision. My eyes shift to follow it. A girl in a shimmery white dress is moving across the floor in the direction of the toilets. Her walk is slow and sexy, effortless, and her bone structure is very fine and delicate. In the dog world she would be a Saluki bred by the Bedouin to race across the desert sand during a hunt. A dog considered too fine to be called simply a dog.

Her skin is very pale and her hair is raven black. It pours thickly down her back like an oil slick. Normally, I would have been put off by the combination of pale skin and long black hair. It reminds me too much of the chalk-white, black-wig-wearing female demons in the Japanese horror flicks that my sister and I used to secretly watch until the early morning hours when we were really young, but something about this woman ...

I exhale smoke.

A strobe light catches her face and my eyes widen.

Whoa! She is far more stunning than I had imagined. In the blue light she looks almost unreal, like a creature from a fairy tale. So pure she cannot be tainted by vulgarity or coarseness even when she is surrounded by it. The quality is so rare I don't feel her call in my cock where most women make their presence felt, but deep in my gut. A tendril of excitement twists up my spine.

I want that woman.

Badly.

I kill my cigarette in an ashtray on my desk and leave my office. I take the stairs two at a time, stride down the corridor, and enter the club. Cool air from the vents above hits my face. Dillon Francis and DJ Snake's track 'Get Low' is playing. I position myself by the Chinese bar with its blue and white porcelain tiles.

An acquaintance grasps my hand and pumps it. 'Hey, Shane, how you doing? Let me buy you a drink?'

'Thanks,' I say with a smile, 'but I've got one coming.'

He wants to talk, but I turn away from him and watch the door that leads from the toilets. My drink arrives and I take a gulp. The door opens. A woman comes out. The door shuts again. I am holding my breath. I let it go in a rush. Why am I behaving like this? My skin prickles, as if it knows something I don't.

The door opens once more and she walks out. Her stride is still a slow sway, but up close she is even more breathtaking. And again I have the impression that she does not belong in this place. As if she is a shimmering water queen risen from a river, able to transform boredom into a feast of the senses.

As she gets closer I have the impression of something exotic. It could be her nose or the straightness of her eyebrows. But blood from distant lands flows in her veins. Her lips are full and painted some spicy color, a mixture of turmeric and chili. Her eyes are elongated and look straight ahead.

She would have passed by without noticing me if I had not shot out an arm and grasped her delicate wrist. Her reaction is strange because it is so deliberate. She stops walking and lets her gaze swing slowly from my hand wrapped around hers up to my eyes. This close, her irises are light green and liquid, the pupils flaring. They are almost ethereal. I have the weird sensation that I am waking her up from a dream. It is disconcerting.

Inside the circle of my fingers, her bones are as fragile as a bird's. I stare into her deeply mesmerizing eyes. They make me want to know everything about her. About what has made her so fragile and otherworldly. They make me want to possess her.

'And who would you be?' I ask, flashing her my most charming smile.

She stares up at me for a few seconds longer. Then she frowns. 'I'm probably not what you think I am.'

What surprises me is that she did not mean her answer to be provocative or flirtatious. That instantly makes her the most interesting woman I have ever met. My cock is pulsing and crushing against my jeans like crazy, so, naturally, I promise myself that I am going to fuck her. I'll be damned, I can't remember the last time a woman had me this strong. I widen my grin. 'What do you think I think you are?'

Her lips move and words quiver out. 'A random pick-up.'

'Wrong. I think you're the most beautiful woman in this club, and I'd like to take you out.'

'Where would you take me?' she asks curiously.

'The woods.' My answer irritates me. *Bravo, Shane. You sound like a fucking serial killer.*

But the first flicker of interest appears in her eyes. 'The woods?'

'Yes. I have an old chateau in France. It is very beautiful this time of the year. At night the fireflies come out.'

She inhales with surprise. 'Fireflies?'

'A sight to behold, they are. I never tire of watching them as they blink around the garden. There used to be more, but there are fewer and fewer of them now.'

'I have never seen fireflies. They seem more like the stuff of myths. How magical to see them for real.'

'Then you must come to Saumur.'

'Saumur,' she murmurs, tasting the name on her tongue.

'I promise you'll love it. There are crickets and bull frogs and wild boar, and occasionally a peacock looking for a mate will wander into the grounds.'

Her mouth parts with wonder. 'Really?'

'Scout's honor.'

'Will I have to sleep with you to see all this?'

I am still holding her hand. I stroke the silky skin on the inside of her wrist with my thumb. 'Not if you don't want to,' I say.

She smiles slowly, sexily. When she smiles she's as beautiful as a field of fireflies.

'We can just be friends?' she asks cautiously.

My eyebrows shoot up. That's a new one for the books. I honestly don't think anyone has *ever* said that to me. 'We can be whatever you want us to be.'

She leans closer, her eyes suddenly alight with mischief. 'Are you wearing mascara?'

I laugh. 'No.'

'You have very fancy eyelashes,' she says solemnly.

'I could say the same about you.' I swear I have never had such a weird conversation with a woman before.

'But I'm wearing mascara,' she says with a grin.

'Do you have a name, mascara-wearing babe?'

'My name is Elizabeth Dilshaw, but everyone calls me Snow,' she says as she gently tugs her wrist out of my grasp.

I don't want to but I let go. 'Really? Snow?'

'Yes. I was born in India where almost everyone is dark-skinned, so when I was born so fair and with such a full head of midnight-black hair, all the nurses started calling me Snow White. The name stuck and I became known as Snow.'

I smile broadly. She did step out of a fairy tale, after all. 'Skin as white as snow, lips as red as blood, and hair as black as ebony.'

'And you are?'

'Shane.'

'Yes, I think I'd like to see the fireflies and have you as my friend,' she says softly.

Izzy Azalea and Rita Ora's 'Black Widow' is playing. There are people brushing past us; I can smell their perfume and cologne. They serve as a backdrop for her. Someone calls my name, but I don't turn to look. 'Can I get you a drink?'

She bends her head and shakes it, and her beautiful hair moves like a silky curtain around her face. 'No, I'm with ... friends. I have to go back to our table.'

I take my phone out of my pocket. 'What's your phone number?'

She lifts her head and tells it to me and I key her number into my phone. Not taking my eyes off her, I press the call button. A bird starts chirping from inside her bag.

'Now you have my number too,' I tell her.

'Yes, now I have your number,' she says slowly.

The moment is strange, surreal even. Full of undercurrents and deeper meanings, it doesn't belong in the middle of a club relentlessly dedicated to the pursuit of the pleasures of the flesh. All the clever words and witty remarks have deserted me. I don't want to let her go.

My phone vibrates in my pocket. I ignore it. 'I'll call you tomorrow,' I say.

She nods slowly. 'Yeah, maybe you will.'

For some odd reason her voice is sad. As if this promise has been made before and never kept, even though I cannot even imagine a scenario where a man takes her number and does not call. She is impossibly intriguing. I resist the temptation to reassure her that I will call.

'Well, then. Nice to have met you,' she says and, turning, begins to walk away.

'Snow,' I call.

She turns around, one charcoal eyebrow raised.

'I will call you,' I promise. It has never happened to me before. I have never cared to reassure anybody that I will call. If I felt like calling the next day, I called. If I didn't, well ... c'est la fucking vie.

One side of her mouth lifts, and then she turns away and carries on in her path, again an incorruptible fairy tale creature. When she disappears from my sight I can't stop smiling. I take a triumphant sip of my drink before tilting my body slightly so I have a view of her table.

And that moment is like that video of John Newman's track, 'Love Me Again'. Do you know it? Where a boy and a girl meet in a dreary club. They escape from her wannabe gangster boyfriend and run out of the back doors. Hand in hand, full of hope and excitement, thinking they have outrun the bad guys, they get out of a narrow alleyway and dash straight into an oncoming vehicle. The video ends abruptly on a black screen.

I guess you are supposed to infer that they die.

Snow's table is Lenny the Gent's table.

The fairy tale takes an unexpected and unwelcome turn. Lenny 'the Gent' is not the wannabe variety but a real gangster. What they used to call a mobster. They call him the Gent because he is always so fucking polite. He would say 'please' or 'do you mind' before he hacked off your face. The Gent is surrounded by beautiful, giggling women vying for his attention, but he gazes at Snow's approach with the kind of hunger that makes me sick to my stomach.

Fucking hell. Straight into an oncoming vehicle!

Snow is Lenny's woman.

When she reaches his table, he stretches out his hand. For a second she hesitates then she opens her bag and gives him her phone. He pockets it, and taking another phone out of his pocket gives that to her. She puts it into her bag and sits down beside him, and he places his hand on her thigh.

I try to make out her expression, but her face is as smooth as a statue. Like a man in a daze I start walking toward her. My mind is blank. Fortunately, I collide with a waitress.

'Sorry. It was my fault,' she apologizes.

'Don't worry about it,' I tell her, my hypnotic trance broken.

I stop where I am standing and look at Snow. She is staring vacantly into her drink, her numb face the perfect frame for her empty eyes. The emptiness is total. I recognize its significance instantly. Her frozen body and expression are an instinct to survive. She has locked herself away in a place where she cannot be corrupted by the baseness and degradation around her.

A nearly naked woman is writhing her flesh close to Lenny the Gent's face, but, like mine, his eyes are glued on Snow.

There is only one way this thing is going to end. Badly. But I don't care. I have always gone where angels fear to tread. The blood expands in the veins of my forearms.

Snow will be mine.

The second mouse will get the cheese.

Three

SNOW

Better keep yourself clean and bright;
you are the window through which you must see the
world.

—Lucien Bernard Shaw

'**A**re you ready to go?' Lenny asks. As if it is ever my decision to stay or go.

I turn my head in his direction and feel like a deer that has stepped out of cover. It stops and stands, motionless, nose to the air, watching, smelling, ready to flee at the least sound. A million years of evolution has taught it how to sniff out danger.

He looks back at me, his eyes totally blank. It is the thing that I find most unnerving about him: how dead his eyes can be at certain moments. Then he smiles and his face fills with human emotions and I forget that momentary disquiet.

'Yes, I'm ready to go,' I reply.

'I'll be coming up with you tonight,' he says, watching me for my reaction.

I become cold inside. The deer would have bolted, but I don't. My face cracks into a smile. 'Of course,' I say quietly.

He stands and holds out his hand. I take it. At the next two tables men are standing up—his minders. We walk out of the club followed by them.

What a mistake it was to talk to that impossibly gorgeous man, to flirt with him and pretend that I could ever go out with one such as him. Shane. Beautiful name. But it was stupid and careless to walk back with some of his warmth still wrapped around my wrist and his cocky smile lighting my eyes.

Lenny knew straight away. He sees everything. Eyes like a hawk. I am his possession. He doesn't use me too often, usually twice a week, sometimes thrice, but I am his, just as much as the hammock he uses only in the summer is. He will sleep with me tonight because he wants to exercise that ownership over my body.

He is actually furious.

We get into the rear of his Rolls-Royce and he leans back and runs his hand along my inner thigh. I inhale sharply. It is an involuntary gesture and his hand freezes. My gaze swings nervously to his eyes. With a cold, hard smile on his face, he moves his hand relentlessly upwards.

I suppose it is my fault, really. If I had not allowed the other man into my head. If I had not come back thinking of fireflies. If I had just been a little better hidden, he would not be doing this now.

'Open your legs,' he instructs.

I part them slightly. His fingers pull away the material of my panties and brush at the seam of my core. I flinch inwardly. Outwardly, my face is calm. I stare straight ahead as if nothing is happening.

'Dry,' he murmurs. 'You're always so damn dry.'

I swallow hard. 'I have lubricant at home.' My voice sounds suddenly panicked. I don't know where the instinctive horror of him comes from. He has never hurt me—at least, not yet. Perhaps, the revulsion comes from the frightening emptiness in his eyes, or the smooth hairless skin on his back. Like a reptile.

'Hmmm.' He takes his hand away and I close my legs with relief.

The car stops outside my building and we get out. In the lift, I know he is watching me steadily, but I cannot look at him. Here the lights are too bright, God knows what he will see. The lift doors open and we step out onto plush maroon carpet.

We walk down the corridor and he opens the door with his own key. It is a small one-bedroom apartment. I live here. He pays the rent and all the bills.

I put my purse on the sideboard and head for the little table that serves as my bar. If I'm going to have sex I will need a very stiff drink.

'Would you like a nightcap?' I ask politely.

'Yeah, pour me whatever you're having.'

I require a drink where I can put lots of alcohol into the mix and no one will be the wiser. 'I'm having vodka and orange juice,' I throw over my shoulder.

'That'll do me,' he says, and slumps onto the sofa.

I've noticed recently that he's changing right before my eyes. His moods are becoming darker and more frequent. With my back to him I prepare our drinks. Mine is three-quarters vodka and a quarter orange juice. I carry our drinks over to the sofa and hand him his. I sit next to him and take a gulp. Heavens, it is strong.

'I have some of your favorite caviar. I'll go and get it,' I say, attempting to stand.

His hand shoots out and clamps around my wrist. My shocked eyes fly to his face.

His thin, cruel mouth twitches. 'I'm not hungry ... for that.'

'Oh, OK,' I mumble anxiously, and take another gulp of my drink. I steal a glance at him and he is watching me with the kind of coldness that chills me to the bone.

'Will you need to finish all of that before you can do anything?' he asks, lighting a cigarette.

I nod and push the ashtray toward him.

He looks at me through swirls of smoke. 'Go on then. Fucking finish half a bottle of vodka before I fuck you,' he says. His words are vicious, but his tone excruciatingly courteous.

So I do. I drink the whole thing and it seeps into my limbs and deadens them. My head gets fucked and I no longer care about anything. I put the glass down carefully and look at him expressionlessly. 'I'm ready,' I tell him.

He stands and, pulling me up, carries my limp body to the bedroom. As bedrooms go it is unremarkable. All the furniture came with the apartment and I have not added anything to it. But it is clean. Very clean. I couldn't bear it if it was not.

He helps me undress and when I am naked he lays me on the bed. He doesn't undress fully. Just his trousers and his underpants. His legs are oddly stick-like compared to his upper half, which is thickly muscled and bull-like. His penis is dark red, erect and ready. The sight gives me a twinge of distaste, but I damp it down quickly.

I know he's not a good man, but I owe him my life.

I stare up at him dumbly as he opens the first drawer and takes out a condom packet. He rips it open and rolls it on himself. Then he reaches into the drawer again and takes out a tube of KY jelly. I watch him with detachment as he unscrews the tube, chucks the top carelessly behind the bedside cabinet, and squeezes a couple of inches of gel onto his finger. He places the tube back on the cabinet surface, and comes up to me. His finger is gentle as it slides in, but the jelly is cold, and my muscles contract in rejection.

'Shhh ... relax,' he urges, thrusting his finger deeper into me.

Don't worry, Snow, the way he tells it, it will not be a long tale of the night. Just a little story. A quick in and out. I turn my face to the side, and he climbs onto the bed and lets his mouth crawl from my neck down to my breasts.

'You're so fucking beautiful. So fucking beautiful. Anybody tries to take you away from me, I'll fucking kill him,' he mutters as he pushes deep into me.

I don't make any sound. I start to feel that familiar feeling of being almost weightless. I know it is actually happening to me, but it feels removed as if it is happening to someone else and I am just watching.

As his body slaps against mine, my mind floats away to my childhood days. I am six years old again. My hair is in two long plaits that reach my waist and there are jasmine flowers woven into them. I can smell their strong fragrance. My nanny, Chitra, and I are standing barefoot at the entrance of an Indian temple.

Together we start ringing the big temple bell. We do so because the priest has given us special permission to help. The bell is made of different types of metal. The sound echoes into the distance to welcome the god and goddess.

Chitra and I walk into the temple together with all the other devotees. We stand with our hands clasped and watch the stone statue of the goddess being washed and dressed. A flame is waved around her then brought to us. We hold our cupped hands a few inches above the flame and touch our warm palms to our faces.

The priest, his mouth stained red with beetle juice, smiles indulgently at me, as he offers me half a coconut filled with a small banana and some flowers.

Chitra and I fall to our knees and let our foreheads touch the cool tiles. While she prays, I turn my face to look at her earnest eyes and think how beautiful she is and how much I love her. I love her more than I love anybody else in the whole wide world.

Then we stand and she bends and kisses me. She never lets her lips touch my skin; instead she presses her nose on my cheek and inhales audibly. When she moves her face away, her breath rushes against my skin. That is her way of kissing.

Lenny climaxes, as he always does, with a shrill scream.

His mouth is too close to my ear and the horrible sound startles me out of my dream. Suddenly, I feel the length of his body on mine, all the rough hairs on his legs and belly scratching my skin. He rests on his elbows and looks down at me with heavy-lidded, blank eyes. I stare back at him wordlessly.

'Poor Snow,' he says. For some inexplicable reason, his pity breaks the protective numbness.

'Don't,' I whisper, and I feel my eyes fill with tears. They roll down the sides of my cheeks 'Please don't.'

'For fuck's sake. I'm sorry, OK? Don't cry. Just fucking don't cry again, OK?'

But I cannot stop. So he pulls out of me, takes the condom off, ties it, drops it to the side of the bed, and holds me while I cry. He cannot fix me, he knows that, but he is the only one who knows.

He alone knows what happened to me that night in that hotel room.

Four

SNOW

He gets out of bed and, standing over me, regards my naked, trembling body. What he is thinking I don't know, but with a sigh he walks away after a while, and comes back with a cream blanket. He covers me with it and, moving to the other side of the bed, props himself up on three pillows and lights a cigarette.

We don't talk while he smokes.

Under the blanket my body gradually warms. I start to feel safe and peaceful again. We have a strange relationship, Lenny and I. But then again I don't know what normal is. My parents had a strange love–hate relationship too. My father loved my mother and she despised him. I don't despise Lenny. I ... am grateful to him. I don't think of the future. Lenny is forty-two. When he found me I was nineteen. I am now twenty.

He kills the cigarette and turns to me. 'You all right?'

'Yeah,' I say softly.

'Want me to stay the night?'

'No,' I mumble.

'I'll call you tomorrow, OK?'

'OK.'

'Do you need any money?'

'No.'

He reaches for his pants and takes a wad of notes out and puts it on the bedside cabinet. 'Here. Go buy yourself something nice to wear tomorrow.'

I don't say anything, not even thank you.

He vaults out of the bed, gets dressed quickly, then comes over to my curled body. He kisses my hair. 'I'll see myself out. Goodnight, Snow.'

'Goodnight, Lenny,' I whisper.

After the door closes behind him I stay still a few minutes longer. My limbs feel heavy and lethargic, but I know from experience that sleep will never come while I have that dirty, sticky feeling between my legs. I force myself to my feet and into the bathroom. I run the shower and stand under the warm cascade.

Water is good. Water cleans.

I shampoo my hair even though I washed it earlier in the evening, and soap every inch of my body. I realize that I am sadder tonight than usual. Is it the loss of Saumur? Or is it the loss of

Shane? I let the water wash away the sadness bleeding out. I only have to do what has proven to work for a year now. Just hold on for tonight. It is always better in the morning light. I have come so far.

I can be like the reindeer moss. Its patience is legendary. Its survival skills are second to none. You can keep it in the dark, freeze it, dry it to a crisp, but it won't give up and die. It simply lies dormant waiting for better conditions. That day will come when conditions will improve for me. Until then I will wait patiently.

By the time I switch off the shower and get out, my fingers are so wrinkled they are like little prunes. I dry myself quickly and, wrapping another towel around my head, I dress in striped pink and yellow cotton pajamas.

I hook up the hair dryer and direct it at my hair before I pad barefoot through my darkened living room. I see my purse lying exactly where I left it. I open it and take out the phone Lenny gave me. It is exactly the same as the one I handed over to him, but when I switch it on it has only one number keyed into it. His.

I feel that strange sense of hopelessness and anxiety try to seep into my body again. But before the feeling can swamp me I put on Vivaldi's *Four Seasons* and return to my bedroom. I find, screw back the cap of the lubricant and put it away.

Using a tissue I pick up the used condom and flush it down the toilet.

Then I go back into the bedroom and sweep the wad of money into the drawer. I shut it with a click, straighten and look around the spotless room. I can still smell the stench of our coupling and Lenny's cigarette. After cleaning out the ashtrays and returning them to their proper places I open some windows.

Cool night air blows in as I stand at the window and look out at the night scene below. A foraging fox trots along the wall that separates my building from the next. It is carrying something in its mouth, probably from the rubbish bins. The woman living in the ground floor flat is always complaining about foxes getting into her bins and the foul smell of the excrement they leave behind.

As if it has felt my gaze, it suddenly turns and looks at me. Its eyes are shining brightly, and I am suddenly struck by its wild beauty. It lives and dies in dirt, but it is full of intelligence and the joy of its own creation. It doesn't compare its existence with other creatures, bemoan its foxiness, or try to be like another. It is simply content to be a fox. It is free.

That is more than I am.

I watch it until it disappears then I turn away and look at my alarm clock. It is nearly four in the morning. I should really get some sleep.

I switch off the light and lie on my bed staring at the ceiling.

Even though I try to keep my mind blank, a face floats into my head. Such beautiful eyes. So blue and so bright. I liked him as well. Something delightfully cheeky and cocky about him. I imagine him to be fun and sexy. I circle my wrist the way he did. He had such massive, strong hands. When he held my wrist I actually didn't want him to let go. I stroke my skin the way he did silkily, as if he was already making love to me.

'Shane,' I whisper into the darkness.

He was gorgeous, but I will never see him again. I feel a ribbon of sadness curl around my heart and I take a deep breath. No, I shouldn't allow myself to get silly. He was not just gorgeous. He was too gorgeous. Too young. Too carefree.

It's not a lost opportunity. He just wanted to have some fun. You can't trust a man you find in a strip-dancing club. Anyway, I am too mangled and broken for him. He wouldn't have the patience to put up with my drama. In the end he would shatter my heart. I try to convince myself that it is a very good thing that his number is gone. A blessing in disguise that I will never see those beautiful blue eyes again.

For almost an hour I try to fall asleep. But sleep refuses to come.

Maybe I should take a pill. I go into the bathroom and take one of my little pills. After a while I feel relaxed and floaty. Nothing matters anymore. I no longer feel sad that I will never again see Shane, or Saumur, or the magical fireflies.

Five

SNOW

When I wake up, the sun is filtering in through the gap I left in the curtains. I sit up and hug my knees. What shall I do today? Last month, for the first time since Lenny installed me in this apartment, I woke up and thought, I have nothing to do. I need a job. I need to meet new people.

But Lenny doesn't like me to meet people. He says I am a bad judge of character. 'Look what happened to you the last time you made a friend,' he points out.

But, more and more, I feel I am fading away within these walls.

After I have brushed my teeth and dressed, I sit in the kitchen and have a bowl of cereal. The apartment is so still I can hear the sound of my teeth crunching the flakes of corn.

The letter flap clatters and I leave my bowl and run to the front door. I pick up three envelopes from the floor. A bill, a menu/leaflet from a local Chinese takeaway, and a letter from one of the boutiques where Lenny has opened an account for me.

The letter I am waiting for did not arrive.

With a heavy heart I put the bill aside for Lenny to give to his secretary, and I open the letter from the boutique. There is a sale this weekend and they are writing to invite me to arrive an hour earlier and join the champagne pre-sale party. I throw the invitation away with the leaflet.

Then I sit down to finish the rest of my solitary breakfast.

When I have washed the bowl and spoon and put away the breakfast things, I walk over to the drawer that I swept the money into last night. I take out the wad and count it. Two hundred pounds. Wow! My tears must have moved him.

He is not usually so generous with cash. He prefers to open accounts for me in different shops that he pays for at the end of the month. I don't know what limits I have in those stores but I haven't yet come across one, even though once, in a state of deep depression, I unthinkingly picked up a dress worth three thousand. However, my credit card has only a two hundred and fifty pound limit.

I keep aside forty pounds. The rest I neatly arrange so that all the heads face upwards. Then I get down to the side of the mattress and gently

unpick the slash I have sewn up. I add the new notes to the growing brick of money. It makes me happy to see it. I have more than half of what I need. Quickly, I sew it back up so it is almost impossible to tell that my mattress is my piggy bank.

Afterwards, I do what I do every day.

I set about thoroughly cleaning the apartment. I vacuum, I brush, I wipe, I wash, I shine and finally I walk around plumping and smoothing the cushions on the sofas so that there is not a single wrinkle in any of them.

The doorbell rings and I look out of the peephole and see the girl from the local florist holding a large bunch of long-stemmed red roses. I open the door and thank her for the flowers. I close the door and I put my nose to them. There is no scent. I take them into the kitchen and remove the wrapping.

There is no card. Cards are not necessary.

I get a bouquet every time Lenny fucks me.

I put them in water and carry the vase to the coffee table in the living room. They are not what I would have chosen, but they brighten up the place. Later I will pop by the florist on my way back from lunch and get myself a fragrant mix of gardenia, honeysuckle and sweet pea.

I glance at the clock. It is lunchtime. So I get into my jeans and a gray sweatshirt with a hood

and go out into the bright sunshine. Usually I buy myself a sandwich and go down to the park and eat it on one of the benches. But today I feel more lost and homesick than I normally do, so I walk down the road, and turn into a little side road.

At the end of it is a small Indian restaurant. I open the nondescript door and enter it. It is a small place with grand ideas borrowed from India before colonial times. Checkerboard black and inky blue floor tiles, fans hanging from a dark-lacquered oak ceiling, an aged brass bar in one corner, cut-glass wall lamps, hunting trophies from the days of the Majarajahs and bitter chocolate, leather love booths and banquettes.

Muted classical Indian music is playing in the background. The smell of cardamom, spices and curry fill the air and I breathe in the familiar scent. The restaurant is deserted. It almost always is at lunchtime. I used to worry that the business was going to go bust, but Raja, the solitary waiter they have working during the lunch shift, assured me that they get very busy at night.

Raja pops his head up from whatever he was doing below the bar, and smiles broadly at me. 'Hello,' he calls cheerfully.

I smile back and take a seat in my usual corner.

'How are you today?' Raja asks when he brings my bottle of mineral water, a basket of poppadoms, and a silver container with condiments and pickles.

'I'm fine, thank you. How are things?' I say.

He nods. 'Very good. Busy tonight. We have a big birthday party.'

'Oh! That's good.'

'Yes, the boss is very happy.'

I smile.

He holds on to the menu in his hand. 'Same as usual?' he asks.

'I think so.'

'OK. Two minutes and I will bring your food,' he says as he walks away.

I go into the women's toilet and wash my hands. When I return to my table, I break a piece of poppadom and, after spooning a tiny amount of sweet mango chutney on it, place it on my tongue. And as it does every time that I do this, the scent and taste take me back in time.

I think of our cook, her wrinkled, cinnamon hand holding out a freshly fried poppadom. But back home we called them appalam. They were hot and, because they were fried in new oil, they did not have any aftertaste. I chew the poppadom slowly. But something is different today. I can't ignore the aftertaste.

It is the beautiful man from last night.

I can't stop thinking about him, and he has infected me with a sense of restlessness and dissatisfaction. I suppose it is to be expected. I lead such an uneventful and dull life, meeting him was like touching a live wire. He invigorated my entire system. And that voice—deep, sexy, cheeky.

I start thinking about him.

He was different from everybody else at the club. Tall with broad shoulders, he alone wore a scruffy T-shirt, worn jeans, and the cockiest grin I've ever seen. A man like him did not need any adornment. He stood alone at the bar. How strange that no dancers tried to accost him. Perhaps it was because he is poor. But he owns a chateau in France so that can't be it. Perhaps he exaggerated. Maybe it's just a run-down farmhouse. Even so I would have liked to have seen the fireflies.

I take a sip of mineral water.

I should stop thinking of him. He is gone. I have no way of contacting him, and he has no way of contacting me. I lean back with that feeling I cannot shake no matter how many times I have tried since last night: I have lost something irreplaceable. Which is madness, really. Of course I haven't lost anything important. That was lost a year ago.

At that moment the door opens and I look up at the intrusion. I have begun to think of this deserted restaurant at lunchtime almost as my own personal space. The door pushes farther in and I freeze with shock.

Impossible! How can it be? What the hell is he doing here?

Inside my body, my hearts starts dancing like a wild thing.

In the daylight Shane's eyes are so bright they are sparkling blue jewels in his face. His mouth is full and sensual, his jaw classically chiseled, and his hair thick and glossy. My eyes pour down his body. He is carrying a motorbike helmet and wearing a blue T-shirt and faded black jeans low on his lean hips. I guess he is what they mean when they say someone is rocking muscles.

I have two seconds before he sees me.

Six

SHANE

I spot her straightaway. She is tucked up in one of the dark brown booths and staring at me with saucer eyes. Her hair is up in a ponytail and her face is devoid of any make-up. She looks even more vulnerable and childlike than she did last night. There is something in her eyes, something that hides and feeds on her.

I know I shouldn't be here.

She's broken. I can see that a mile off. Injured people cling. They are needy. I'm not the kind of guy she needs. Someone like me, I take what I want and I walk. I've never looked back. Never promised anyone anything. My way or no way. But she poses a challenge. A threat. And a promise. And I cannot walk away from her. This is just something I have to do.

I go up to her table and sit opposite her.

'What are you doing here?' she gasps.

I grin. 'Having lunch with you?'

'How did you know I'd be here?' Her voice is breathy. It gets under my skin. Everything about this woman gets under my skin.

'I paid someone to follow you last night, Snow.'

She inhales sharply. 'Why?'

'Because I promised you a trip to Saumur and I didn't know how else to contact you.'

It's amazing the effect my words have on her. Saumur and the fireflies shimmer like a magical promise on her lovely face.

'If you had me followed then you must know that I'm with some—'

I place my finger on her lips to silence the rest of her words. She could have moved back, but she didn't. Her lips are so warm and soft, it sends my dick rigid against the zipper of my jeans. Jesus. I have it bad for her. Her eyes close, but they hold closed for a second longer than it takes to blink. Why, she's savoring my touch. I stare at her. Her eyes open. The green is a few shades darker.

She blushes.

And suddenly I know: she is a sexual innocent.

She must be the most sexually unaware woman I've ever met. She's with Lenny, and it is clear that in exchange for the use of her body he is giving her some kind of protection, or perhaps it

is some kind of a financial arrangement, but it is clear that she has never been touched by a real man. I think about her screaming my name while my cock is deep inside her and immediately my cock, already straining uncomfortably, starts throbbing painfully.

I clear my throat. 'Do you still want to see the fireflies?'

She takes a deep and shuddering breath.

SNOW

I shouldn't involve him in my mess. I know how cold and wicked Lenny can be, but my head nods and he removes his finger.

'Would you like to go on Friday night? I'll bring you back by Sunday.'

'I ... I can't do it at the weekends.' In spite of myself, my voice becomes sad. 'Actually, I can't leave the country at any time. He ... er ... expects me to be around all the time.'

There is a slight tightening of his jaw, but his eyes are expressionless. 'Lenny is busy this weekend.'

My jaw sags. 'You know Lenny?' I breathe, taken by surprise.

'It's a small world, Snow.'

'Then you must know what he is.'

'Yeah, I know what he is,' he says, but he appears unimpressed.

I lean forward. 'He's a gangster. He's killed men before,' I say fiercely.

There is no change in his voice. 'I know.'

I drop back to the chocolate chair back. 'Are you not afraid of him?'

He shakes his head slowly, never taking his dirty, cocky, arrogant gaze off me.

I stare deep into his eyes. The flecks inside them are almost violet. I feel transfixed by them. as if he has a strange power over me. 'Who are you?' I whisper.

'Good afternoon, sir. Can I get you anything?' Raja asks.

His voice startles me and I jump.

Shane doesn't look at Raja. 'What's good to eat here?' he asks me.

'The Neer dosa with chicken curry, I think,' I say awkwardly.

'Is that what you're having?'

I nod.

He glances up briefly at Raja. 'I'll have two portions of that and a bottle of beer.'

Raja shuffles away, his eyes brimming with curiosity. From now on, Raja will never look at me in the same way again.

'I'm not a gangster, if that's what you're asking,' Shane says.

'So, what are you?'

He shrugs carelessly. 'I'm just a regular guy. I own some businesses.'

'And how do you know Lenny?'

'My brother used to do business with him.'

'Is your brother a gangster?'

'He used to be.'

'And you? Were you one too?' I ask.

'No.'

'What are you doing here?'

He grins irresistibly. 'I'm doing what the fireflies do when they flash. I'm sweet-talking you.'

Raja comes with the beer and a glass, and Shane ignores the glass and takes a mouthful straight from the bottle. 'So: are you on for Friday?'

'I don't think you understand. Lenny will kill you if he finds out.'

'I don't think you understand. Lenny is sorted.'

'How?' I demand.

'Let's just say he's had an offer he just can't refuse.'

'What kind of an offer? I thought you said you weren't a gangster.'

'I'm not. But I know people Lenny wants to trade with. As to what kind of an offer, you're better off not knowing Lenny's business.'

I frown. 'You're not going to get him into trouble, are you?'

His jaw tightens. 'Lenny's old enough and ugly enough to dig himself into trouble without any help from me.'

'But it's not some kind of trap you're luring him into?' I insist.

His face softens. 'It's not a trap. It's just business.'

And immediately I know. He is telling the truth. I hardly know Shane but I trust him. 'OK, I believe you.'

'Good.'

'What time Friday?' I ask.

He throws his head back and laughs, a triumphant, satisfied laugh, and my gaze travels helplessly down his strong, brown throat. He's special. I know then that we are not going to be just friends, even though this is exactly the kind of man my mother warned me to avoid at all cost. *Men who are too beautiful have too much choice. And a man with too much temptation is like a pig in shit. It will roll around in it all day long.*

Our food arrives, and Shane watches me ignore the fork and knife as I tear the crêpe-thin Neer dosa with the fingers of my right hand, then dip it into the creamy chicken curry, bringing it to my mouth.

'Does it taste better like that?' he asks with a crooked smile.

'Actually, yes,' I admit. 'You can wash your hands in the men's toilet.'

'No need,' he says, spreading his fingers out in front of him. He has beautiful hands. They are large and masculine, the nails square. 'I've eaten things off the floor and survived.'

I watch him rip the delicate white dosa, dunk it in the curry and put it into his mouth. He chews thoughtfully then raises one impressed eyebrow. 'It's good,' he pronounces.

I smile. 'I think so. It's a dish from Mangalore.'

'Do you come here often?'

'Yes, as often as I can.'

He looks around at the deserted restaurant. 'Is it always this dead?'

'Yes, every time I have been here. Most of their business is at night. But, to be honest, I like it like this. It's got vellichor.'

He takes a pull of his beer. 'Vellichor?'

'A place that is usually busy but is now deserted. You know, like that strange wistfulness you get in used bookshops. The dusty cries of all those forsaken books waiting for new owners.'

His lips twist. 'And you *like* that?'

I shrug. 'It suits me—my frame of mind.'

'You're a very strange girl, Snow Dilshaw. But I like you.'

God knows why, but I flush all over.

'Tell me about yourself,' he invites, finishing the first plate and pulling the second plate toward him.

'What do you want to know?'

'Everything. Start with where you are from.'

'I grew up in India. My mother is English and my father is Eurasian.'

He makes a rolling gesture with his left hand. 'Must have been an amazing childhood.'

I shrug. 'It was different.'

'Tell me what it was like,' he asks.

'My father was an industrialist, a very successful one. He traveled a lot, and since my mother insisted on accompanying him everywhere, my two older siblings and I were left in the care of our many servants. Until I was almost five years old I actually thought my nanny, Chitra, was my mother. She did everything for me. I even crept into her room and slept in her bed when my parents were away.'

He raises his eyebrows in shocked disbelief. 'Wow, you thought your nanny was your mother?'

'Yes, I did. I loved her deeply.'

Shane stares at me with such shock and curiosity it is obvious that he must come from a

very close-knit family where there is no doubt who the mother is.

'That's sad,' he says.

'Yes, finding out that the beautiful, perfumed, blonde woman with the chilly eyes and milky pearls that whispered against her silk blouses was my real mother was very confusing. Of course, I was in awe of her. Everybody was. In a land where everyone was dark-haired and mostly dark-skinned, she seemed to be very special. No matter where we went everybody stared at her.

'I remember once the two of us were waiting to be picked up by our driver outside a shop and there was a street procession passing in front of us. Basically all manner of society was being presented, schoolchildren, teachers, soldiers ... One of the groups was singing, blind beggars holding onto each other for support. But as they passed us one of them broke years of professional disguise to swivel his supposedly blind eyes and stare at my mother.'

Shane frowns.

'So even though I could see clearly that she was very special, I never took pride in being her daughter. I guess even as a small child I already perceived a lack of love in her. Sometimes it even seemed she could hardly bear to be in the same room as me.'

 50

'I'm sorry. That must have been terrible,' Shane says softly.

'I don't know that it was. I think growing up in a fatalistic society just makes you accept the unacceptable more easily. Once I asked Chitra why my mother loved me so little. She looked at me with her great, big, sad eyes and said, 'She might be an enemy from a past birth.'

Shane's eyes fly open. 'Wow! That's some heavy shit.'

'Not really. Chitra is a Hindu and she believes in reincarnation. According to her even though you have no recollection of your past lives, your spirit recognizes your enemies and your lovers from other lifetimes, and reacts accordingly.'

'What about your siblings though? Was it the same for them?'

'If I was my mother's enemy from a past life then my brother, Josh, was a great love. When I was six I heard her tell him, "I dreamt of you every night when you were inside me." There was just nothing he could do wrong. Once he stood on the dining table and holding his little penis sprayed the whole room with his pee. It even hit our cook and she had to run to her quarters and bathe. But when my mother was told about it, she only pretended to scold him. He ran off to his bedroom to sulk. I still remember how my mother had gone upstairs and sat in his room for ages to cajole him into coming downstairs for dinner.'

'Let me guess, he turned into a nasty little boy who pulled your hair and made you cry.'

I smiled. 'Pulled my hair? He took it a few steps further. He set it on fire. It was the only time I saw my father lose control. He put the fire out with his bare hands and afterwards he tore a branch from a tree and whipped my brother with it until my mother came running out of the house screaming hysterically and threw herself over my brother's body. I can still picture my father standing over them panting and wild-eyed. But enough about me, what about you? Tell me about you,' I urge.

'We are gypsies. My mother is from a Romany gypsy family and my father is an Irish traveler.'

'Oh wow! That's really interesting. You must have had some childhood too.'

'I did. I had a wonderful childhood. At least, until my father died. Then it all kind of fell apart for a while.'

'I'm sorry,' I say.

'It was a long time ago,' he says, and quickly changes the subject back to me. 'So, when and how did you end up in England?'

'I ran away from home when I was nineteen,' I say shortly.

 52

His eyes fill with curiosity. 'How old are you now?'

'Twenty.'

He frowns. 'You've only been in this country for one year.'

I nod.

'How did you get mixed up with Lenny?'

I shake my head. 'I can't talk about it.'

He stares at me, his eyes unreadable ice chips, and I drop my gaze

'But you are with him willingly.'

I nod.

'I want you to memorize my phone number and address.'

He tells it to me and makes me repeat it.

'If at all you need me, just call me or come directly to my home. There's a spare key under the mat. Ring the supervisor's bell and tell him your name and he will let you in. OK?'

'OK.'

Seven

SNOW

When I hear the letter flap clatter back to its closed position the next morning, I run to the door to find two letters on the floor. One is a utility bill. The other I hold in both hands, my stomach clenched with excitement. With shaking hands, I tear it open and my eyes graze the first paragraph.

Oh my God! They accepted me!

I hug the letter quietly to the middle of my chest and feel a tiny fountain of joy bubbling inside me. The reindeer moss sees the water and knows things are about to improve.

If only there was someone I could tell my happy news to, but there is no one. I have no friends in England, and I have cut all ties with everyone in India. Of course, I can't tell Lenny because he wouldn't approve at all.

When I pass the mirror, I look at my reflection and almost don't recognize the woman standing there looking back at me. Why, I look so alive. And then I am full of defiance. Why shouldn't I celebrate my good news with someone?

I pull on a light summer coat and run out of my apartment. I skip down the flight of steps and onto the pavement. I think about taking a taxi, and then I decide that, from now on, I'm going to save every penny. I am closer than ever to my goal.

I walk down to the Tube station in a happy daze. In the carriage I smile to myself. A woman catches my eyes and, instead of looking away, smiles back. I grin at her. She smiles again then looks away.

Shane, it seems, is only nine stops away from me.

The magazine seller outside the station points me in the right direction, and I happily float towards where he indicated. Shane's building isn't quite as exclusive or as nice as Lenny's, but I didn't expect it to be.

I know Shane doesn't have much money.

He drives a motorbike, and when I asked him outright how he knew Lenny he vaguely mentioned running a few businesses. In fact, I imagine his chateau, if it is not a farmhouse, to be a bit of a run-down job, but I don't care. He is my friend.

I stand outside his apartment block with my finger hovering over his bell and have a moment of doubt. He did tell me to come whenever I felt like it and that he is almost always around before lunch. *What if he's not in, or he has a woman friend over?* The thought is slightly sickening. With an odd flutter in my tummy, I ring the bell.

Shane's voice comes through the speaker. He sounds aggressively surprised.

'What are you doing here, Snow?' he demands.

'You said I could visit if ... if ... I wanted to,' I stammer.

The buzzer sounds and I push the door open. I cross the foyer toward the lift, but all my earlier enthusiasm has evaporated to nothing. He didn't sound happy to hear from me at all. I get into the lift and press the button for his floor. When the floor indicator passes the first floor, I hit my forehead with the heel of my hand.

Idiot!

This is not India where people just drop in on each other without calling ahead. I remember now, how it used to enrage my mother when my father's Indian relatives would simply turn up and call at the gate whenever they felt like seeing my father. It was their custom, but not hers.

And Shane is British, like my mother. I should have called first.

Suddenly, I feel tearful. The little fountain stops bubbling and reindeer moss withdraws into itself again. Oh God! I've ruined everything. The lift door opens at his floor and I rush to press the button to close the door. For good measure, I hit the button marked G a few times too. Hurry up and close, I pray, but as the doors start to shut, a huge male hand curls at the edge of one of the closing doors.

'Whoa,' Shane says appearing fully at the entrance of the lift. 'What the fuck? Were you going back down?'

I shrink back. 'I'm sorry. I should have called first. It was rude of me. I forgot. These English customs; I'm not used to them. You might have guests, or you might be busy.'

He stares at me incredulously for a second. 'You came to visit me?' he asks.

I nod miserably.

He holds the door of the lift open, and reaching in pulls me out by my wrist. I bite my lip to keep from crying, but the tears are already stinging at the backs of my eyes. I can't believe I am now going to cry, to add to my humiliation. I swallow hard and start blinking the tears back. Oh God, he's going to think I am the biggest cry-baby in the world.

For a moment he seems frozen with astonishment. Then he reaches out suddenly and pulls me towards his hard body.

'I don't have guests and I'm not busy,' he says into my hair.

Like a fool, I start crying in earnest. 'I don't know why I'm crying. I have no reason to cry. I'm such a colossal idiot,' I babble.

'I love it that you dropped by,' he says softly.

'Really?' I sniff.

'Abso-fucking-lutely.'

The little fountain in my heart starts bubbling again.

'I'm sorry if I sounded unwelcoming,' he says softly. 'I didn't know what to think. You took me by surprise. I was not expecting you, and I automatically thought something bad had happened to you.'

I wipe my eyes with the backs of my hands. 'No, I'm sorry. I don't know what's wrong with me. Crying like a fool for no reason.'

'Forget it,' he says kindly.

'OK,' I agree, smiling gratefully.

'Come on,' he says and takes me to his apartment.

The first thing I notice are the toys scattered on the floor.

His smile is mocking. 'In case you're wondering, they're not mine. They're my niece's

and nephew's. I'm babysitting for the next two hours.'

I listen, and the apartment is pretty silent. 'Where are they?'

'Sleeping, thank God.'

I chuckle. 'How old are they?'

'Liliana is four going on thirty-four, and Tommy is a three-year-old who, uniquely, channels monkeys. He climbed the cupboard the other day to reach for a packet of sweets.'

'Oh,' I say with a laugh.

'They'll be awake in an hour and you can meet them then.'

He wants me to stay and meet the children. 'I'd love to,' I say shyly. 'So, they are called Liliana and Tommy.'

'Well, he's still called Tommy,' he says dryly, 'but, she decided last week that she no longer wants to be known as Liliana, but Margarite Hum Loo.'

I laugh. 'Margarite Hum Loo?'

'Yes, and you can't shorten it and call her Margarite either. It has to be the full whack or nothing.'

I smile. 'Why that name?'

'No idea. You can ask her yourself when she wakes up.'

'I will,' I say still chuckling.

'I'm just about to make myself a meal. Join me?'

'Thanks, but I'm not hungry.'

'You'll regret it.'

Laughing, I follow him to his kitchen. It is done up in warm tones of honey and yellow.

'What will you have to drink? Milk? Juice? Water?'

'Juice will be nice.'

'Orange, apple, or—Liliana's favorite—mango crush.'

'I'll try the mango crush then.'

He takes a glass out of a cupboard and pours a thick orange-red liquid into it.

A cat comes to rub its face on my legs. 'You have a cat,' I exclaim, surprised.

'Yup. That's Suki,' he says, scooping rice into an opaque plastic cup. He pours it into a silver colander.

'Do you need some help?' I offer.

'Let's get the rules clear right from the start. This kitchen is my domain,' he states.

'Good, because I can't cook to save my life,' I say.

Sipping my drink, I watch him rinse the rice under the tap, drain it, and pour it into a pot. He pours bottled water onto it, salts it, puts a lid on it, and leaves it to cook.

'You sounded happy when you rang my bell,' he says, fishing out a live lobster from a pail of water with ice cubes floating in it.

'I was,' I say distractedly as I stare at the lobster. Its claws are tied, but all its little legs are waving frantically. 'I mean, I am. I received some good news this morning.'

He picks up a big knife and puts the lobster on the chopping board. 'Yeah?'

My eyes widen with horror. 'You're not going to kill that lobster and eat it, are you?'

His hands still. He looks up at me. 'Yes, why?'

I puff air out of my lips. 'I mean, it's alive. Wouldn't you feel bad to eat something you've killed with your own hands?'

He rubs his jaw with the edge of the fist that is holding the knife. 'Don't you eat lobster?'

'Yes,' I admit uncomfortably, 'but I couldn't eat it if I saw it alive a few minutes before.'

He laughs. 'We all have to die, Snow. This guy has had a good life at the bottom of the ocean, and I'm giving him a quick death. I wish my death could be so quick.'

'I just can't get my head around it.'

He grins. 'That's because you're a hypocrite, Snow. You'll eat it after someone else kills it for you, arranges it neatly on a Styrofoam tray, pulls a bit of cling film over it, and sticks it on a supermarket shelf.'

'Afraid so.'

'Right. Look away now. I'm about to say his last rites.'

I turn my head and hear a crack then a squelching noise before the knife hits the chopping board. I turn back, and the lobster has been neatly halved lengthwise. Some of its legs are still waving. Then they all slowly stop. Something about its still body makes me remember when I wanted revenge so bad I wanted to kill, and not just a lobster, but human beings. When I could have killed with a song in my heart.

'Shane?'

He looks up at the different tone in my voice. 'What?'

'Could you kill a human being?'

His eyes narrow, and he looks dangerous.

'If he's hurt you—I mean really, really hurt you, or someone you loved ...'

He doesn't hesitate. His voice rings strong and sure in that kitchen, with the rice boiling and the dead lobster lying on the wooden board. 'Yes. I'd kill for those I love.'

I nod slowly, and for a few seconds we gaze at each other. His eyes burn with fierce intensity. No more is said, but I suddenly feel safe, safer than I have ever felt with Lenny. My muscles are

singing with renewed vigor, and I feel as if I could do anything, be anything.

Eight

SNOW

'**W**hat made you decide to pay me a surprise visit?' he asks, as he begins the task of scooping up and discarding the yellow-green tomalley from the two halves of the lobster.

'I'm really sorry; I realize now I should have called. It's not the done thing in England to turn up unannounced at someone's door.'

He lifts a lemon from a fruit bowl on the kitchen table, washes it under the tap, and cuts it into wedges. 'It's done, but usually by people selling things you don't want, and suspicious girlfriends trying to catch their boyfriends in compromising situations,' he says dryly.

'You can add a new category to your list. Foreign-born women who have just received great news.'

He looks up from the lobster, his eyebrows raised expectantly. 'You have great news?'

I nod excitedly.

'Spit it out then.'

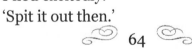

'OK, here it is,' I say with a happy grin. 'My greatest dream for as long as I can remember was to become a pre-school teacher. To give back to other children what my nanny gave me. To instill in them a thirst for knowledge. But my mother did not want me to become a teacher. In her opinion, it was a badly paid, thankless job, and, no matter what I did, I could never change those children's lives one iota. I guess that's the real reason I ran away to England. I knew if I wanted to chase my dream, I had to leave India ... and, since I had a British passport, I came here.

'But here, in England, all teaching colleges require you to have work experience before they will accept you. Soooo ... I applied to do some voluntary work at some local schools, and this morning a letter arrived from one of them to tell me that I've been selected.'

'Am I looking at the happiest teacher-in-training ever?' he asks, his blue eyes crinkling up.

'Pre-school teacher-in-training,' I correct. 'I only ever wanted to teach small children.'

'I think you'll make a brilliant pre-school teacher.'

'You mean it?'

'Of course. How could you fail to be when you are so enthusiastic and eager? When you see education as passing down the magic,' he says, placing a cast-iron griddle pan on the stove and switching it on.

As we carry on talking, he drizzles the two halves with olive oil and seasons them—salt, pepper. I watch his beautiful hands take a pinch of paprika and, hovering over the lobster, he rubs his fingers together. A sumptuous, exotic red mist settles like crimson dust upon the gray flesh of the crustacean. Out of nowhere, a thought snakes into my head. How great it would be to have those big, powerful hands on my body.

With a pair of scissors, he snips off a sprig of parsley from a pot growing on the windowpane, chops it finely, and drops it into an earthenware bowl. He uses the heel of his hand to break up a garlic bulb, and chops four of its cloves. That goes into a blue earthenware bowl with two thick sticks of butter and a sprinkle of chili flakes.

He pours a little olive oil onto the hot pan and places the lobster halves flash side down. The flesh sizzles. Very quickly, he flips them over and pours cognac in two quick strips over the seared flesh. Two long blue flames leap up angrily from the pan.

'Wow! Impressive,' I say.

'You think that's impressive? Wait till you see what else these hands can do,' he teases.

My face flames as bright as the lobster shells.

The rice cooker pings at the same time that he takes the lobsters off the fire.

He turns to me. 'Would you like some?'

My mouth is salivating with all the delicious smells, but I shake my head resolutely. I saw that lobster alive. Hypocrite or not, I couldn't. I'd be eating the moment of its death.

'Last chance,' he offers.

'Thanks, but no,' I say firmly.

He opens the rice cooker and spoons the rice onto an enormous, white, square plate. He takes the lobster halves and lays them on the rice. Carefully, he spoons the melted butter mixture over his meal.

He looks up at me. 'So, you're just going to watch me eat?'

'Yes. If you don't mind.'

'Hmm ... Want a double chocolate chip cookie instead? They're very good.'

I hesitate. 'Um.'

'Her majesty, Lady Margarite Hum Loo baked them.'

I smile. 'She did?'

'She's an awesome baker,' he says persuasively.

'In that case, OK.'

He opens a tin and brings it to me. They are in the shapes of animals.

I take a cat. 'Thank you.' I bite into it. 'It's actually delicious,' I say, surprised.

'Bring the whole tin with you,' he says, and leads the way to his dining table, which has been set for one.

He raises an eyebrow. 'How about a glass of Pinot Blanc?'

I shake my head, fascinated by the care he has taken to cook his own meal. Only a true gourmet would go to such great pains to prepare a feast for one, but he seems unaware of how unusual his behavior is.

He fishes a bottle of wine from a bucket of ice, and pours himself a glass of wheat-colored liquid. Then he sits down and lifts his knife and fork. I watch him cut out a piece of lobster and, in a sensual act of pure pleasure, slip it into his mouth, and suddenly I'm salivating like Pavlov's dog. My cookie seems to be a childish indulgence when I watch him savor every mouthful. As if each mouthful was a unique work of art that he has been given the privilege of experiencing.

I watch him eat, and it is a joy to do so. We talk and we laugh. He is easy and funny. There are only two or three bites left on his plate when there is a shrill scream from somewhere in the apartment.

'Good timing, kids,' Shane says good-naturedly, and stands up.

'Shall I wait for you here?' I ask.

'No, you don't want to miss this,' he says with a laugh.

I follow him to the entrance of a room painted in bright colors with two cots and lots of toys.

'It was *not* an accident!' a beautiful, blue-eyed little girl with her hands on her hips screams furiously at a boy who has his arms crossed.

'What's going on here?' Shane asks calmly.

'He,' she fumes, throwing a fierce glance toward her cousin before bringing it back again to Shane, 'banged me on the head with his train while I was sleeping.'

Shane moves into the room. 'Let me see that head,' he says.

She touches the top of her head gingerly and cries pitifully, 'I've been treating him happy and he just wants to kill me.' She takes a shuddering breath, and, opening out one palm beseechingly toward him, demands. 'Why? Why?'

Shane gets to his haunches in front of her. 'Of course, he doesn't want to kill you, sweetie. He's your cousin.'

'Yes, he does. Yes, he does,' she insists, striking the sides of her little body violently. She points at Tommy dramatically. 'He just wants me to die out here.'

Shane busies himself with gently feeling the top of her head. 'Now, why on earth would Tommy want to kill you?'

She thinks for a minute. 'So he can have all my toys,' she says triumphantly.

Shane shakes his head. 'He's a boy. He doesn't want your dolls and cookery set.'

She appears to lose interest in Tommy's motive. 'Is there an egg on my head?' she asks anxiously, instead.

'Maybe a very small one,' Shane agrees.

'I'm never sleeping with him again. Don't make me, Uncle Shane,' she pleads.

I have to turn my head to hide my smile. How Shane is keeping a straight face is beyond me.

'Why did you bang her with your train while she was sleeping, Tommy?' Shane asks the little boy, who has so far said nothing.

He scrunches his shoulders up to his ears. 'It was an accident. I wanted to kiss her, but the train fell from my hand, and ... and ... banged her head.'

Shane turns to Liliana. 'See? It was an accident. He just wanted to kiss you.'

'I don't believe him. He's a'—she frowns to think of the right expression—'juvenile delinquent.'

Shane's lips twitch. 'Do you know what? I kind of believe him. You're very, very kissable.'

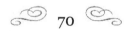

And he kisses her on her cheek, twice, loudly. 'Don't you sometimes look at your new baby sister and want to kiss her too?'

She looks at Tommy from the sides of her eyes. 'Yes, Laura's cute,' she admits.

'Can you forgive him?' Shane asks.

She stares mutinously at Shane. 'I'll have to think about it.'

'All right then. Think about it while you have lunch.' He turns his gaze to his nephew. 'Tommy, what do you say when you accidentally hurt someone?'

'Sorry,' he pipes up immediately.

'Good boy. Now, why don't we all go into the kitchen and have some lunch?'

Tommy, relieved that he is not going to be punished, nods eagerly.

'Who's that?' Liliana asks, noticing me for the first time.

'That's Snow. Say hello.'

'Hello, Snow,' she says, wiping her tears, her rage forgotten.

'Hi, what's your name?' I ask with a smile, simply because I want to hear her tell me her new name.

'Margarite Hum Loo,' she replies solemnly.

'That's a pretty name. What does it mean?' I ask equally solemnly.

'It doesn't mean anything. I just like it because it reminds me of a seahorse, or a mermaid, I'm not sure which yet.'

I smile at the purity of her innocence. It's been a long time since I was in the presence of children. It is like bathing my soul in clear, pure spring water. It makes this morning's news even sweeter.

I turn to Tommy. 'Hello, Tommy.'

'Hello,' Tommy says shyly.

'He's a cry-baby. He cries all the time,' Liliana denounces scornfully.

'Excuse me,' Shane interrupts, 'but you used to cry when you were his age too.'

'I only cried for milk; he cries for everything.'

Both Shane and I crack up.

'Are you Uncle Shane's girlfriend?' Liliana demands suddenly.

I look at Shane, but he just looks at me innocently.

I clear my throat. 'I'm Uncle Shane's friend,' I say primly.

'Don't you want to be Uncle Shane's girlfriend?' she asks curiously.

I feel myself flush and Shane grins evilly. 'Answer the child then.'

'Well,' I say.

'I know what. You can marry him if you want and then you can kiss like mummies and daddies.'

Shane bursts out laughing, and even I have to smile.

The next hour is the best fun I've had in years. Shane and I prepare thick homemade fish fingers that Liliana's mother has sent, shelled peas, and mashed potatoes. The kids are a barrel of laughs, but my first impression of Tommy as a helplessly little baby is quickly dispelled. He turns out to be the naughtiest little imp.

After lunch, Shane puts on the Whip/Nae Nae record and Liliana, who knows all the moves, starts dancing. Disgusted with the noise and activity, the cat retreats into the kitchen.

'Again,' Liliana cries when the track ends.

God knows how, but on the third run the bossy boots manages to make both Shane and I join in. I have been out of circulation for so long, I don't know any of the steps, but Shane, like Liliana, knows them all. He looks real good doing it too.

We all stop when the phone rings.

'Can I answer it, Uncle Shane?' Liliana asks.

'Go on. It's probably your daddy anyway.'

She rushes to the phone, picks it up, and says, 'Hello, Margarite Hum Loo speaking.'

'Daddeeeeee,' she squeals. She listens for a while, then asks, 'What time are you coming? OK. Hi, Mummy. Yes, I was very, very good. Tommy wasn't, though. He banged my head really hard. On purpose. I was very brave. There was a very big egg on my head, but it's gone down now.'

I turn toward Shane with widened eyes at the lies she was telling.

'Don't worry, everybody knows what a terrible shit-stirrer she is,' he whispers with a wink.

Her mother must have asked about lunch because she says, 'Yes. Fish fingers, mashed potatoes, and peas.' She swivels her eyes toward me. 'No, but Uncle Shane's girlfriend is here. Yeah. Yeah. I don't know.' She takes a big breath. 'Mummy, did you buy anything nice for me? Yay! OK, see you soon. I love you, Mummy. Bye, bye.' She puts the phone down and skips over to us.

'Mummy and Daddy are coming.'

'I guess I'd better go,' I say.

'You don't have to,' Shane says immediately.

'No, I should go. It's getting late.'

'Are you sure?'

'Yeah, I'm sure,' I say with a smile.

'I'll call you a cab.'

'Thanks, Shane.'

In less than five minutes, the cab calls up that he is waiting downstairs.

'I really enjoyed my time here,' I say.

'Hold on. We'll all come down with you.'

So, all of us pile into the lift and go down. As Shane shuts the door of the taxi, I see a silver Bentley drive into the forecourt. I turn back to watch it, and I see a tall man with very similar coloring to Shane, and a beautiful woman with a slightly Oriental feel to her features get out of the car. The woman is holding a baby in her arms and Liliana is jumping up and down with excitement. As soon as Shane lets go of her little hand, she races to her father and throws herself at him. He catches her, lifts her high into the air, and whirls around while she squeals with delight.

Then the taxi turns into the road and I can no longer see them.

Nine

SNOW

It is nearly 7.00 p.m. and the light that fills my apartment is livid and deep, half storm-purple and half the fiery orange eyes of a hawk. I've been wandering aimlessly within these walls ever since I returned from Shane's house. Hearing myself breathe. Jumping at the sound of the water in the pipes.

Feeling something. Dread and excitement.

A hot, damp wind pushes in through the window and I stop and gaze at my surroundings as if seeing it all for the first time. Everything is still and silent and bland. There are no cherished paintings, family photographs, or lovingly collected little objects of beauty. The walls are magnolia, the furniture is plain and brown, and it is all as clinically clean as an ICU unit in a hospital.

Which is strange considering that this place has been my salvation, my solace, and my sanctuary. My hiding place from the world outside. The world that is always waiting to hurt me. I listen to the silence, and it feels heavy and oppressive.

I turn my thoughts to little Liliana, the shit-stirrer.

'Margarite Hum Loo,' I whisper, and just saying her made-up name aloud in the stillness makes me chuckle.

I try to imagine her in her own home with her parents. It is clear that they adore her. The image that comes to my mind seems warm, bright, full of laughter, and infused with the smell of Liliana and her mother baking a new batch of cookies.

I think of Shane. Of course, he will not be at home now. He will probably be in Eden. I try to picture him walking around, talking, laughing, and I feel sad that I am not part of his life. I realize I miss his mischievous sense of humor, his handsome face, his wolfish grin, and his warm, sparkling eyes.

But I stop myself short. I cannot be part of his life. No matter what it looked like this afternoon, he is a playboy through and through. I saw that a mile off. No one that good-looking can be trusted. This is just a flirtation for him. Soon he will be gone. Looking for greener pastures.

My thoughts inevitably return to my mother. She would be so disapproving if she ever met

Shane. Not that she ever will, of course. She always wanted her children to marry into money.

'What can you do with good looks?' she used to say. 'You can't eat them. They won't pay the bills. All they are is endless trouble. Finding phone numbers in their pockets, going through their credit card bills, and worrying every time they're a little late home.'

So my sister, Catherine, married into money.

When she was twenty-three she met Kishore, a nondescript guy with curly hair. He was thirty and from a 'good' and powerful Indian family. They fell in love over a plate of marsala tosai, she signed a six-page harshly worded pre-nup contract, and they got married in one of the biggest society weddings in Calcutta. Political figures and Bollywood celebrities attended the glittering occasion.

Now she has given him three kids, he cheats on her all the time, sometimes even openly, but she won't leave. She won't give up the mansion, the servants, the swimming pool, the invitations to all the best parties, and the overseas shopping trips.

My brother, on the other hand, has told my mother in no uncertain terms that he will marry only for love. It is the only time that we agree on an important issue.

My brother and I don't get on. From the time we were children, he didn't want me around. I never understood why he resented me so much. He had everything. He was the favorite of both my parents and got absolutely everything he ever wanted.

Even when Papa lost all his money and all that was left was the house, which fortunately he had transferred into my mother's name, and the money he had stashed away in her account, I was immediately pulled out of Calcutta International school. It was decided however, that there was enough money to pay Josh's school fees and eventually to send him to America to finish the last part of his education.

Our very large house was sold. Some of the proceeds went toward Josh's education fund, and some was put toward buying a smaller house. When Josh flew away, I was left in the house with my parents, the cook, the gardener, and a cleaning lady who came in daily. All my fine school friends had dropped away one by one. They were either too busy, or had left the country to finish their education. Papa locked himself into a room and let the TV blare. Without my brother and with the loss of her grand lifestyle, my mother became a very unhappy woman.

For a long time after our slide into disgrace, staff from my father's offices and factory used to

come to the front gate pleading for their unpaid wages. Once, I asked my mother why we didn't just pay them at least something.

'Elizabeth,' she said tight-lipped. 'If you had your way, you'd have us all begging in the streets with them, wouldn't you?'

As time passed, Papa's unpaid staff grew more and more desperate. They started shaking the gates and shouting insults. My mother used to stand at the window behind the curtain, and look down at them as the gardener chased them away by hitting their fingers with a broomstick and scolding them.

In fear of their anger, my mother arbitrarily decided she did not want me to finish my education, even at the local school. I was very upset, but I didn't want to go against her, since things were already so fraught at home. So I sat in my swing and read. Tons of books. I read the classics. I read translated works. I read Indian poets. But my life seemed meaningless. I felt like a prisoner. Trapped and without a future. I wanted to live.

I don't know what made me decide one day to run away. Perhaps because I could not see my mother ever allowing me to pursue my dream of being a pre-school teacher. I opened Papa's safe— I had known the combination since I was fifteen— and stole the money I needed. My passport was

ready from the time I was first sent to international school. I took a taxi to the airport and got on a plane.

I was nineteen when I arrived in London. It was autumn and the air was chilly, but I remember I was so excited and so filled with adrenalin I did not feel the cold. In my T-shirt, I traveled to Victoria Station. From there it was easy. I got into the Tube station, bought a ticket, and took the Victoria Line, then got off two stops up at Oxford Circus.

Central London's Oxford Circus was a shock. The bustle, the energy. I could not believe it. The world seemed a big, beautiful, bright place, and I was so happy. I walked to the YHA hostel. I had checked them out on the Internet and I knew they had beds for £18.00. It was a lot in rupees, but I expected to find a job as soon as possible.

The YHA was a fun place decorated with brilliant jewel colors. It looked more like a kindergarten than a budget hostel. And I loved it. There were two beds in my room. They had bright apple green pillowcases and duvet covers. One was already taken. I put my bag on the other and thought I would burst with excitement.

There was free Wi-Fi, so I went down to the Internet room. It had purple beanbags, which I thought made the place look funny and warm. I sat down at the computer and sent Papa an email telling him that I was in London. I apologized for taking the money from the safe, but I promised him that I would pay the whole thing back as soon as I got myself a job. I told him I loved him and my mother and then I signed off.

When I went back to my room, my new roommate was already there.

'G'day,' she called. I had never heard the greeting before. Later, I would learn that it was short for 'Good day'.

Suddenly, that old flicker of discomfort is back. And so is that sensation of gnawing apprehension. I sigh deeply and close my eyes. Her face is so vivid that it could all have happened yesterday. I know I'll never forget her as long as I live. *I'm fine. I'm fine now. I survived.*

I go to the kitchen and switch on the kettle. I don't want to remember any more. Not today. I don't want to have to take those pills. I want tomorrow to be a fun adventure. I want to see the fireflies. I want to run away from here. From Lenny and the sickening, unspoken agreement that I have to pay his kindness back with my body for as long as he wants. Which could be forever. I put a tea bag into a mug.

The phone rings. I stand in front of it and let it ring twice more before taking the call.

'Hello, sweetheart,' Lenny says.

'Hello, Lenny.'

'How are you?'

'I'm fine.'

'Good. Look, I've got business over in Amsterdam tomorrow, so I'll pick you up and take you to dinner tonight.'

'Uh. Not tonight, Lenny. I'm really very tired.'

There is a malevolent silence. 'Oh yeah? What have you been up to all day?' His voice was deadpan, cut from rock.

'Nothing. I cleaned the flat, had lunch at a cafe, and then I went shopping. You know how shopping always exhausts me.'

'Did you get something nice?'

'Yes, I did.'

'What?' There, there's the reptile lazily sunning itself on a warm stone suddenly striking. He's caught me out. When his secretary goes through all the boutique accounts and the credit card bill, there will be no purchases with today's date. He will know I lied. I haven't lied to him before.

'A red dress,' I say. And then quickly add, 'I used the money you gave me the other night.'

'Good. Wear it when I take you out on Monday night. I'll be back by then, and we'll do dinner somewhere nice.'

I grip the phone hard and keep my voice light. 'That'll be nice.'

'All right. Call you when I get back.'

'Have a good trip.'

I switch off the phone. I'm playing with fire. Things are unraveling too fast. I almost got caught there. Lenny is unpredictable, his violence legendary. A ruthless, wild raptor. If he even scents another male trespassing on his territory, I will see the incandescent, uncontrollable fury that I have only glimpsed so far.

Once, a drunk man touched my bottom in a club. It could have been an accident, but I jumped because it had startled me. Lenny saw my reaction and he turned and calmly nodded to one of his henchman. The big brute immediately went forward and kicked the shit out of him right in the middle of the club.

I was so shocked I froze, but when I got control of my limbs I turned to Lenny and cried, 'Stop him! Stop him!'

And Lenny clicked his fingers and his other henchman stopped the assault.

I looked at the man, bleeding and groaning, and then I looked at Lenny, and there was absolutely no expression on his face. It was nothing to him. And I was afraid. For the first time I became afraid of Lenny. And I knew he had not done that to punish the man, but to frighten me.

I don't love Lenny. I never have. I just let him use my body because I didn't know what else to do. I was so broken, and he had taken care of me. I had no one else. When he put his hand on my thigh that night, I couldn't bring myself to stop him. And then, before I knew it, he was on top of me and we were having sex.

But it has to stop.

Even if it means my dream of becoming a pre-school teacher is delayed, I have to take back control of my own life and find a job to support myself so I am no longer beholden to him. Perhaps I could rent a room cheaply. Better that than let him use my body anymore. I wasn't strong enough before, but I know I'm ready now. I know I have to act soon. But there is a tight feeling of apprehension in my body that sets my teeth on edge. Secretly, I am afraid of Lenny.

I go into the kitchen, butter a slice of brown bread, and put together an open tomato and cheese sandwich. As I cut the little cherry tomatoes, I think of Shane cooking, the passion with which he prepared his meal, the enjoyment he took from every bite, and it occurs to me that I live without tasting life. My whole existence is a meal without salt.

I walk to the dining table with my sandwich and my cup of tea. I lift up a slice of tomato, put it in my mouth, and let the fresh zest of its juice burst into my taste buds. I wait for the flakes of sea salt to melt on my tongue. Next, I take a bite of bread and cheese. The cheese tastes milky and smooth as I roll it slowly together with the nutty, rich taste of the buttered bread. I savor it the way Shane relished his meal. With my eyes closed, my meal is no longer a humble sandwich, but a complex of things of many scents, flavors and textures.

I can see that just by being on the outside edges of my life, Shane is already subtly changing me. Yes, there is a lot of terrible pain trapped inside my body, but when I am with him, it hides away, as if it is afraid of him. It is afraid he will banish it away forever.

That evening I listen to music and go to bed early, but I am too excited about my trip with Shane to sleep.

Finally, just when I have fallen asleep, I am awakened by the sound of a key in my door. I freeze with fear. Then I hear the familiar sound of Lenny's footsteps. He comes into the bedroom and silently walks over to the bed. He stands over my prone body and watches me. I keep my breathing even and deep, and pray that he will not wake me up.

To my relief, after a few minutes he quietly slips out of the flat.

After I hear the door shut, I sit up then go over to the window. From the darkness of my window, I watch him walk to his car. The driver opens the back door and Lenny gets into it. Feeling unnerved, I return to bed. It has been a long time since he did that. He used to do that a lot when he first found me, when I was almost mad with grief and horror. I wonder why he did that today.

Does he on some level sense that another man has strayed into his territory?

Ten

SNOW

Shane comes to collect me at 9.00 p.m. because that is when Lenny's plane takes off and there will be no more calls from him after that. A man in a peaked cap opens the back door of a blue Mercedes and I slide in. Shane introduces him as the driver of the family's company car.

'Mostly only my brothers use this car. I can get anywhere faster on my bike,' he says.

'We're not going to Heathrow Airport?' I ask when I notice the car going on a different route.

'No, we're flying out of Luton,' Shane says.

'Oh,' I say, and settle back against the plush seat while Shane gives the man instructions to bring his car to the airport on Sunday. I don't listen. A ball of anxiety sits at the base of my stomach. I feel as if I am cheating on Lenny, even though I don't love Lenny and he cheats on me all the time, and anyway, I am not going to do anything with Shane. Shane and I are friends, and we are just going to see the fireflies.

At the airport I am in for a shock. We are walking toward a private plane!

'Wow! Whose plane is that?' I ask, astonished.

'My brother bought it about two years ago for the family's use.'

'Is he the ex-gangster?'

'Yeah. Jake was a gangster, but don't judge him too harshly. He had no choice. He did it for us. It was a great sacrifice for a man who wanted to be a vet.'

'You love him very much, don't you?'

'We're blood. I'd give my life for him.'

And his eyes shine with sincerity.

Then the pilot is introducing himself to me and we are walking up the steps into the jet. It is another world. The inside of it is beautiful, with heavy, wooden doors, red, luxurious carpets, and huge cream seats facing each other with tables in between. There are fresh flowers everywhere and it smells of perfume. Farther along, closer to the cockpit, there are two single beds with furry slippers tucked at one end. The table we are invited to occupy has a white tablecloth spread over it and is set as if in a fancy restaurant.

We sit and the smiling air stewardess pops open a bottle of champagne.

I can't help being wide-eyed with wonder. 'Oh my God, how amazing,' I gasp. 'This is exactly what I imagined it must be like to be a film star.'

He laughs softly, his handsome face indulgent, and we clink glasses then drink.

Fruit and tiny little canapés are served on a mirrored platter.

It takes us an hour and forty minutes to arrive in Cannes, a town so exclusive that there is no commercial airport and only private jets are authorized to land. There are no queues, Immigration and Passport Control, or baggage to worry about. Instead, our passports are checked by two policemen, and then we step onto the runway.

'Welcome to France,' Shane says.

I marvel at how easy and smooth travel is for the rich. 'I can't believe we're actually in another country.'

'Come on. We've got dinner reservations,' he says, and leads me to a waiting car.

Full of excitement, I look around me as the palm-tree-lined boulevards swish by as we get into the town. I gaze in awe at all the beautiful old buildings. In twenty minutes I am ushered into one of Cannes' famous seafront restaurants, Le Palais Oriental. It is brightly decorated with blue seats, white tables, and mirrors on the ceilings.

The place is in full swing, heaving with belly dancers and huge groups of noisy party-goers. We are greeted by a friendly Moroccan waiter who shows us to our table. The tables are low, and Shane has to sit with his knees spread far apart. He catches my grin and acknowledges the funny side. I love that he is able to laugh at himself. There is something so endearing about a man like that. My father couldn't. My brother will never be able to, and Lenny will tear your head off before he'd even contemplate doing such a thing.

Shane and I order tagine of lamb with prunes and couscous, which our cheeky waiter claims is terrific because it is cooked on the bosoms of angels.

We drink mint tea and watch the dazzlingly graceful belly dancers as they advance, retreat as they snake their arms sinuously in the air, and shimmy their hips so hard and fast their luxurious costumes swim about their feet. I feel an instant affinity with them—the colorful costumes, the sun-drenched skin, and the bells on their bra tops remind me of the beautiful Indian dancers of my childhood.

Like those Indian dancers, they twist their bodies into shapes that express joy, laughter, sadness, grace, lust. This story is one of entrapment and beauty. One woman wears a veil and over it her dusky black eyes flash enticingly. Not only her body, but her eyes speak.

I look around me and there are different reactions to them. To some, these women are cheap meat, but there are others who see what I do. All dancers are dreamers. There is no such thing as a sinful dancer.

'I've never seen a belly dance in the flesh,' I tell Shane.

'Do you like it?' he asks.

'It's simply beautiful,' I say, watching a woman in a blue costume. Her personality and her sensuality flow through the timeless moves her body makes.

'I agree.'

I turn to look at Shane. He is watching me. 'The one in the blue costume is so seductive.'

'Yes, she's so seductive,' he says softly, but he does not turn to look at her.

When the lamb comes, it is succulent, and the couscous could indeed have been cooked on the bosom of an angel. We eat our food and drink our wine, and slowly the beat of the Arabic music makes me tingle, and my body moves in tune with it.

'Do you want to dance?'

I shake my head. 'Perhaps I could dance under a moonless sky, or if I was on my own and no one could see me.'

'Great: Moonless Sky is my chosen Red Indian name,' he says cheekily.

'Forget it,' I say.

'Never say never.'

We leave the restaurant late, our bellies full and the scent of adventure beckoning us as we drive to Shane's chateau. In thirty minutes we arrive at a set of arched black iron gates. We drive up a road for a few minutes in total darkness and then, suddenly, we have reached our destination.

Saumur.

My mouth drops open with astonishment. This is no farmhouse or dilapidated chateau! How is it possible that Shane could own something so magnificent? Built from pink stone and trimmed in white, it rises from the ground in a truly imposing and majestic structure.

'Wow,' I exclaim opening the car door. 'But this is a palace!'

'How astute of you. It used to belong to an Iraqi prince, so it's architecturally more royal palace than chateau.'

The gravel crunches under my feet as we walk up to the chateau. He unlocks the tall door and switches on the light and it is breathtaking. I look around in awe. My father was very rich once, but, even then, our mansion house was nothing like this. I have to seriously re-evaluate Shane's financial worth. And to think I had been expecting a ruined chateau or a farmhouse! God, it never crossed my mind that he could afford such extraordinary splendor. This pile must be worth millions and millions of pounds.

'All this belongs to you?'

'Yes,' he says staring curiously at me.

'You're so young. How could you be so rich?'

'I have my brother to thank. He started us off early. He got us into the property market, investing in Internet start-ups, bought us all citizenships in Monaco, and put us into every tax saving scheme available.'

I look around in wonder. 'It's absolutely stunning, Shane. You're so lucky.'

'Come, I'll show you the best part of the house.' He winks at me. 'Just in case you want a midnight swim.'

Stunned by the grandeur of the place, I follow him through the rooms with their high ceilings and the lovely marble floors. In the main salon there are stupendous art deco chandeliers and superb antiques. He leads me toward the pool, which has been uniquely situated in the center of the property.

I gasp when we reach it.

It is like suddenly finding yourself in a different world—the sumptuous, luxurious, precious, lost world of an Oriental potentate. Lit by softly glowing lamps, it must be seen to be believed. Massive and round, it is surrounded by tall double Corinthian marble columns that form a veranda around the pool. The stone columns are slightly submerged, giving the illusion that they are rising from the water.

The roof is covered in wisteria, throwing the reflection of the columns and dripping plants into the still water. There are white orchids growing in large bronze pots and loungers with cream cushions.

Made speechless by the unrivaled luxury and beauty, I walk toward the edge of the pool. There are rose petals floating in the water.

I hear him come up behind me. I turn around and look up at him. 'Wow,' I whisper.

His eyes are hidden by shadows. There is a slight tension in his body. 'Feel like a midnight swim?'

I am suddenly wary. 'I didn't bring a swimsuit.'

'There are swimsuits in the changing room, I believe,' he counters.

'I didn't come here to sleep with you,' I say, and my words hang between us. Both of us know that's a lie.

'Pity. Still, I'm only inviting you for a swim.'

I bite my lower lip. 'OK, let's swim.'

In the changing rooms, I find some plain black bikinis. I get into one and, after slipping on

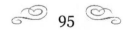

a toweling robe, nervously go back out to the pool. The air is warm and scented with the smell of the countryside. His back is to me and he is naked, but for a pair of briefs. He turns slightly when he hears my approach, and smiles.

And he takes my breath away—he's the sexiest, most delicious thing I've *ever* seen. I gape at him like a silly teenager with a crush. The air changes between us. I feel goosebumps scatter quickly on my skin like millions of insect legs. A shiver goes through me, and between my legs a strange throbbing begins.

I breathe in deeply. What the hell am I doing?

I force my eyes away from him. If I'm planning to sleep with him, I should have drunk more alcohol at the restaurant.

'Could I ... er ... have a drink?'

He turns fully then. Tattoos. Muscles. Ripped body. And a beast of a cock, barely held in check by his swimming trunks. All as if carved from glowing marble. There is no fear or shame in his face. He is the most self-assured, beautiful thing I have ever seen. Powerful male sexuality radiates from every pore of his impressive form. My mouth feels dry and my body does something it has never done before.

It aches for him.

Eleven

SHANE

She stands in the glow of the lamps with absolutely no idea of just how fucking beautiful she is. She looks like she's made of porcelain, or fairy dust. I want to go up to her, strip her naked, and ravish her right there on the cold tiles, but I can see that she is so nervous, her knuckles show white where she is hanging on so tightly to the edges of her robe's front.

'Sure, you can have a drink. What do you want?' I say, ignoring my raging hard-on, and sauntering over to the concealed bar to the left of me. She trails behind.

'Vodka and orange juice,' she says.

I pick up a bottle of Grey Goose and a tall glass. 'Say when,' I tell her, and begin to pour.

I am nearly halfway up the glass and she is still staring at it. I carry on pouring, my eyes on her face.

'When,' she says.

I stop pouring and put the bottle on the bar. She lifts her eyes to mine. What kind of strange, sexy creature have I got standing in front of me? No woman has captivated my interest like she has.

'You can fill it to the top with orange juice now,' she says.

I don't move. 'You'll drown if you drink this much alcohol before you get into the water,' I say softly.

'Oh! I guess I should have asked you to stop pouring earlier.'

'What's the matter, Snow?'

'Nothing's the matter.' She bites her lower lip. It is sweet, glossy, and plush. A whore's mouth in an angel's face. I picture her lips on my abdomen and going lower still. My cock hammers and heat churns in my balls. Fuck, my dick is begging me to throw her against the nearest wall.

'Is this what you have to do before you let Lenny touch you?'

Her eyes fly open, and she takes a step back from me as if I have struck her. 'You have no right. You know nothing. Do you hear me? Nothing!' she cries and then she begins to run.

My reflexes are fast, propelled by the hellfire of lust burning in my blood. I catch her easily and spin her around to face me. She gasps, sharp and sudden, and looks up at me with startled, wide eyes. Her robe is gaping open, and I can see the soft curve of her breasts as they rise and fall with her agitation. Hell! I want to fuck her senseless. I can feel myself pulsing.

'I'm sorry. I shouldn't have said that,' I apologize. My voice is tight with frustration.

'No, I'm sorry. It's my fault. I overreacted. I'm just nervous. You're the only friend I have. I don't want to fight with you.' Her voice is wobbly.

I let go of her forearms and flash her a good imitation of a grin. 'So, let's not fight then. How about a swim?' I say, and, turning away from her, dive cleanly into the pool. With slow strokes I swim away from her. I'd need to do fifty laps to burn off this sexual frustration.

When I reach the other end, I turn back to look at her, and she is sitting at the edge with her legs moving languidly back and forth in the water. In these surroundings she is like a fantasy figure, a figment of my imagination. I experience a strange sense of possession. The urge to mate with her is primal, strong and rabid. If I was an animal, my fur would be bristling, my tail out and wagging stiffly, and my ears erect.

The drive to mount a woman, possess her and claim her as mine is an unfamiliar one. Sure, I could write a whole fucking encyclopedia about the impulse to mount a woman, but to possess and claim her? I exhale the breath I am holding and, swimming back to her, grab her feet. They are small and soft.

She giggles. 'That's ticklish.'

'Are you coming in, Miss Dilshaw?'

She doesn't stand and take off her robe the way any other woman with a body as dazzling as hers would have. Instead, she slips it off her shoulders awkwardly while still sitting, and pushes it off her hips and thighs just before she slides into the water. I catch her in my arms.

Her body is narrow and slippery. She gazes up at me, her lips slightly parted, and her eyes so dilated they are almost black. And it's clear I'm not the only one who fucking wants it bad. She wants it too.

'You can let go of me now,' she whispers.

'Give me one good reason I should.'

'Because I want you to,' she says.

'Liar,' I counter softly. 'Here's what I think you want. I think you're aching for the taste of my cock.'

'Mighty sure of yourself, aren't you?' she scoffs, although bright red is crawling up her neck and into her cheeks.

'Shall we put it to a test?'

She looks alarmed. 'What do you mean?'

I move my head closer and she jerks back.

'What's the matter? Don't trust yourself to resist even a little kiss?' I taunt.

'I trust myself,' she says, and, holding her chin high, closes her eyes like a schoolgirl expecting her first kiss. This is unfamiliar territory! It's been a long, long time since any woman behaved in such a virginal way. If I wasn't bursting out of my trunks to get to her, I would have found it funny.

I pull her toward me, bend my head and touch my lips lightly to hers. Her reaction is explosive. She moans, her hands snake around my neck to twine in my hair, and she practically melts into me. The water laps around us as her mouth opens and her nipples are like little pebbles burning against my chest.

I kiss her full and hard, my tongue pushing into the warm softness of her mouth. And there is not a damn thing tentative about the way she sucks on my tongue. She looks like a little spring flower, but she kisses with the kind of wild, reckless passion that blows my mind. She does it with the kind of desperation of someone starving.

I wrap my hands around her waist and push her upwards. Water cascades down her beautiful body, as I lift her onto the edge of the pool and place her firmly on her butt. I haul myself out. Getting on my haunches, I untie her bikini top. It falls away easily.

'Shane,' she whispers, my name catching in her throat.

Her breasts are small and perfectly formed, the areolae, shy rose buds. She gazes up at me, her eyes enormous, the eyelashes wet, and her delicious mouth swollen and red. My lips brush the side of her neck and she leans her head to the side and offers me her throat. It is a call to mate as much as it is when a female wolf lifts her rear and exposes her vulva to tell her alpha that she is in heat. My tongue trails down the silky skin. I've done this a thousand times before, but this time my movements are jerky with urgency.

I lay her on the cool tiles and wrap my lips around her nipple. She groans and closes her eyes. My hand slides down her body and moves toward her bikini bottom. I hook my fingers into it and suddenly she starts struggling under me. I lift my head in surprise.

Her hands move to cover her breasts.

'I'm so sorry,' she says.

I feel a surge of searing temper. This is fucking bullshit. I'm too old to play these cocktease games. I grab her wrists and pull them apart and hold them high over her head so her breasts are exposed to me. She does nothing to stop me. Then I look deep into her frightened and excited eyes.

'Well, I'm fucking not,' I grate. I don't hide the feral hunger in my eyes as I let my gaze roam her whole body, lingering lustfully on her breast,

as if I own it all. And in my mind I do. She will be mine if it's the fucking last thing I do. 'I will have you, Snow Dilshaw. Fucking count on it. Not tonight, but you will be mine. And you know it too. You just like dragging things out. But you're wetter than you've ever been, aren't you?'

She says nothing, just stares up at me.

So, I slip my fingers in that last scrap of cloth between her and me, and brush my fingers between the soft lips. They are fucking soaking. I smile. I take my fingers out and suck them. Her eyes widen with surprise.

What is it about her? She is like no other woman I have been with. Even at a time like this, I can't be angry with her. All I want to do is wrap her in my arms and tell her it's going to be all right.

I stand and pull her to her feet. I pick up her discarded robe and tie it around her waist. And the strangest thing happens to me. I had a raging hard-on and yet at that moment I could have been belting little Liliana into her coat. I feel only a fierce sense of protectiveness toward her. Anybody touches her or tries to hurt a single hair on her head and I'll break their fucking backs.

The day will come when *I* will yank her hair and she won't be afraid of what comes next. She will just call my name, and tighten her muscles around my cock as I thrust it deep inside her. She's mine. She just doesn't know it yet.

'Come on, I'll show you to your room,' I say.

I need to put some space between us. I don't completely trust myself with her. I need to be level headed.

Because this one's a keeper.

Twelve

SNOW

I wake up, confused by the faded splendor of my surroundings. And then I remember where I am ... and what happened last night. And I touch my lips wonderingly. No one has ever kissed me like that. So dominant and possessive, as if he owned me. And I have never felt so alive, almost high. Like that time I was buzzing from drinking too much cough medicine. Heat and lust had pooled between my legs and I longed for him and yet I stopped him.

I think of Lenny saying, 'Before I'm finished with any man who touches you, he'll be wishing I had killed him.'

The thought makes me turn and bury my head in the soft, fragrant pillow, away from the wrongness of what I am doing. Sharp guilt slashes through me. It makes a bright new wound. I am betraying Lenny who has never been anything but kind to me when I was broken, and, to make matters worse, I am endangering Shane.

Lenny will have him for breakfast. Shane is a playboy; Lenny is a psychopath. Right now, just lying in this stupendous bed alone, I am cheating on Lenny and implicating Shane. Last night ... Oh God, if he knew.

Oh God.

Show some freaking spirit, Snow.

I sit up suddenly, with a new resolve. No, I won't betray one whole year of kindness for one stolen night of dark pleasure. In my own way I care about Lenny and I'll never forget what he did for me. I won't do this to Lenny. I will leave him in a good way. A way that I can be proud of. Without betraying him. Without anyone getting hurt.

I feel empowered by my new resolve. I won't have sex with Shane. I'm not some slut who can't control herself. Today, I will be very careful not to get into any kind of situations where we are both half naked again.

Today, I will be more guarded.

But the resolution makes me feel trapped. The future stretches bleak and pointless. Excruciating, actually. What about what I want? A wretched knot of nerves deep inside me shudders painfully. *Don't think about it now, Snow.*

I square my shoulders and, kicking away the fragrant sheets, leave the splendid room fit for an Oriental potentate. I wash in a fabulous green-veined marble bathroom. Water plinks from the polished gold taps onto the ancient stone.

There are glass jars of sweet-smelling salts and I drop in handfuls and watch them bubble and fizz. The air fills with their perfume. The longing for the unattainable feels only like a faint ache. I am used to that feeling. I brush my teeth as the bath fills. I undress and slip into the warm, silky water.

'Ahh ...'

I lean my head back and sigh. I don't allow myself to think of anything. When the water cools, I step out of the bath, dry myself on a soft lemon-scented towel, and pull on an apple green T-shirt and a pair of skinny jeans. I stop and look at myself in the gilded mirror. The color of my top makes my eyes look good.

I make the bed before closing my bedroom door and going downstairs.

As I walk down the grand steps, I try to imagine what it must be like to actually live here. There can be only one word to describe it: magnificent. I wonder who else lives in this vast property. Someone must be cleaning the house, the pool, the grounds. Whoever they are, they are doing an admirable job. There isn't a speck of dust to be seen anywhere.

As I get to the bottom of the stairs, an unsmiling woman appears in the archway leading to the other end of the house. She has salt and pepper hair that is neatly tied into a bun at the back of her head, and she is wearing a black dress and heavy shoes with gleaming buckles that I associate with Victorian times.

'Bonjour, mademoiselle,' she greets. Her voice is as somber as her attire, and her lips have barely moved.

I am pretty certain she is saying 'Good morning,' and that the reply should be 'Bonjour, madam,' but I'd be stuck after that. The extent of my French is 'Bonjour,' 'Bonne nuit' and 'Merci.' 'Sorry, I don't speak French,' I admit with an apologetic shrug and smile.

'Ah, oui. Monsieur Eden est à l'extérieur,' she says formally, and points in the direction of the pool.

'Oh, merci,' I say.

'Je vous en prie,' she replies, which I presume must be 'You're welcome' to my 'Thank you.'

I smile politely.

She nods again gravely, and retreats into the shadows behind the arch.

I walk out to the pool. In the daylight, it has lost its magical appeal. It seems newer and more nouveau riche, but it is stunningly beautiful all the same. I go beyond the submerged pillars and see

Shane working shirtless in the garden. His body is magnificent in the morning sun. I walk up to him.

I shade my eyes and call out, 'Good morning.'

He turns to look at me, and I find myself inhaling sharply. Damn, the man is edible.

'Mornin',' he says, and wipes the sweat from his brow with the back of his hand. He sticks the shovel he was using into the ground and takes a few steps toward me. I swallow hard. Dear me!

As he approaches, I see everything I did not see in the soft lighting of the pool. His chest is a mass of glistening, rippling muscles, and his shoulders are covered in beautiful tattoos. Sweat is running off his body in rivulets. My heart swells and I feel almost intoxicated, but I try to appear unaffected. He stops about a foot away from me and I can actually smell him, and he smells damn good. Wow! Who would have thought that sweat could smell so tantalizing? Oh, God. I can't believe I'm crushing on him like a schoolgirl.

'Um ... what are you doing?' I babble.

'I'm planting some rose bushes,' he says.

'Mmm ...' I say, my eyes sliding hurriedly away from his body and finding about five pots of rose bushes on the ground. And all my high and mighty resolutions crumble to dust. I want to feel his velvety skin on mine and to taste his tongue again.

'Don't you have a gardener?' I ask because my skin is sizzling and I can think of nothing else to say.

'I do, but I like working with the land,' he says.

'Oh, OK,' I say, my gaze following a drop of sweat as it travels down between his taut pectorals. *I could lick that off him.* The air between us buzzes with desire. *Mine.* The undeniable truth is: To hell with it all. I want this man with a burning need. I want to rest my chin on his hard chest and watch him sleep. And when I feel like it, I want to kiss him awake.

'Are you going to stand there all day staring at me?' he teases.

I flush all over. I am so distracted by his big, golden body, it is embarrassing. 'I'm sure I wouldn't be the first one,' I mutter, taking a step back.

'Give me ten minutes to finish up here.' He raises one glorious eyebrow. *God, how good-looking is this guy?* 'Want to have that swim or maybe walk around the garden before breakfast?'

'OK,' I say unsteadily, and am turning away when his hand catches my arm.

I look up into his face. His eyes are crinkled up against the sun and flame blue in his tanned face. 'You look beautiful this morning. I could stand here all morning staring at you,' he says softly.

I can't help it: the heat creeps up from my throat and up to my cheeks. Suddenly, the desire in my head is out in the open, in the darkening of his eyes, in the tightening of his jaw.

'Now, on your way, before I throw you on the ground and show the rabbits how it's done.'

I stumble away quickly. When I am halfway to the house, I turn around and see him standing where I had left him, just staring at me. After that, I don't turn around anymore.

Once past the house, I decide not to swim but to explore the gardens. An elderly man in faded clothes and a battered hat is trimming some bushes in the far corner of the property. He lifts his hand to me in a wave, and I return the greeting absent-mindedly. I guide my feet out beyond the garden, which is haphazardly crammed with all kinds of flowering plants.

There are butterflies and birds aplenty, but it is not the kind of properly manicured garden I would have expected for a house like this. Still, it has a charm all its own. The type of charm that sinking rusty old tram cars in the ocean produces after ten years. That's when it becomes a gloriously colorful reef and the home of hundreds of diverse schools of fish.

As I walk through the garden, I sense the true elegance of allowing nature to take its own course. It is like being in a lost, secret garden. In some places the weeds are taking over, but, even then, there is rich beauty to it. Bushes and creepers have been deliberately allowed to become overgrown to help bury the vulgarity of superfluous statues and stone arches. A sort of balancing of scales.

I like it, but it makes me wonder why someone would buy a stupendously beautiful, but totally nouveau riche chateau like Saumur and allow the grounds to go their own wild way like this.

A fat, ash-gray cat with yellow eyes comes and meows by my feet. I reach down and tickle her behind her ears. She rubs her head against my legs before wandering away to curl up on an old, sunlit bench.

As I venture farther, I realize that some of the property is thickly planted with bushes and low-hanging trees, but that a great part of it is pure meadow. Not far away I can see a wide expanse of water glistening in the sun. There is a Moroccan style tent by the edge of the water. Inside there is a bed with lots of jewel-bright red and green cushions.

For a while I sit at the edge of the water and look out at the glinting surface. It is serene and peaceful, but my mind is in turmoil. I have never wanted anybody the way I want Shane, but I am not a free agent ... yet. Lenny is still in the picture, and it would be wrong and ugly of me to betray him, and ... yet, I want Shane. The desire is so strong I don't think I will be able to resist it for much longer.

But, as I sit motionless and contemplate the silent beauty of the water, a profound transformation takes place in me. There are no mobile phones, no police sirens, no car horns, no emails, no birthdays to forget, no queues, no terrorists, no wars. All the stress, noise, fears and distractions that form part of my everyday life seem to belong to a different world.

The sun warms my skin and reflects off the water, and still beauty and peace in the air trigger ancient genes that humans must share with all the other creatures we have evolved with. My body relaxes, my pulse slows, my body feels charged, and I feel as if I have come home.

I hear my name being called and turn around to see Shane walking toward me. Freshly showered, he has changed into a clean T-shirt and blue jeans. His hair is still wet. With the sun behind him, I can't see the expression on his face.

I stand and brush my bottom with my hands. 'The lake is beautiful,' I say.

'Well, I like it.'

'Why have you allowed the place to go to seed like this?'

He looks down at me. 'I bought this place only because I heard of the sightings nearby of fireflies. And then I set about making the environment irresistible to them. They love moisture, tall grasses and low-hanging trees that they can hide in during the day, and an abundance of insects, slugs, and snails.'

'Will we see them tonight?'

'I'll be very disappointed if we don't. We'll come out after dinner. They're usually around about nine-ish.'

'You really love them, don't you?'

He grins. 'My madness is I have no time for things that have no soul.'

'Actually,' I admit, 'I like it wild and overgrown too.'

'Then you'll definitely like the owner of this place.'

'Is he the one who's built like a god?' I ask cheekily. Being cheeky with a man is something I would never have done before I met him. I'm the boring one. Never say boo to a cat.

'That's the one,' he says, and something in his eyes lights up.

I laugh, and in that moment I'm not the girl with the terrible past. I'm just a girl flirting with an irresistibly sexy man.

Thirteen

SNOW

We have breakfast at a rickety wooden table under the shade of a massive old oak tree. There are croissants, pastries, cold country butter, homemade jams, and slices of watermelon. An unsmiling Madam Chevalier pours thick, strong coffee into small cups for us. It is too bitter for me, but Shane has no trouble downing his. I decide to stick with orange juice. When she goes back into the house, I whisper to Shane, 'Is she in a bad mood?'

'Nope. She's always like that,' he says unconcernedly, and bites cleanly into a croissant.

'Really? Why?'

He shrugs. 'Fuck knows. Probably disapproves of what I'm doing to the grounds.'

I stare at him. 'And you don't mind?'

'Snow,' he explains patiently, 'this woman cooks using a recipe book that is one hundred years old. As far as I'm concerned, she can be as sour as she likes. Don't judge until you try her Soupe à l'Oignon Gratinée.'

I shake my head. 'I don't care how good a cook she is; I don't think I could ever live with disapproving staff.'

He grins roguishly. 'Here's something you might not yet have picked up: Madam secretly likes me.'

'Shane Eden, you are incorrigible.'

'I'll take that as a compliment,' he says with a low chuckle.

After breakfast, the elderly man I had seen pruning the bushes ambles toward us with a hearty smile plastered to his ruddy face. Shane introduces us, then tells me that Monsieur Chevalier is taking us to Cannes' indoor market. He is a much friendlier chap than his wife, and, because he doesn't speak a word of English and Shane's French seems to be pretty basic, he compensates with a lot of nodding and grinning. We get into his beat-up truck and he drives us to Forville Market.

It is a large red-brown building that oddly reminds me of the Red Fort in Delhi. Inside, it is vast and cool. Vibrant with shoppers and a seemingly inexhaustible array of produce, it is a treat for the senses. There are stalls dedicated just to mushrooms! All kinds, shapes, colors, and scents. Other stalls specialize in dried meats, fruit, flowers, vegetables, cheese, wine, olives, pastries, bread, spices, honey. And everything looks so fresh and clearly locally produced. It is the opposite of the sterile environment of the supermarket where everything is sanitized, homogenized, and sold under a plastic covering.

Shane buys the ingredients for our dinner: a rack of lamb, baguette sticks, onions, vegetables, pineapple. The sellers all seem to know and like him. One asks about the fireflies and says he wants to bring his son to see them during the week. He tells Shane mournfully that the fireflies have stopped coming to his land. He blames the pesticides.

When we get outside, Monsieur Chevalier packs everything into the back of his truck. The plan is for him to drop us off at Le Suquet, a quirky, hilly town overlooking a harbor, before setting off to Saumur to deposit the market produce with his wife.

Le Suquet is the old part of the city so it is full of quaint, narrow streets full of old-fashioned shops. It is charming, and I fall in love with it, but it is here that I notice that women simply can't stop staring at Shane. Everywhere we go, he gets ogled at. And I mean really ogled at. When we stop at a little café with tables spilling out into the sideway and order pissaladière, a beautifully simple and delicious pizza with onion, olives, and anchovies, the waitress actually totally ignores me, and flirts outrageously with Shane.

'Are you a model?' she asks him in English.

He says something to her in French, which makes her glance at me, shrug, and start taking the order.

'Well,' I say when she walks away, 'she certainly thinks you're God's gift.'

He crosses his arms. 'Says the woman who's got most of the population of Le Suquet staring at her like zombies with working dicks.'

I snort. 'Zombies with working dicks? Excuse me? There were girls walking backwards after they passed us just to keep admiring the other side of you.'

'Well, darling, while you were looking at the women walking backwards, I've had to endure the painful sight of men blatantly stripping you with their fucking eyes.'

I lean back. 'You're serious?'

'Damn right I am. It's fucking annoying.'

My eyes widen. Can it really be that Shane Eden is jealous? The thought is like a bolt of lightning in my heart. 'Are you jealous?' I ask incredulously.

'Yes,' he admits gloomily.

'I love it when you look all brooding and moody. It's kinda sexy.'

He perks up. 'Did I just hear you describe me as sexy?'

'Yeah, I think I might have.'

'Well, that's what's called progress.' His voice is warm and full of laughter.

'By the way, what did you tell the waitress just now that made her look at me?' I say casually, taking a sip of my perfectly chilled rosé.

'I told her I was gay but that she was welcome to you.'

I almost choke on my drink. 'What?' I burst out.

He laughs.

'You don't care if people think you're gay?'

'Nope. It's extremely useful in certain circumstances.'

'Couldn't you have just told her you weren't interested?'

'Girls like her don't give up easy; she'd have been slipping her phone number into my hand as we left. And that would have just made you get all jealous and pissed off.'

'I'm not jealous,' I deny.

'Oh, you're jealous all right, Elizabeth Snow Dilshaw. You're the kind of woman who would try to make a man wear a chastity belt.'

His statement surprises me. He hardly knows me. 'What makes you say that?' I ask curiously.

His eyes are like mirrors, giving nothing away. 'Experience,' he says cryptically.

'Well, you're wrong. I have never been jealous in my life. Not with Lenny, and certainly not with you. In fact, I found it amusing that all those women were looking at you.'

'That's really great to know, because they don't make chastity belts in my size.' He grins. 'Too large.'

'I wouldn't have cared if the waitress had slipped you her number,' I say.

There is mischief in his face as he reaches out, grasps my wrist, and strokes it with what seems to be a seductive promise. It is intimate, delicious, and wonderful. Pleasure ripples over my skin, sizzles into my muscles, and instantly I feel strong desire swirl inside me like dead leaves picked up by the wind and helplessly drawn into another's world.

The expression in Shane's eyes changes, becomes so lust-drenched that I am undone by the look. I lick my lips. And we find ourselves lost in our own world. We stare at each other hungrily. Desire shimmering between us like some invisible magic. My blood heats up and I feel wetness pooling between my legs. God, it never crossed my mind that I could be so sexually aroused while sitting in a restaurant just looking at a man.

The waitress comes with the food, and, standing over us, clears her throat loudly.

I snatch my hand away. She plonks the pizza in the middle of the table, slaps a small plate in front of each of us, and stalks off.

I giggle at Shane.

'I told you what she's like,' he says.

We both laugh.

The pizza is beautifully simple and delicious. Once Shane has paid our bill, we walk out and start walking uphill. It is hot, and the hill is steep, but we get to the top. We stand outside the majestic old church, Notre-Dame d'Espérance, and look down at the stunning view over the bay.

'Want to go into the church?' Shane asks.

'OK.'

We pass through the old doors, and inside it feels like we have entered a different world. Even the air is cold enough to make me shiver. The stone walls give the impression of damp chill, and the air is hushed and still. Our footsteps echo. Afternoon sunlight falls dustily from high stained-glass windows into the dim interior and lays in milky shapes of color on the floor. It is deserted except for a woman with a black shawl on her head, bowed in prayer in one of the front pews.

She does not turn to look at us. I look at the vast, high-ceilinged space in awe.

'Vellichor much?' Shane whispers next to me.

I glance up at him. 'No, I love it. This is far better than any used bookshop.'

He looks at me strangely. 'Are you messing with me?'

'No, I'm serious. Ever since this place was built, people have been coming here bringing all their pain, sadness, hopes, gratitude, and joy. The stones have absorbed it. Hundreds of years of human emotion. Can you not feel it?'

He stands very still for a few moments, then looks down at me. 'Nope.'

'Shame,' I whisper, and move forward.

He follows me. 'Have you never been to a church before?'

'No. My mother is a non-practicing Christian so she never took us to church. However, I begged and harassed my nanny until she gave in and took me to the temple with her in secret.'

'How old were you then?'

'My first trip was when I was five.'

'Are you a Hindu then?'

'No. As a child I didn't go to the temple to pray. I just loved my nanny so much, I couldn't bear to be parted from her for any length of time.

Plus, I enjoyed the trip because it was colorful and the priest allowed me to ring the bell.'

We find ourselves at a side altar with burning candles, and Shane turns to me. 'Do you want to light a candle?'

'What does it signify?'

'It's a symbol of your prayer that carries on burning even after you are gone.'

I remember Chitra lighting oil lamps and asking her why she was lighting them, and I still recall her answer. Sweet Chitra. I miss her so. *It is a way of asking for something from God. The fire lifts your prayer up to God,'* she said.

I look up at Shane. 'Yes, I'd like to leave a prayer here.'

He drops a note into the donation box slot and takes two candles out. He passes one to me, and we stand side by side and light our candles solemnly. I watch Shane place his in its holder, and I close my eyes and pray. I pray like I've never prayed. I pray to any god, Hindu or Christian, who will listen. I ask the stones to absorb my prayer and keep it safe after I am gone and even when the candle burns out. I pray for a bright, silent intercession from the heavens that my actions harm neither Lenny nor Shane.

I open my eyes and see another candle about to sputter out. It seems to grasp desperately for its last breaths of life. I cannot watch it die. I look up

123

at Shane. He is watching me avidly. 'Can we buy another candle?'

His eyebrows rise, but he puts another note into the box and takes another candle out and gives it to me. I light the candle using the fire of the prayer that is about to sputter out, and plant it next to it. I watch the new flame take over and then I turn to Shane and smile. 'Shall we go?'

We go out into the afternoon air. It is warm and full of the smell of the sea.

'Feel like an ice cream?' he asks.

'Lead the way, sir.'

'Step this way, madam, for the best ice cream ever,' he says when we reach a sweet little shop with a green and yellow signboard and cast iron metal tables and chairs outside. There is a bell at the door that chimes prettily when we enter the shop. It is obviously a mom and pop business. The ice cream counter curves around the entire shop in the shape of a U. A man with a walrus mustache is standing behind it. He knows Shane, and talks to him in French.

'You can have as many flavors as you want in a cone,' Shane tells me.

There are so many unusual flavors it is difficult to choose, but in the end I decide on four different types of chocolate: Ecuadorean dark chocolate, Mexican chocolate with cinnamon, Rocky Road, and white chocolate with ginger.

Shane has salted Turkish pistachio, grape nut and black raspberry. Shane pays for our ice creams, the man gives us napkins, and we carry our treasures out into the sunshine to sit at one of the tables outside. I carefully lick the white chocolate ginger bit first. It is delicious.

'Good?' he asks.

'Very,' I say looking up at him through my lashes.

'Are you flirting with me, little rabbit?' he asks, his lips covered in ice cream.

I remember how they felt and tasted last night, and feel a rush of something through my body—what, I do not know, but it is exciting. I like that about him. The way he makes me feel so alive. 'Maybe,' I say boldly.

His grin is wolfish, his eyes full of light. 'Works every time,' he says.

'What?'

He takes a lick of his ice cream. 'Feed a girl ice cream and she gets an appetite for love.'

'I said maybe,' I remind pointedly.

He chuckles and looks at me with lazy eyes, his whole body relaxed. 'Maybe, definitely, what's the difference?'

The sun is warm on my skin, I am with the most dazzling man on earth, and suddenly I feel bold. I lean forward and lick his ice cream. 'This is maybe,' I say softly. Then I stretch forward and, going close to his face, lick his lips. 'And this is definitely.' I lean back and try to look nonchalant. 'See the difference now?'

Something flashes in his eyes. Suddenly he doesn't seem so tame and friendly anymore. It's like waking a sleeping tiger; I can't tear my eyes away from him.

He smiles slowly, invitingly. 'I'm a bit of a slow learner. Would you mind if I run through that again?' he asks.

My heart begins to race. I can't believe I started this. What on earth was I thinking of? And yet, I can't back off now. 'No,' I say huskily.

'So this, then, is maybe,' he says, and, bending down, kisses me, his lips gentle, but persuasive and insistent.

I try to keep my head, I really do, but, by God, the blood is drumming in my ears and all kinds of winged insects are fluttering in my stomach. The man can really kiss! He lifts his head. I gape at him stupidly. His eyes are heavy-lidded.

'Now, let's try definitely.'

He takes my lips again, but this time his mouth is more sensuous, more—far more seductive, urging mine to open. His tongue slips in. Waves of dangerous pleasure sweep through my body and stir my blood awake. I begin to respond to him. *Oh God!* I think dazedly, my whole body feeling like it is blazing with need. I want him inside me!

He ends the kiss, and I feel his face move away from me.

'I think I got the difference now,' he drawls, his eyes languorous.

His hand reaches out and straightens mine so my ice cream cone is no longer tilted at an almost horizontal angle. I look at my hand as if it is separate from me. There is a puddle of melted ice cream on the sidewalk. I turn back to face him. His face is deliberately neutral. He stretches like a sun-warmed cat.

'We should be getting back,' he says, and stands.

We walk down the hill in a kind of pregnant, expectant silence. Neither acknowledges it, but both of us know. This is just the beginning. There is no denying this thing burning between us.

Monsieur Chevalier is leaning against an old wall, smoking a cigarette and waiting for us. He drives us back to Saumur in good spirits. The men talk in their own way with hand gestures and half-understood French, and I hang my head out of the car and breathe in the scent of France.

Who knows if I will ever come back here again?

Fourteen

SNOW

We agree to meet in the great Salon at seven. I have an hour to soak in the bath and dress. I get into a two-piece dark grey cocktail dress. It has a high scoop neckline with cut-in shoulders. The crop top is encrusted with floral beading with a keyhole opening at the back and a scalloped trim along the midriff. The short flaring skirt is layered with organza fabric and stops just below the knee. I slip into beaded high heels and pull my hair into a knot at the nape of my neck. I line my eyes, brush the mascara wand a couple of times over my eyelashes and color my lips a deep red.

The effect is sophisticated and sleek.

Feeling nervous and excited I go down to the salon. Shane is already there. He must have heard my footsteps on the marble floors because he is standing by the window, a glass of some amber liquid in his hand, looking at the entrance. I stand at the doorway for a second. Both of us drink in the sight of the other. This is the first time I have seen him dress up and he is, well, there is no other way to describe it, breathtakingly, extraordinarily handsome.

'Will you walk into my parlor, said the Spider to the Fly,' he says.

'Oh no, no, said the little Fly, 'for I've often heard it said, they never, never wake again, who sleep upon your bed!'

He walks up to me. 'I promise I'll eat you and you'll live to see the day,' he murmurs, his breath whispering into me.

I find myself blushing. He touches my cheek and my throat feels suddenly parched.

'What will you have to drink, pretty little fly? Vodka and Orange?'

'No,' I say. 'I'll have a glass of wine.'

'We're having a Beaujolais with our starter. Want a glass of that? Or would you prefer champagne?'

'The Beaujolais sounds lovely.'

'Make yourself comfortable,' he says and disappears out of the room. I walk to the window he had been standing at and look out. It faces the side I have not explored. An open meadow borders a forest. I wonder if that is where the wild boars live.

I hear him come up to me and I turn around to face him. He holds out my drink.

'Thank you,' I say softly.

He lifts his glass. 'Here's to the fireflies.'

I lift mine. 'The fireflies,' I repeat, looking into his eyes and knowing that we are not drinking to the fireflies.

First course is Madam's famous Soupe à l'Oignon Gratinée made to a century's old recipe. As the dish with a thick golden crust is put in front of me, Shane explains the laborious technique that Madam used to make it.

'Baguette toasts, half an inch thick, are spread with butter and layered with grated Emmental cheese, sautéed yellow onions, and tomato purée. Over this construct she gently pours salted water. The dish is then simmered for thirty minutes and baked uncovered for an hour at 350 degrees.'

'No wonder it looks almost like a cake,' I say.

'Bon appétit,' he says.

'Bon appétit,' I reply and dip my spoon into it. The inside is so thick and thoroughly amalgamated it is impossible to discern the cheese from the onion or the bread. I put it into my mouth and catch Shane looking at me.

He raises his eyebrows and waits for my verdict.

I exhale and widen my eyes. 'It's to die for.'

He grins, happy, wholesome, irresistible. 'That's exactly what I think.'

When the soup bowls are cleared away, Madam serves pineapple tartare, finely diced raw pineapple mixed with salt and a hint of chili. It is the perfect palate cleanser after the richness of the starter.

Outside it gets dark and Madam lights candles. I notice that no lights have been turned on anywhere in the house.

'Is there no electricity this evening?' I ask.

'Lights affect the fireflies. It interferes with their mating process so we keep it to a minimum during this season.'

In the flickering candlelight the dressed up Shane seems like the perfect host, sophisticated, charming, and urbane. A beast that can only be admired from afar. I almost wish for the Shane in the T-shirt and jeans that was just good fun.

A spruced up Monsieur Chauband wheels in the main course. 'Gigot d'Agneau Pleureur,' he announces proudly.

'It translates as a crying lamb gigot because the meat is cooked in an oven, slowly, on a grill, with sebago potatoes and vegetables placed on a rack underneath it. The meat's juices, the tears, fall on the vegetables and cook them,' Shane explains.

I bite into a piece of meat and it is tender and succulent.

'Tell me about your father. You never talk about him,' Shane invites as he pours red wine into fresh glasses from a bottle of Merlot that Monsieur brought in.

I pick up my glass and take a sip. The wine is robust and fragrant. 'I told you a lot about my family and my childhood, but you told me nothing about your family or your childhood. What was it like being from two different types of gypsies?'

He spears a capsicum on his fork. 'I actually know very little about my Romany heritage. My mother doesn't speak much about her family. All I know is when she fell in love with my father, she had to elope because my grandfather was so furious with her. Not only had she chosen someone outside the clan, but she had chosen a well known gambler. On the day she got married he disowned her. She could never again go to see her family. Even when her sister died a few years ago her family were forbidden to tell her.' A shadow of sadness crosses his face. 'I know my mother misses her family very much, but there is nothing anyone can do while he is still alive.'

'That's so vindictive. Didn't you say your father has already passed away?'

'My father was murdered, Snow.'

My eyes widen in shock. 'Your father was murdered? How horrible!'

His face tightens with an old anger that cannot be forgotten. 'Yes, he made the stupid mistake of stealing from his boss. Unfortunately he was not just any boss, but a mean gangster. So Jake, being the oldest, was forced to go and work for the man who slit our father's throat from ear to ear, and pay off the debt.'

'Oh my God,' I gasp.

'Yes, it was a very traumatic time for us, our family fell apart after my father's death. For a very long time Jake was lost to us. He put food on the table and paid all our bills, but everyday he became colder and more unreachable. I think he hated himself and what he was being forced to do. My poor mother used to cry at night when she thought no one could hear, and my brother Dom became an angry rebellious stranger. Only my sister Layla, because she was so young, remained mostly unaffected by our tragedy.

He pauses and takes a sip of wine.

'Then one day for no reason, Dom turned over a new leaf and that made my mother a bit happier, but things really turned for the better when Jake was nineteen. That was when he fought back and took over the organization. Once he had done that he streamlined everything, moved away from all the illegal aspects of the business, and concentrated all his attention on gambling dens and strip clubs. He started to make a lot of money, and I mean really a lot.' He pauses and smiles, a clean, gorgeous, heart-throbbing smile. 'That's when he got both Dom and me in to act.'

'So you got into strip clubs and gambling dens too?'

'Not gambling dens. Not even Jake does that anymore. Our family invests mostly in property and aspects of the entertainment sector: restaurants, gentlemen's clubs, and normal clubs.'

'Hmmm ... so you must meet a lot of beautiful girls.'

'Yes, I do,' he says with a cheeky grin. 'But when you own a candy store you don't actually eat all the sweets in it.'

'This reminds me of a joke,' I say so lightly, it trips off my tongue.

'Yeah?'

'A woman treats her husband to a strip club on his birthday. At the club the doorman says, "Hey, Jim. How are you?" The wife looks at Jim and asks, "How does he know you?" "I play football with him," he tells her. Inside the bartender asks, "The usual, Jim?" Jim turns to his wife, "Before you say anything, dear, he's on the darts team." Next a stripper comes up to them and touching herself sexily says, "Hi, Jim. Do you want your special again?" In a fit of rage the wife storms out dragging Jim with her and jumps into a taxi. And the taxi driver says, "What's up with you, Jimmy Boy? You picked up an ugly one this time." Jim's wife gave him a very nice funeral though.

Shane throws his head back and laughs and I do too, a little, but when the laughter dies down, he looks at me teasingly. 'You won't have to give a nice funeral, Snow.'

'Don't worry, I'm not holding it against you, but I could tell the moment I laid eyes on you that you're a playboy.'

He fixes his gaze on me. 'I'm not going to pretend I'm some saint. I'm a man and I have needs, and sure, there are always women willing to satisfy them, but I happen to want you.'

'So that's what I've become. Part of the horde of women always willing to satisfy your needs.'

He stares at me curiously. 'Don't you think we'd be real good together?'

'I have not thought about it,' I lie.

'I think we'd be earth-shatteringly good together,' he says softly.

My heart thumps in my chest.

'You know you want me too.'

I open my mouth to protest and he raises his hand. 'There's no reason to be ashamed of your body's urges, Snow. When you're ninety you're never going to think oh hell, I wish I hadn't slept with that Shane guy. You're going to regret every opportunity you didn't take.'

'So sex with you has become an opportunity, has it?' I scoff.

'Don't knock it until you try it, sweetheart.'

'Just because you're handsome—'

'First I'm sexy, now I'm handsome too ...' he says, a playful glint in his eye.

'In an obvious playboy sort of way, of course,' I say.

'Of course. What other way is there?' he drawls.

Before I can respond, Madam Chaumbond appears at the door, her demeanor, formal. 'Etait-il bon?' she asks, her voice carrying over the vast space.

Shane turns to me. 'Madam would like to know if you enjoyed your food.'

'It was incredible,' I say sincerely.

He turns to her and translates.

And in the small smile of satisfaction that she permits herself, I realize that Shane is right. She does have a soft spot for him. It was there all along in the big portions, the care with which she served him, the details she lavished on the food.

'Bon,' she says with a dignified nod, and withdraws, her black clothes swallowed by the shadows that have lengthened around and inside Saumur.

Shane picks up his wine glass and turns to me, his eyes glittering. 'Are you ready to go into the forest with the big, bad wolf, Snow?'

'You've got your fairy tales mixed up, but yeah, I'm ready.'

Fifteen

SNOW

The air is fragrant with the smell of flowers.

Carrying torchlights we set off for the dark forest. It feels cooler under the canopy of leaves.

'It will rain later tonight,' Shane says.

'How do you know?'

He glances at me. 'The weather forecast.'

'Right,' I say embarrassed. I got caught up in the idea that we were in a magical place far away from civilization. Besides, there are, after all, people who can tell it is going to rain by the 'feel' of the air or by looking at animal behavior or observing the sky.

We take a path that is so narrow it will only accept one person at a time. I follow Shane's broad back until we come upon a clearing with a spooky log cabin. It's exactly how I had imagined the witch's hut that Hansel and Gretel found in the forest would look.

Shane opens the wooden door and we are standing in a rectangular room roughly about fourteen feet by ten with a wooden board floor. The planks make a creaking sound as Shane walks on them. A large blackened stone fireplace is set into the back wall. A fire is lit, but it is low with bits of charred wood and plenty of ashes.

'What's up with that?' I ask shining my torch towards a huge black cauldron hanging to one side of the fireplace.

He grins. 'Authenticity. You can't have a witches hut and no cauldron.'

'Right,' I say with a smile and shine my torch all around the room. There is a single bed with a blue and yellow bedspread at one end, and a small wooden table and four chairs in the middle. The wooden shelves have stuff on them, an axe, nets, knives, tin boxes, bowls, worn books, mortar and pestle, wooden spikes, dark gunny sacks. I guess they are a hunter's utensils.

Shane opens a box of candles and lights some. There are windows, but their shutters are closed. Strands of mushrooms are drying from a string hung across the firewood. There is the smell of earth and burning wood. In another corner there are bunches of herbs hanging from the ceiling. There is a large rocking chair next to the fireplace. It has an old cushion on it.

'Monsieur Chevalier uses this cabin a lot during the truffle hunting season,' he explains with a smile. 'I think it gives him a break from Madam.'

I chuckle quietly.

He takes a brown bottle from a shelf and hands it to me. 'Mosquito repellent made of herbs.'

I rub it on my hands and legs and it smells pleasantly of lavender.

He snatches a couple of blankets and a basket and we set off again. We reach another clearing where there is a round flat surface with a green plastic covering. Shane flicks the covering off it and reveals a round bench with a flat round mattress and lots of cushions on it.

'Go on. Climb aboard,' he urges.

I get on the mattress and lie back. The sky is alive with stars. He switches off the torches and lies next to me. I can hear sounds in the forest, foraging animals, insects, and I can hear him breathing next to me. My whole body tingles with hyper awareness. He turns his head and looks at me. His eyes are gleaming in the dark. I inhale suddenly.

We're going to have sex in the forest.

And then it happens. A tiny light comes on close to my head. Startled, I gasp and jerk my head around. Why, it is a firefly. The little creature flashes and then goes dark. And then flashes again. Magical.

'Look Shane,' I whisper in wonder.

'Look, mate. This one's taken, go flash elsewhere,' he tells the firefly.

I laugh, a laugh of sheer joy and enchantment and reach up with my cupped hands.

It darts away.

'Oh,' I say disappointed, but I realize that others are dancing into view. They glow and flicker in trees and in the air, and slowly they light up the whole forest like a Christmas tree giving enough light that I can make out Shane's features. Between the blades of the tall grasses and dandelions, hundreds of lights twinkle as if all the stars in the sky have fallen to earth.

'It's the most beautiful thing I've seen. I'll never forget this night as long as I live,' I whisper in an awed voice. 'Thank you, for bringing me here.'

'The show's not over yet, honey. I've still got a bit of flashing to do myself,' he says lazily.

The words die in my throat when I see his shadowy face loom over me before warm soft lips are kissing me.

SHANE

We Irish believe in faeries. The Irish fairy is not like Peter Pan's Tinker Bell. An Irish fairy can take any form she wishes, but prefers the human form. Our elders claim that they are beautiful, powerful and impossible to resist, which really, is a crying shame, because most Irish faeries love to bring misfortune and bad luck to the mortals who come near them. At that moment in the glow of the fireflies, Snow looked like an Irish fairy.

Beautiful, powerful and impossible to resist.

And I don't resist. The air is laden with sexual longing, I have a raging hard on, and her white skin and luscious black hair are spread out before me like an irresistible siren's call. Come misfortune, treacherous rocks, and bad luck. I'll deal with you later. Her mouth is warm and sweet, scented with honeyed apricots she ate earlier. Her top has a metal hook, a hole and four little buttons at the back. All in a row. Piece of cake to undo.

I pull her towards me so she is lying on her side and unbutton them. I slide my hand in and stroke her silky back.

SNOW

The fireflies are still twinkling and shining around us, but I cannot look at their magic. I can only look at the beauty of Shane's face. My blouse whispers as he tugs it off.

I smell him, his cologne, his sweat, his desire. It is all male. I can't help but look at his cock. It is so massive, so thick, and the tip is already dripping.

'My God! You are so big,' I whisper.

'Yeah, and it's all going into you. Every last fucking inch.'

Between my thighs I am wet and aching for the feel of his hard cock deep inside me.

In a daze I reach out a hand and curl it around the thick shaft and I open my mouth. Because it's him. Because I want that liquid that's dripping from the tip. He puts his hands on my shoulders and I wrap my mouth around the shaft and slide down the smooth shaft. His hands are strong and aggressive. Nothing like Lenny.

He strips me quickly until I am buck naked. He pulls back and looks at me with hunger in his eyes. His fingertips slide over my body, possessively. It feels good. I want him to know that it feels good so I moan.

He stops. 'I'm nearly ready to explode, but first I will take care of you,' he says assertively.

He slips his hand down my hips and opens my legs, but my body knows what it wants. I lift my hips and offer my wet pussy to him.

He sinks a thick finger into me. I gasp with pleasure.

'You're so swollen and wet,' he says, his eyes dark with desire.

The smell of my own desire floods my senses making me flush with excitement.

His huge cock pushes against me before slowly, inexorably pushing in. For a moment it hurts so much it feels as if I am tearing apart and I claw at his shoulder. But this pain is different from any other kind of pain I've endured. It's a ... good pain.

'You're too tight. The pain will pass,' he tells me. His face is rough with a mixture of lust and concern.'

'I know,' I gasp.

'Want me to stop?'

'No,' I growl. I want him inside. My body is not too tight to take him. I grasp his firm buttocks and pull him hard towards me. His cock breaks me open. The shock of the pain steals my breath and makes me freeze as he slides in.

He goes so deep I can't catch my next breath. He pulls back and thrusts in. Again. And again. I groan. His large hands grip my hips and of their own accord they move back and forth. Shane's mastery and technique is evident in every move and touch and soon I start to relish the pounding my pussy is taking and the pain has transformed into warmth and pleasure. Pure, real pleasure. My eyes widen with surprise. I never thought sex could be like this.

'Oh Shane,' I beg. 'Don't stop.'

He answers by grabbing both my wrists and putting them high above my head. He looks down at my breasts with hunger. I feel them bounce and jiggle as he continues to thrust into me. I feel helpless. He controls everything. I am his to do whatever the hell he wants to do to me.

Then he is swooping down and taking my nipple in his mouth. Lenny has taken my nipples in his mouth more times than I can remember, but it never ever felt like this. My body arches with pleasure. His tongue flicks the tips. All the while he is thrusting deep into me.

And then it comes. The promise that began from the moment Shane held my wrist when we first met.

The orgasm.

The thing I have never experienced. And it blows my mind. I cry out his name. I am so shocked by the experience I don't even realize that he had been holding on for me, and as soon as he

sees me climax, he pumps me so hard the platform bed we are lying on starts to shake with every hard slam.

He doesn't scream like Lenny when he climaxes, he roars and carries on thrusting through it until that last thrust when he holds himself, throbbing and pulsating deep inside me. Breathing hard he looks down on me. I lie limp under him, my thighs trembling and my toes curled.

I am his.

I feel sore and tender, but I don't want him to pull out of me. I want more. I want a repeat. I want another climax. It felt so good.

'I want more,' I whisper, without any shame whatsoever.

His eyes flare. 'You can't handle more, Snow,' he mutters.

'I can,' I insist.

He kisses my forehead and tries to pull out of me, but I grab his buttocks. 'Don't,' I plead.

He smiles. 'Aww, sweet Snow. Don't fret, I'll give you a different kind of more,' he teases gently.

He pulls out of me, removes the condom, while I lay with my legs open and wait. He comes back and puts his head between my thighs and begins to suck my clit. The shock of his hot mouth between my legs is like an electric bolt.

I start to crest again and dig my heel into the bed, my muscles stretching, my neck arching uncontrollably.

Sixteen

SNOW

'You want me again?'

I wake up and look straight into Shane's sleeping face. Curiously, I watch him slumbering He looks so young. One could fall in love with a face like this. Last night is like a dream. I remember it in a daze. My head swims to think of how wanton I have been. Me saying, 'You want me again?

Three times, I asked him that. That makes a total of six times.

A secret smile is curved on my mouth when his long, sooty lashes lift. We stare at each other, the smile dying on my lips. Passion flames deep inside me. His gaze moves from my eyes to the curve of my cheeks and lingers on my mouth, now provocatively parted. An invitation.

Breathlessly I watch fire leap into the blue depths.

He rolls his body over mine. Resting on his elbows his mouth comes down on my own I wind my arms around his neck and pull him even closer. His fingers rake through my hair, forcing back my head. My mouth opens in hungry response as our lips touch. The kiss seems endless. As if neither of us can satisfy our need for each other. I feel my body sizzle with need.

He lays on his side, tugs the sheet off me, and lets his eyes rove down my body. Trembling and impatient I slowly open my legs. Another invitation.

'Fuck, Snow. You intoxicate me,' he says hoarsely.

My mouth is dry with heady excitement. 'Do I?' I whisper throatily.

'I took one look at you and all I wanted to do was possess you. It didn't even matter that you were with Lenny. I couldn't walk away and leave you. I just had to have you. Any risk was worth it.'

'You've got me now.'

'Yeah, I've got you.'

I watch dreamily as his head moves down my body trailing a velvety hot tongue on my skin, fluttery, half formed kisses, or whispers, hard to say what they are really. My body lifts off the bed to meet those whispery, whiskery things. But it all changes when he buries his mouth in my throbbing pussy.

He devours me as if he is starving.

Squirming with intolerable pleasure, I reach for the edges of my pillow on either side of me and grab them tightly. His tongue runs down my slit all the way underneath me until I feel the tip touch my anus. I freeze with shock. No one has ever put his tongue there before. I have a sudden lightning thought – Oh God! If my mother knew she'd be horrified.

And suddenly a flash. I remember the tearing, piercing pain. No, not again. The thought is terrifying and my legs struggle to close, to stop him, but he forcefully keeps them open with his powerful hands. I raise my head and shoulders in a panic.

He lifts his head and looks at me.

'I got to have all of you, Snow. Every last inch. I'll lick what I want and fuck what I want.' His voice is calm. His expression is as unshakable as a granite hill.

I open my mouth and nothing comes out.

'I won't hurt you,' he says quietly.

Instantly all the fear falls away from me like an unwanted coat and a strange excitement shivers up my spine. I don't want him to stop. I like the idea of being totally at his mercy and submitting to his power.

He pushes my thighs closer to my body so that he has total access to everything, and he returns to his task of claiming every last inch of me. Holding my cheeks firmly open, he presses his tongue against the ring of muscles. I groan, half with embarrassment, half with electric pleasure. He pushes again.

As his tongue pushes in, his finger enters my wet sex. I writhe with pleasure. Very gently he withdraws the finger and pushes that slick, honey coated finger into my ass. He raises his head and looks into my wide eyes.

'Do you trust me?'

I nod.

'I'm going to fill your sweet little asshole with my cock.'

Another lifetime ago I would have protested. Would have said, 'Never.' But not now. Now I want it. I *need* it. I nod again.

He smiles and reaches for a bottle of pure pomegranate oil sitting on the bedside cabinet that he told me he used for sunburn. He unscrews the top, flips it to the surface of the cabinet and, holding it over my exposed pussy, tips the bottle. A thin red stream of oil hits me and he uses his other hand to smear it all over the quivering flesh of my sex.

The movement is sensuous and slow, like a massage, as if he is anointing my sex. It reminds me of the dedication with which the priests bathed their deities. With reverence. As if what lies between my legs is precious beyond compare.

He dips a different finger, his middle finger, into my pussy and uses that to insert into my oily anus. One by one he uses all his fingers until that entire region feels like a hot mess of saliva, my own juices, and oil.

I sigh with the incredible sensations.

He introduces his thumb. It is thicker, but I am so relaxed and so open to anything he wants to do to me, it slips in easily. He drives his thumb in and out of me. My neck arches. I am ready.

He gets on his knees and I see his cock, massive, twitching and throbbing, wanting in. I feel no fear. The lower half of me is like an uncovered bowl. Exposed and waiting to be filled. He reaches for a condom, rolls it onto himself, grabs me under my thighs and with one swift thrust slams deep into my dripping pussy.

I shudder with pleasure as my muscles clench around him like a closing fist. My blood rages through me. He pulls out and fills me again and again. Plowing in so deep I cry out with each thrust. When I think I am about to break apart he pulls out of me and rests the tip of his cock against the tight muscles that he has worked so long to loosen.

He locks eyes with me.

The head of his cock presses hard against the ring of oily muscles and slowly, slowly he starts to enter me. His thumb had been pleasure but this,

this was sheer pain. I wince and grip the pillow. 'You're too big,' I groan.

'Breathe deeply and relax your muscles. Do what your body doesn't want you to do,' he instructs.

I frown.

'It's telling you to push out. Pull me in.'

I take a deep breath and will myself to relax, my quivering, tense legs becoming limp.

When I exhale he senses the give in my body and seizes the opportunity to gain another inch into me.

I cry out at the knife-like pain of the intrusion, and he stops and waits for my body to adjust to his girth. I take another deep breath and as I exhale again, the massive shaft lodged inside me takes another inch of me.

Every time I exhale and he feels my muscles relax, he takes that lull to force his way in again. I gasp with the sensation, but he just keeps going, deeper and deeper into my body until his balls are touching my skin. His cock is firmly wedged all the way inside my bowels.

Then he stops and smiles. The slow smile of a conqueror. He's got what he wanted.

There are tears in my eyes, but it doesn't hurt anymore. Just feels tight and stretched. I close my eyes.

And he begins to thrust his cock in and out of my ass. Part of me hates the sensation and another part of me wants more. But the more he rams in and out, the more the strange, dark pleasure takes over my body.

'Harder,' I hear myself cry. 'Fuck me harder.'

He pumps faster and I feel as if I am drowning in sensations. My skin feels alive. Another part of my brain is shocked at my own salaciousness. My whole body is alive with nerves that I never knew existed. I even feel his cock pulsing inside me.

Staring at him boldly, I clench my muscles with all my might and he groans. It is a powerful feeling that I can affect him this deeply. His movements become more frantic. And then I feel it, his cock swelling inside me. As hard as I can, I milk that cock. And he responds by throwing his head back and roaring while jerking and spurting and spitting inside me.

He pulls out of me and lays me back on the bed. I watch him take his condom off and then he turns to me and, hunkering over me aggressively, impales two fingers into my pussy. I gasp and he jams them as deep as they will go.

My body stretches into a bow as he rhythmically pumps his fingers in and out of my wetness. He is doing it so hard I can hear the squelch of my juices. I watch his brown hand go in and out of me in a daze of sensations. His other hand moves lightly over my clit, his face submerged in concentration as if he is an artist working on a masterpiece.

'Squirt for me, pretty pussy,' he says.

'Shane,' I call. My voice sounds broken. And then a wail, a shocking animal-like sound comes from deep inside me as I fall over the edge into the abyss of pure pleasure. He holds me as I clench, shudder and gush over his fingers. I open my eyes and he is gazing down at me possessively. He bends down and licks the tears from my eyes.

'Sleep for a bit now, Snow,' he says, and there is an almost hypnotic quality to his voice and, closing my tired eyes, I fall into a tranquil, dreamless sleep.

I wake up to the sound of people talking. I sit up naked and look around me. The sheets are soiled with oil and stains of our coupling. Wrapping myself with the top sheet, I walk over to the window. Shane is below. He has been working in the garden again. His body is glistening with sweat. I watch him quietly talking to Monsieur Chevalier.

Suddenly he looks up and sees me. For a while we simply look at each other. Then he waves.

'Wait for me. I'm coming up,' he says, and starts striding towards the swimming pool. I turn away from the window and face the doors. He bursts through the double doors like a force of nature or an untamed tiger. Wicked eyelashes and curving, wet, seriously sexy muscles. His mother built him beautiful and then he went and added all those gorgeous tattoos too.

'You're awake,' he says.

'Yes,' I reply shyly.

He walks up to me and pulls at the sheet. At first I hold on to it and then I stop resisting. The sheet comes off in his hands and I stand naked in the afternoon light.

'You're perfect,' he whispers thickly, his eyes smoldering with need.

Seventeen

SHANE

I watch the way the light falls on her pale and fine-boned body and marvel at her fine beauty. Her limbs are as delicate as a porcelain doll. Even when I fuck her I sometimes feel myself hold back in case I hurt her. I see the stains of what I did to her earlier on her inner thighs, and I become a slave to the pull of desire for her. I can't help it. I just want to fuck her over and over again. She's like no other. With her nothing is enough.

I run my palms over her nipples and see them become thick with arousal.

'Are you wet?' I ask her.

She bites her lip and nods. 'Shane.'

'Snow.'

'What are we doing?'

'I don't know what you are doing but I'm ruining you for any other man.'

I bend and, putting my hands under her knees and back, I lift her nude body into my arms and carry her to the connecting bathroom. I set her down in the shower. I take off my jeans and step out of them. Her eyes are wide as she stares at my erect dick. It is almost purple with need.

Why I need her cunt so much is a fucking mystery to me. With every other woman I immediately lost a little bit of my desire for her as soon as I fucked her. And every time we'd fuck I'd lose more and more until I wanted her no more. But not with this one. With this one, I cannot get enough. It is like pouring oil on fire. The more I get the more I want. I stand immobile. I have never enjoyed a woman's eyes on me like I do hers. When she watches me, I actually feel a high.

When her gaze leaves my erect cock and rises up to meet my eyes, I step into the shower. I switch it on and warm water cascades on us. I take the bar of soap from the metal holder and I hold it out to her.

'Soap yourself up for me. Show me,' I instruct.

She takes the soap and runs the bar across her chest, under her arms, around her neck then— God, would believe, shyly—between her legs. Soap suds slide down her inner legs. She raises her arms and bends her elbows to do her back. She does the crack of her ass. Then she does her thighs and legs. She picks up her foot to do it and reveals the delicate, pink folds of her sex. I stare at them transfixed. She puts the foot down. Raises the other. Shows me another eyeful. Water rains down on my cock, making it bounce. It is so fucking hard it is tingling.

I bend down and take her nipples between my teeth. Water runs into my mouth, changing the normal sensation of having a woman's nipple in my mouth. I've been in the shower with hundreds of women. I've taken all their nipples in my mouth. But when I take hers I don't feel that it is a simple exchange of pleasure: I make you come and you make me come.

No, I feel like eating her alive, consuming her. I feel like going on my knees and fucking feasting on her pussy for days. I feel like never letting anyone else have her. I feel like keeping her forever. I feel like she is mine. And yet of all the women I have been with she is the least mine. In fact, she belongs to someone else. Fucking Lenny.

It is a kind of frustration that makes me bite her breast. She gasps. I lift my head.

'Why did you do that?'

'Did you not like it?'

'I don't know.'

I take the nipple back into my mouth and suck hard enough to cause her pain. She makes a small cry.

I lift my head. 'Do you want me to stop?'

'No,' she whispers, her eyes wide and dilated.

I take her other nipple in my mouth and suck it gently. After pain, pleasure. She moans. I turn her around so she is facing the tiled wall. Very firmly I tilt her hips upwards. Then I get on my haunches. I turn her body to watch me. I grab the flesh of her cheeks and blow on her sex. She shivers with anticipation. I bury my face between her cheeks and ... I feast. This time I can't help it. I suck, I lick, and I bite the plump flesh. Even her pitiful whimpers don't stop me. I ravish her like I have never ravished another. I suck until she shudders in ecstasy.

My cock is hot and hungry. I feel the blood surging urgently through it.

I pull her out of the shower and position her in front of the sink.

'I want you to watch me fuck you in the mirror. Hands on the sink, legs spread, ass sticking out,' I tell her as I open a drawer and take out a condom. While she stands gripping the sink hard, legs apart, and pushing her cute little ass as high as it will go, I open a drawer and find a bit of rubber.

'Play with your clit,' I tell her.

She takes her right hand off the sink and starts moving it in circles. Her back arches even more causing her ass to go higher and her whole sweet pussy to hang between her legs. My favorite pose for a woman.

Perfect. Just fucking perfect.

I grab her hips and slide into her. I slide so far in her eyes widen in the mirror. I fuck her hard from the back, our wet bodies slapping, our eyes locked on each other in the mirror. The sound of the two of us echoes through the bathroom like an erotic sexual symphony. Our wet flesh slapping, the sink creaking, her groans, my grunts and finally her strange animal-like cry as she comes hard on my dick. Whoa. There's no holding back after that. I explode deep inside her. I don't immediately slide out of her, I stroke her hair and, pushing it away from the back of her neck, kiss it.

I look up and her eyes are sparkling, her cheeks flushed, her mouth slightly open and panting. 'Another last one for the road?' I ask, hopefully.

And she giggles like a fucking kid.

SNOW

Lunch is served outside. There is the scent of citrus in the gentle summer breeze. We have pan-fried duck confit served with potatoes roasted in duck fat and bowls of tomato salad. The duck is

extraordinarily succulent and tasty. Shane tells me the preparation of the meat takes Madam up to thirty-six hours.

Afterwards, Madam serves me chocolate soufflé with a cherry on top of it and brings a cheese board for Shane. I break through the chocolate crust and spoon the soft creamy chocolate filling into my mouth.

'Mmmm … very, very delicious. Want to taste?' I ask.

He moves his face closer. The crisp male cologne on his skin mingles with the scent of the dark chocolate and makes me feel almost drunk. Swallowing hard, I feed him a spoonful. He catches my wrist, chews, and swallows. He bends and slides his tongue along my collarbone. My eyes widen.

His bright eyes flash. 'You're right, very, very delicious,' he murmurs.

And though he has done all kinds of things to me and we are lovers, heat rushes up my neck.

And those sinful, sinful lips that have been on every inch of my body, twist with amusement. 'You're blushing.'

To my horror I flush even more.

He chuckles. 'Do you know you blushed through our entire first time?'

'How could you tell? We did it in the pitch dark,' I retort.

'Snow,' he says caressing my name like a kiss. 'You were at least two shades darker.'

'And you ... you ... panted through our entire first time,' I lie.

'Sometimes you make me feel so cheap,' he says with a sexy grin.

'I doubt any woman could make you feel cheap,' I reply.

He moves closer to me and for a heart stopping moment he hovers over my mouth. A pulse throbs at his throat and sexual energy glimmers off him like a heatwave. His fingers seek the hem of my skirt and push it upwards.

'You are a strange combination, Snow. Enormous, butter-wouldn't-melt eyes and a slutty mouth built for suckin' cock,' he says, lust thickening his voice. 'All I want to do is fuck you all the fucking time.'

And to my shock I actually feel like standing up, wrapping my thighs around his hips and impaling myself on his big, hard cock. Wet lust quickly flowers between my legs at the thought.

But he pulls away from me with a frown. 'What do you want to do this afternoon, Snow? Go back into town? I could take you around the sights if you want. Or take you shopping.'

There is so little time left of our weekend together. I may never see him again. I don't want to waste these last few hours in town and certainly not shopping. 'I want to stay here. I want to swim with you, and then … I want to end up in your bed.'

His strong hand reaches down and curls around my wrist and he pulls me up. We run up the grand curving staircase up to his bedroom where he flings me on his bed, rips off my clothes, and thrusts into me urgently, as if he can't wait another second.

'Your pussy fits around my dick like a fucking glove,' he growls.

He does not stop all afternoon until sweat runs down his curving muscles and I am so exhausted and sore I have to beg him to stop.

Eighteen

SNOW

We arrive in London at ten past nine and clear Customs as simply and easily as we had in France. We reach the car park quickly and come to a stop in front of a muscular red Camarro with white racing stripes on the bonnet. I know hardly anything about cars, but this one is one of those fire-breathers specially built for dangerous speeds.

'Is this *your* car?' I ask incredulously.

'If it's not, then we're about to become car thieves,' he says, holding open the passenger door for me.

'Very impressive,' I say, sliding into its plush black leather interior.

'She's a babe,' he says closing my door.

Shane is very quiet in the car on the way to my house and in the tense silence I start to feel a knot of apprehension in my belly. All this while, seduced by the magic of Saumur, I had let myself totally forget Lenny, but now I am afraid that even though Shane said he had arranged it that Lenny will not call during the weekend, what if he did? I hate the thought of having to tell a whole pile of lies. But more than any of that is the sinking feeling that France was just a dream. It's over.

This is reality. This is real life.

But I simply don't want to go back to how it was before. I don't want to feel Lenny's body on top of me, using me to relieve his sexual urges. I feel sick even thinking about it. I am not the woman who left for Saumur. I've changed, and significantly.

We reach my apartment and I look down at my hands clenched hard in my lap. The silence is unbearable and I am dying to ask him if I will see him again, but what if this is it? If this is all our liaison is supposed to be?

'You can turn on your phone now,' he says, his voice empty and hard in silence.

I nod and look at him.

He seems so distant. Is he eager to get rid of me? Could it be that this was all an elaborate ploy just to sleep with me? Surely someone who looks like he does, doesn't need to go to these unnecessary lengths. And yet he is so cold and unreachable it is as if he can't wait to get rid of me. I feel tears start pricking the back of my eyes. I won't cry in front of him again. I always knew he was conquering the world one pussy at a time so I shouldn't be so hurt and I'm not so broken that I don't have my pride still.

'OK, thanks,' I say quickly and reach for the door handle.

His large hand curls round my arm. I turn to look at him and he says, 'Oh Fuck.' And pulls me into his arm. 'Don't cry, Snow. Just go back to your apartment and he'll call in the next thirty minutes. Just be normal and all will be well.'

I look up at him with confused eyes. 'How do you know when he will call?'

He runs an agitated hand through his hair. 'Because I arranged for two prostitutes to keep him busy until you were safely home.'

My mouth drops open. 'You did what?'

'It was the only way I could be sure he would not call while you were away. It was the only way I knew to keep you safe.'

I take a deep breath. 'You did that for me?'

He turns away from me and, staring ahead, grips the steering wheel. 'It's no big deal, Snow. Just go. And answer his damn call and … be as normal as you can, OK?'

'OK,' I whisper and, getting out, I slam the door closed and run into my apartment building without ever looking back. As I get through my front door I hear his car blast away, the tires screeching madly around the corner.

SHANE

I take my foot off the gas as I come up to the next red light. Fuck. My fingers drum on the dashboard. I rest my elbow on the window of my car and squeeze my temples. I always knew she was something special. I turn my eyes and catch the gaze of a man in a seven series BMW. He shakes his head with distaste because I am unconsciously revving my thunderous V8 engine impatiently and it is annoying him.

'What the fuck are you looking at?' I snarl, and the little coward immediately stares straight ahead.

The light turns yellow and I hammer the gas pedal and fly off the mark. Up ahead I see a U-turn sign. I could take it. But that would be madness. Gritting my teeth I keep my foot on the accelerator. I pass it. I can't believe how angry and resentful I feel. Soon I hit the motorway. For twenty minutes I drive. I know he will have called by now.

I hit the music and Lana Del Ray's Summertime Sadness comes on.

My car eats up the miles and in my head I see only the expression on her face when I left her. I have just given her back to him. What the hell was I fucking thinking of? I feel bitter, as if I have been cheated. What I really want to do is drive back to her place right now and take back what is *mine*. Fuck the consequences. But a sane inner voice stops me. *It is you who made these arrangements. This is the safe way. This way you get the girl and keep Lenny off both your backs.*

My mind turns to her in the forest.

How sweetly she gave herself to me. I could have done anything to her and she would have let me. And the way she had looked at me with those big, green eyes full of trust and innocence when I took her little ass and made it mine. And then I think of that ugly fuck, Lenny, touching her. And I feel fire burn in my belly.

Fuck it.

I'm not fucking giving her up to him. Not even for one day. Fuck the safe way. Change of plan, asshole. She's mine. She was mine from the moment I laid eyes on her.

SNOW

I close the door and the house is as silent as tomb. I take my little suitcase into my bedroom. The flowers I bought on Wednesday are dead. I put the suitcase on the bed and go back out to the

living room. I sit on the sofa and put my mobile phone beside me and wait.

When the phone rings I jump. I take a deep breath and wait for the third ring before I pick it up.

'Hello.' He sounds like he is drunk or high. I've seen him take cocaine from the dining room table before. He's even offered it to me, but I didn't want to and he said, 'You're right. Maybe you shouldn't. Your head's fucked enough as it is.'

'Hello,' I say. My voice is beautifully normal. It appears I am just as capable of deceit as Lenny is. Still, Lenny never promised me fidelity. That was never in the cards.

'How are you, luv?'

For some reason that endearment grates on my nerves. I'm not his luv and I never will be. 'I'm fine,' I reply.

'Good. I'll be back tomorrow morning. Don't forget I'm taking my girl out to a fancy restaurant tomorrow night.'

I feel a stab in my chest. I'm not his girl. He's been with two prostitutes. Not that I care or ever cared. I just don't want to sleep with him anymore. I don't want to go out with him. I don't want him to touch me. Ever again. I hear myself say, 'OK.'

'Right, I'll call you when I touch down. Goodnight, Snow.'

'Goodnight, Lenny.'

I kill the call and lay the phone down on the table. Tomorrow night looms on the horizon. What on earth am I going to do? Oh God! I cover my face with my hands. What a mess.

My phone rings again making me jump. I pick it up and look at the screen.

Number withheld.

My heart starts beating fast in my chest. I accept the call.

'Hello,' I say cautiously.

'Will you have dinner with me tomorrow night?'

My heart soars with joy. He called. He called. It isn't over. Then reality hits. My heart sinks like a heavy stone inside my body. 'I can't go. I've already agreed to meet Lenny for dinner.'

'Yeah? Well, poor old Lenny won't be able to make it for dinner with you tomorrow. He will be otherwise tied up.'

I feel a wild rush of joy flash through every cell and nerve in my body. It comes out as a mad giggle even as I wonder what exactly he means by tied up. More prostitutes? More business deals that Lenny simply can't say no to?

'Snow,' he calls softly.

'Yes,' I whisper, gripping the phone hard.

For a few seconds he is quiet. 'Wear something pretty tomorrow.'

'I will,' I say, and I am smiling from ear to ear.

'Goodnight, Snow.'

'Goodnight, Shane.'

Oh my God. We're having dinner tomorrow.

I place the phone on the table and, jumping up to my feet, do a totally mad dance around the coffee table.

'Yes. Yes. Yes.'

It seemed as if he couldn't wait for me to get out of his car so I thought he didn't want me anymore. But he *does* want me.

I stop suddenly. And what of the next day? What will I tell Lenny when he wants to have dinner with me on Tuesday? Or Wednesday? How long can Shane keep him busy? How will I escape from Lenny?

Monday passes with interminable slowness. Lenny gets into Heathrow at nearly midday and calls me from the back of his car. He sounds upbeat, but ends the phone call by saying that something has come up and he won't be able to make dinner today.

'That's OK,' I say quickly. 'I need an early night anyway.'

'Why?' he asks immediately, his voice suddenly different.

But I am a better liar than I could ever have imagined. 'I didn't sleep very well last night.'

'Nightmares?' he asks quietly.

And instantly I feel like a bitch. What I am doing is so wrong. I am cheating on someone who has only ever been good to me. I have to do something about my situation, and fast. I close my eyes and, taking a deep breath, I lie. 'No, not nightmares. I think I ate something that didn't agree with me. I kept going to the toilet.'

'Ah well, in that case it's for the best that we are not doing dinner today. Rain check for tomorrow?'

'Tomorrow,' I repeat softly, guiltily.

Nineteen

SNOW

More than an hour before Shane is due to pick me up I start panicking. I don't know why I am more nervous today than I was even when he was taking me away to France. Then I had no expectations. Now my feelings are involved. I really, really like Shane.

I practically pull nearly all my clothes out of my wardrobe, and still feel that nothing I have is suitable for tonight. Everything is either too short, too long, too tight or just too meh. I want to look perfect for Shane.

A bath, I think. A bath always calms me right down. I chuck a soap bomb into the water and wait for it to fizzle out before I pour a good one fifth of a bottle of oil into it. I lie in it and take deep calming breaths, but even that doesn't relax me. The turmoil is inside my tummy.

Impatiently, I wash my hair and get out of the bath. I wave the hair dryer at my head and brush it until it is as sleek as the coat of a black panther. Wrapped in a towel, I go back into the bedroom and stand in front of the clothes strewn all over my bed.

Red. I'll wear red. I slip into red, satin and lace matching underwear. I hook on suspenders and carefully pull on sheer nearly black stockings.

I look in the mirror. Not bad.

I put all the other clothes back into the wardrobe and slip into my red dress. It is a fitted, tailored thing with buttons all the way down the front that makes it look like I am wearing a long, tight jacket that comes to the middle of my thighs. Because it has long sleeves I will only need to carry a light coat for when it gets colder.

I paint my lips in a similar shade to the dress and carefully pull the mascara wand a couple of times over my eyelashes. Then I sit on the bed and pull on shiny black, patent leather boots. I find a little red clip in a drawer and I slide it into my hair. Finally, I dab perfume at my pulse points.

I find my red purse and put my lipstick, my credit card, a wad of tissue, a couple of mints, and as I always do, my little pill container with a few of my pills in them. That done, I kill the rest of the time by pacing the floor restlessly.

When Shane arrives he calls me on my mobile and waits for me downstairs. I go down and for a second he does not see me. He is leaning against the glass, his hands jammed into the pockets of his black jeans and he's staring at the floor. He looks remote and preoccupied. As if the weight of the whole world is on his shoulders. I start walking towards him. He looks up and straightens, stares at me with such an odd expression that I stop walking, my stomach sinking, and I ask, 'What is it?'

He shakes his head and a small smile lifts the corners of his lips. 'Everything's good. You look amazing.'

Shane takes me to a restaurant called Lady Marmalade. It is only when we get there that I realize that Lenny has taken me there before. I debate whether to tell him and I decide that I will, but later, when we are seated, I will casually mention it then. It's not like it is important.

We walk in through the doors and a man in a navy suit rushes out to greet Shane. He claps his hand on Shane's back in a familiar manner and Shane calls him as Mario. There is only one word to describe the man's behavior: effusive. His eyes turn to me and quickly travel down my body the way Italian waiters do, half-professional, half-over-the-top-leering. With great enthusiasm he shows us to a table in the middle of the restaurant. Almost immediately, waiters start dancing around us, flicking napkins open, flourishing menus.

I am still studying my menu when a tall, broad man strides up to us.

'Hey,' the man says to Shane, his face lit up with genuine pleasure. He looks very much like Shane, but he is a little older, and while Shane's looks are more classically handsome, this man is more aggressive looking with a strong, stubborn jaw.

Shane looks up and smiles at him. 'What the hell are you doing here?'

'Bloody cheek,' the man says with a laugh. 'I'm on my way out actually.'

Shane turns towards me. 'Snow, meet my brother, Dom. Dom, meet Snow.'

Dom turns to me with a smile which freezes on his face. He frowns as he tries to remember. I recognize him at the same time he remembers me. I've seen him once before. Then it suddenly comes to me. He owns this restaurant. He came to say hello to us when I was here with Lenny, but it was months ago, and I was so spaced out on my pills then that I did not really take note.

'Hello, Snow,' he says. His voice has lost all its humor and cheer.

'Hi,' I say awkwardly. I look at Shane and he is staring quizzically at me.

'I've been here before with Lenny,' I explain quietly, my heart sinking.

Shane nods slowly, his eyes betraying a spasm of fury, then he squashes it down and turns to his brother.

'Look,' Dom says tightly, 'it's none of my business, but—'

'Then don't fucking get involved,' Shane cuts in. His voice is cold and clipped.

I stare at him in shock. I have never seen him as anything but cheeky and charming, but Dom doesn't appear to take any offence at his brother's openly hostile tone.

'I'll talk to you tomorrow,' he says quietly. There are deep worry lines on his forehead. Unlike my brother who can't even stand to be in the same room as me he must love Shane very much to care so deeply that his brother is going out with Lenny's girl.

'Sure. I'll call you,' Shane says distantly.

His brother turns towards me. 'Goodnight. Enjoy your meal,' he says formally.

'Thank you,' I whisper.

He turns away and takes two steps before turning back to look at Shane. 'I'll be waiting for your call.'

Shane nods.

His brother walks away and Shane turns back to me. 'I suppose you've lost your appetite.' His voice crackles with aggression, but his gaze is innocuous.

I nod slowly.

The expression on his face changes and he looks at me wistfully. 'Why didn't you tell me?'

Seeing the look of disappointment in his eyes as if I have betrayed him, is unbearable. Tears sting the backs of my eyes. I feel as if I have ruined everything. Unable to look into his eyes I gaze down at my clenched fists. 'I'm sorry,' I tell my hands. 'I was going to. Really I was. I just didn't want to spoil our evening.'

I look up and he is leaning back against the chair and looking at me expressionlessly.

Mario appears at Shane's elbow, his large smile quickly faltering at the tension he finds between us. 'Something to drink perhaps?' he suggests uneasily.

Shane doesn't look at him. 'Can you give us a minute, Mario?'

'Certainly,' Mario says, and with an expansive gesture, backs off.

Shane sighs. 'Do you want to stay, Snow?'

'Are you going to carry on being angry?' I ask anxiously.

His mouth twists ruefully. 'I'm not angry now.'

'It sure looks like it to me,' I say miserably.

He reaches a hand out and gently traces his knuckle along my jaw line. 'My poor Snow. Did you have fun here with Lenny?' he asks.

'No.' My voice is strangled.

'No tequila shots upstairs?'

I shake my head.

Shane laughs suddenly. 'Then you haven't really been to Lady Marmalade at all,' he declares, and raises his hand. Mario must have been hanging around watching because he materializes at our side like a genie out of a bottle.

'Give us the works, Mario,' he says.

Mario raises his hand like the conductor of an orchestra and says, 'Bravo.'

So the evening begins. A bottle of champagne is popped and glasses filled. Shane is funny and cheeky and sexy all at once. We eat the insanely good food and then he takes me upstairs where there is a bar and a dance floor. We do tequila shots at the bar and then Shane whirls me off to dance. We join the conga line of someone else's party and I laugh until my stomach aches.

'If I die tomorrow, I'll die happy,' I tell him.

He pulls me towards him. 'I won't. Not while you're with him. Even dead I don't want him to have you. He doesn't deserve you,' he growls.

I stare up at him, shocked by the passion in his voice.

Mario gives me a little box of chocolate truffles as we are leaving. 'I noticed that you liked them. Have them for later,' he says with a nod and a wink.

'Thank you,' I say, surprised and touched by the gift.

In the car, Shane tells me that we will be dropping by Eden.

'We'll have a quick drink there. There's something I have to do at the office.'

We are nearly there when my phone goes. I freeze with fear.

Shane stops the car at the side of the road and switches off the music.

'Take the call,' he says tautly.

'What if he is calling me from my apartment?'

'He's not.'

'How do you know?'

'Just trust me.'

He takes my purse from my lap, pulls my phone out and gives it to me.

I click accept and Lenny says, 'Did I wake you?'

'No,' I say, and even to my own ears my voice sounds shaky.

'Are you all right?'

'Yes. Yes, I'm fine.'

'Where are you?'

Paranoia grips me. I swallow hard and try to keep my voice neutral and casual. 'In my bedroom.'

'Are you just about to go to bed?'

'Yes.'

There is a pause, then he says, 'I have a surprise for you.'

'Oh.'

'I'll give it to you tomorrow night.'

'All right.'

'Sweet dreams and don't let the bed bugs bite.'

'Thanks. And goodnight, Lenny.'

'Goodnight, luv.'

I disconnect the call and put the phone back into my purse. Shane starts the car and drives on. He doesn't say anything. The atmosphere in the car is so tense I feel it pressing down on me.

Twenty

SNOW

Inside Eden, the manager comes forward to help me with my coat, but Shane forestalls him, lifting my coat away from my body and tossing it carelessly on the counter. He places his hand on the small of my back in an unmistakable gesture of ownership and leads me into the club.

Flushed and tense with nerves, I let him guide me into the club. Music throbs around us and I am conscious of almost everyone staring at me because I am with Shane. Some of those looks are filled with malice and envy. Their faces swim before me. I force my spine straight and hold my head up high.

A blonde woman dressed in a powder blue suit hurries towards us. Her face is wreathed with a friendly smile that encompasses both of us. 'Hello,' she greets.

'Briana, meet Snow, my girlfriend. Snow, this is Briana, the housemother of this club.'

'Hi,' I say, taking her cool hand and feeling suddenly shy. I feel as if I am floating on cloud nine. I can't believe that Shane introduced me as his girlfriend. It feels strange and fantastically wonderful.

She turns to Shane. 'She's simply gorgeous.'

Shane moves closer and slides his arm around my waist. He looks down at me, his eyes gleaming with triumphant ownership. 'Yes, she is rather ravishing, isn't she?' he murmurs.

'Would you like to stay and have a drink?' Brianna asks.

'I'm actually here to pick something up from the office.' He turns to look at me. 'Would you like to stay for one drink?'

'OK.'

'Come on,' Brianna says and leads us to a booth in the corner. We sit down and a waitress comes with a bottle of champagne and fills our glasses. When she is gone we clink glasses.

'To us,' Shane says.

'Is there an us?' I ask softly.

'Yes, there is an us,' he says, and his voice is terse, almost brutal.

'To us,' I whisper.

He raises his glass to his lips and watches me over the rim with a dark, brooding look. A muscle twitches in his cheek. The atmosphere between us grows tense again and I feel myself start to tremble. I have never seen Shane angry. I don't know why he is, but I know he is seething under the surface. It all started when Lenny called.

'Come here,' he says with an edge to his voice.

I put the glass down on the table and, licking my lips nervously, shift closer to him leaving six inches between us. He ruthlessly jerks me sideways towards him so I tumble off the seat with a surprised gasp and land in an ungainly fashion in his lap. My hands searching for balance are both gripping his body. He puts his hands on my hip and thigh and pulls me closer to him so my body is molded to his and my thigh is pressed against his erection.

'I want you like hell,' he whispers into my neck. 'I want to fuck you, right here, right now.'

'No, please, Shane,' I protest, even though I am already embarrassingly wet at the thought. It is amazing how he can arouse me with a look, a touch, a suggestion. 'Can't we wait till we get to your place?'

'I'm sick of waiting. I'll have you now and you'll fucking enjoy every minute of it,' he says, his face hard.

I shake my head, staring at him with a jumble of excitement and horror. My body seems to be flaming with heat and my heart is beating so fast I feel it like a flutter in my chest. 'We are in a public place,' I whisper.

'Snow?' His eyes are as hungry as a wolf in the night.

'Yes,' I say.

'That wasn't a request.'

'This is madness. There are cameras, aren't there?' I cry.

'They get turned off when I get into a booth.' His face is dark with desire. A horrible thought enters my head. Does he bring all his women here and have sex with them here? Is that why there are no cameras here?

'No,' he says violently. 'I don't fucking don't do this with all the others.'

He kisses me then, so brutally I taste the salt of blood on my tongue. Shocked by the intensity of his mouth, I automatically try to push him away.

'Don't fight me, Snow,' he grates harshly. 'I need this.'

I look into his eyes and I see that he is telling the truth. For whatever reason he needs to take me here in this public place where anyone could come by and see me taken like some cheap slut. The fight goes out of me. I lie in his arms while his fingers snake into my dress and push aside my panties. There is nothing I can do.

He is going to make me climax here.

SHANE

Her eyes are wide open with surprise and affront, but she's practically vibrating with excitement and anticipation. Like biting into a ripe summer cherry, my fingers sink effortlessly into her tight, little pussy. The sound of her helpless whimper turns my blood to fire. I feel the kind of feral hunger that makes me insane with need. My cock pulses hard, right on the edge of something.

If I don't get into her soon I will fucking explode.

I want to lay her on the table, tear her clothing off and bury myself so deep inside her that it obliterates the memory of that sick bastard. She doesn't know, but I still see him in her eyes. She still thinks of him. She doesn't want to 'hurt' him. She feels 'grateful' to him. And the worse part of all: she feels 'guilty' when she's with me as if she still belongs to that sicko. I hate that. Fucking hell, she's mine.

'Open your eyes,' I tell her. My voice throbs with fury.

Her eyes fly open, large and guileless. When she is aroused her eyes become brilliant and shiny. I had a cat once with eyes like that. Beautiful.

Staring into her fabulous eyes I add another finger. Her pale legs tremble open further. She gasps, her body arching slightly.

'Have you ever been finger-fucked in a club, Snow?'

She shakes her head.

With a little laugh I realize that I don't need to fuck her, I just want to lay claim to her. Make her submit sexually to me anywhere, anytime. I need to dominate her and get it through her head that she belongs to me, mind, body and soul and I won't tolerate even the ghost of Lenny's memory.

Every time I see him in her eyes, I'm going to fuck her until he is completely gone. My other hand roves possessively over her body. I unbutton the first two buttons of her dress and slide my hand inside it. I run my palm caressingly over her nipples. Through the thin silky material of her bra, they are like small stones under my palm. I push up the bra cup and pinch her nipple. She groans softly.

Using my thumb, I gather the slickness from the tender pink folds and begin to relentlessly circle her clit. She rocks with sudden hunger.

'I love your body, little rabbit,' I tell her, thrusting my hand harder and harder as she starts to quake, her exposed breast jiggling.

She buries her head into my neck. 'I'm going to come, Shane,' she gasps. It is almost a plea.

Asking my permission to come. I like that. It's fucking horny. I pump her even more furiously and her poor little pussy clenches around my fingers. Then she goes over the edge beautifully.

I let her hide, her body shuddering, and her muscles locked around my fingers. I hear her heart thudding hard against mine.

'I don't ever want you to go back to Lenny,' I state harshly.

She pulls away from my neck and stares up at me, her face a confused oval of white. 'I can't do that. I owe—'

'Owe? What do you owe, Snow?' I ask, my voice is a vicious snarl.

She shakes her head and tries to wriggle away from me, but I grip her hips hard.

'I'm the man with my fingers buried inside your pussy, and that's the way it's going to be every night from now on,' I tell her thickly. And, staring insolently at her, I begin to move my fingers in and out of her in a show of my total control of her body.

She stares at me helplessly, her eyes darkening again with spiraling excitement.

'What do you owe him, Snow?' I ask softly.

'I can't tell you,' she says hoarsely.

'Why not, Snow?'

She bites her lip with consternation and mounting arousal.

'Are you afraid of him?'

'No, not really, but I can't talk about it. It's too dreadful to talk about.'

'Sweet Snow,' I groan. 'You're too fucking sweet to be true.' And, bending my head, I kiss her hungrily. Her fingers cling to my shoulders and suddenly I have the ugly searing thought. Did she cling to him? Did she ever come alive under his hand and his mouth? My tongue pushes into her mouth roughly, my teeth hurting her soft flesh. I hook her tongue, bring it into my mouth, and suck it so hard she whimpers and tries to fight back, her clenched fist striking my forearms, then grabbing my hand and trying to pull it out of her pussy.

I pull my mouth away and her rage dissolves at the expression on my face. So full of lust it startles her. We stare at each other as I continue to pleasure her. She comes with a strangled cry of submission. I caress the delicate bones in the curve of her spine.

'You're never seeing Lenny again,' I say firmly, and slipping my fingers out of her, I pull her bra cup over her breast, button her top and pull her dress over her thighs.

She drops her eyes. 'I'll come back with you tonight, but I'll have to see him again. I have to explain.'

'No, you fucking won't. I'll take the fight to him. I knew what I was doing when I decided to hunt you. I knew there'd be consequences to pay. And I'm ready to pay them.'

She licks her swollen mouth nervously. Unshed tears glimmer in the depths. 'Lenny is dangerous, Shane. I can't let you confront him. Please, I'm begging you. I know how to handle him. He won't hurt me.'

'No fucking way. I wouldn't trust him with you for a minute. I'll rot in hell before I let that psychopath anywhere near you again.'

She looks at me desperately. 'Maybe we can run away together.'

I laugh mirthlessly. 'Run? I come from a long line of bare-knuckle fighters, Snow. We don't fucking run. We fight for what we want. I'm not scared of him. If I was, you'd be in his bed now. I want you and I'll fucking fight to the death for you.'

'Oh, Shane. I'm so sorry. I never meant to get you into such a rotten mess,' she cries.

'Fuck, Snow,' I say in wonder. 'You didn't get me into this mess. I'm my own man. *I* got me into this rotten mess and I'm not one tiny bit sorry. I'll fight anyone for you.' I touch her lovely, sad face. 'He should never have had you in the first place. He's got no soul, Snow.'

She hugs herself as if she's cold and stares at me intensely. 'You don't understand. He'll let you win a bare-knuckle fight. He'll even clap you on the back, congratulate you, and tell you the best man won. But he's a vindictive man, Shane. He never forgets. When you think it's all fine, he'll send his attack dogs.'

I smile. 'Ah, Snow. You didn't think I was going to challenge him to a bare-knuckle fight, did you? You only do that when you're fighting a man. He's not a real man. He has no honor. You'll just have to trust me when I say I *do* know men like him. I know exactly what makes them tick and exactly how to approach them. And he's not the only one with attack dogs.'

She stares at me. 'You have a plan?'

I nod. 'I have a plan.'

'What is it?'

'The less you know the better.'

'Is your plan dangerous?'

'Not to me it's not. I'm pretty sure I've got it all covered.'

She looks scared. 'Promise?'

God, she's so beautiful she takes my breath away. I smile slowly. 'Promise.'

She smiles back tremulously.

'Listen, I've got to go upstairs and get something, and then I'm taking you home. Want to come up with me or wait here for me?'

She smiles shyly. 'You've made a mess between my legs. I need to go freshen up. I'll just nip into the Ladies while you're up.'

'Don't clean too hard. I plan on making one hell of a bigger mess when we get home.'

'I like it when you make a mess,' she says and, leaning forward, kisses me lightly on the tip of my nose. It's sweet.

'Go anywhere you want inside the club, but don't walk out of it. It's dangerous for a woman outside.'

'I have no intention of going out,' she says with a heartbreaking smile.

Twenty-One

SNOW

I am washing my hands when the woman walks in. She stands next to me and looks at herself. I cannot help but stare. Blonde, and well over six feet tall in her high, white shoes she's unbelievably beautiful. Her eyes are deep blue and she is wearing flash eyelashes, the tips of which she has dusted with silver. It has a very dramatic effect when she blinks. To my surprise she smiles warmly at me and I smile back.

'Hi,' she says. 'I saw you come in with the boss.' Her accent is quite strong, possibly Russian.

'Yes,' I say shyly. It's going to take some time before I get used to thinking of Shane as my boyfriend.

'I'm Nikki,' she introduces.

'You can call me Snow.'

'Snow. Beautiful name for beauty.'

'Oh, thank you, but you're the real beauty here.'

She waves my compliment away modestly. 'It's all make-up. You should see me in the morning.'

'I don't believe that for an instant,' I tell her. And that's the truth. She would be beautiful without any make up. She's perfect in every way. Tall, blonde, big breasts, stunning.

Haven't I seen you here before?' she asks opening her little clutch purse.

'Not really,' I say awkwardly.

She takes her lip gloss and unscrews it. 'Yes, I have. I never forget a face. In this business you need to have a good memory.' She smiles. 'You know, which customer likes which move ...' She lets the sentence hang and applies a layer of gloss onto her bee stung lips and then turns to look at me again.

'It's been nice meeting you. Maybe I'll see you around,' I say.

She narrows her eyes at me. 'Ah, I remember now. You're Lenny's woman.' And she smiles happily. 'I knew I had seen you before. Lenny is a good customer of mine,' she says with a knowing wink. 'But between you and me you've done well to dump him for Shane. Lenny's very generous and all, but Shane's brilliant in bed, isn't he?'

I freeze. 'I beg your pardon.'

'Oh don't worry. I'm not jealous or anything. We finished ages ago. I know all about his,' she makes air quotation marks, 'have cock will travel' rules. He's had at least twenty women since we broke up.'

'What?'

She widens her eyes. 'Oh, I didn't mean to shock you or anything. I didn't know you thought it was serious. Take it as a friendly warning, dahling, it's never serious with Shane. He's a total manwhore with a frisky donkey dick, but that's what makes him so good in bed. Look, don't worry about it. Just enjoy it while it lasts. Just don't let him break your little heart. Good luck, sweetie.'

I think of Shane. The way we made love. *Have cock will travel!*

My throat clogs. I'm so fucking pathetic. *You don't eat all the candy from the candy shop.* Again and again I make the same mistake. I trust the wrong people. He doesn't eat all the candy just the best pieces.

But he told me I was his. I belonged to him.

The air suddenly feels chilled. Her words are like frost covering my heart. Gooseflesh crawls on my skin. I feel cold. So cold. Even colder than when I stumbled out of that hotel room.

God, how stupid I've been. Of course a man as beautiful as he is will have loads of women after him. Of course he is a player. Look how he chased me even after he saw me with Lenny. I can't believe I never saw it until now.

There is no puzzle to put together. A child could have worked it out. I was just too idiotic, too unhappy to see it. And there I was besotted, thinking he was the other half of my soul. He is just a courteous, charming player. Disgust crawls over my skin. I feel humiliated and used, again. All I want to do is run away.

Malicious amusement at my naivety glints in her eyes. Unshed tears scorch the backs of my eyes. I won't give her the satisfaction.

'Leave me alone now,' I say. My voice is strangely detached.

I drop my eyes to my hands. They are still wet. I need to dry them. I walk over to the hand drier and hold my hands inside the machine. Hard jets of air blow on them. I hear the door open and close and I crumple. For a second I stand where I am with my back to the door, the poison spreading into my body, and then I walk to it and stand just inside it. Afraid to open the door.

Oh, my poor heart. It still wants to believe.

But the cold truth was undeniable. She is right. I always knew he was a playboy, but I could not help myself, and after a while I started to believe in him. But if this stunning creature couldn't keep him, what hope have I?

I have let Shane break my heart.

I open the door and the beautiful night creatures are going about their fun and laughter.

Nothing has changed for them, but for me it feels as if I am dying. I start walking towards the entrance. I can make out Nikki. Her face is turned towards me, her claws sheathed, but her eyes filled with dark interest. I feel every cliché: the ground dropping out beneath my feet, my whole world shattering before my eyes, and our life together vanishing in a cloud of smoke.

My stomach twists and I start hurrying to the door. As I get closer, my feet speed up even more. Soon I am running. People are turning to stare, but I don't care anymore. I just want to be out of this ugly place with its ugly, ugly people doing ugly, ugly things to each other. Tears soak my eyelashes and run down my face.

He's just a habit. A very bad habit. But even the worst habits can be broken. I will survive. I survived the hotel room. This is nothing.

But tears keep pouring down my face.

I run out of the club and suddenly find myself in the deserted parking lot. The night is so sultry it is almost muggy, but I feel cold and numb. My life seems like a dream that I'm walking through with my eyes closed. Making mistake after mistake after mistake. Ignoring every clue.

I look around me in confusion. How will I get home? I have no money. My hands are shaking. I bow my head to think and when I lift it, suddenly, and bewilderingly, I am surrounded by men. Where did they come from? Who are they?

I peer at them and they look like they are part of a stag night party because one of them is wearing a pair of felt antlers. He comes up to me and touches me. I freeze. Another touches my hand.

'Come on, love. Give us a kiss.'

One of them takes a note out of his pocket. 'Go on love, he's getting married tomorrow.'

Another one says, 'Come guys. Leave her alone. She's scared shitless.'

'Fuck off, Larry. It's just a bit of fun,' says the guy who took the note out of his pocket. And the rest of them laugh.

Somewhere in my head I realize that they think I am one of the strippers. That they are not going to hurt me. They just want to buy a kiss for the groom, but a kind of paralysis has swept over me and my whole body is in lockdown. I cannot move a muscle.

Only my eyes swivel over them in terror. And then the fear comes.

I am so exposed. So utterly vulnerable. They could take me. There are six. I want to scream. I want to run. But my body does nothing. I can't understand what is happening to my body. I am frozen I have become petrified. Like those tree fossils from millions of years ago. It is incomprehensible and terrifying.

My purse has fallen on the floor and all the contents have fallen out. One of the guys comes really close to me. 'What's wrong, sugar? Are you all right? We're not going to hurt you.'

His breath reeks of alcohol.

I look at him wordlessly.

'Hey, look at that. She can't move.'

He starts to laugh. Tears start rolling down my face. Daringly he touches my breast. And yet I can do nothing. He sniggers. 'Shit, this chick is like a statue. We could take her home with us.'

The other guys crowd around me curiously. It is exactly like it was before. I was frozen and tears were escaping fast from my eyes and no one cared. They just went on doing whatever they wanted to me.

Suddenly there is a great roar and wind whooshes by me. I stare in shock as Shane punches the guy with the antlers and kicks the guy who wanted to take me home, to the ground. I have never seen the primal animal inside him, and I stare transfixed.

He is so achingly beautiful. Like an animal. No rules. Perfectly unfettered, free to extract whatever punishment he wants. There is no pretense, no nod to what is socially acceptable. He just surrenders to the beast inside him.

In the commotion the other men are screaming, 'What the fuck?'

'Hey, we didn't mean her any harm.'

'We didn't fucking do nothing,' is the cowardly defense to Shane's fury and fists.

Two of them turn and run away. The bouncers appear and Shane is putting his arm around me.

He bends his knees and looks into my face. I just stare at him. He is white about the mouth. His hand is bleeding. He cups my face with his hands.

'Are you all right?' he asks. His voice confuses me. It is strange and different. As if he is speaking a different language.

I take a shuddering breath and open my mouth to say, yes, but no words will come out. I close my mouth.

'It's OK. It's OK. I'm here,' he says and crushes me to his chest. I am trembling so hard he pulls back and looks at me worriedly.

I know the bouncers are all around me, but I don't see them. I know Shane is holding me, but I can't feel it. Some one is picking up my things from the ground and putting them back into my purse. Shane gives his car keys to someone who brings the car right next to us. Shane opens the car door and puts me in it. We drive back to his home in complete silence. Once we get there he comes around and lifts me bodily from the car.

'I can walk,' I croak.

'It'll be faster this way,' he says. In the lift I feel his eyes staring down at me, but I keep my head bent.

Inside the apartment he lays me on the couch and goes to the liquor cabinet. He pours us both brandies. A super large one for him, which he throws down his throat, and a smaller one that he brings to me. I take it and curve my hands around the cold glass. He sits opposite me. His face is still pale under his tan.

'Do you want a hot drink?' he asks.

I shake my head.

'Drink up,' he instructs.

I take a gulp and the alcohol runs through my body like fire.

'Finish it,' he says.

I do it and he leans forward and takes the glass from my hand.

I look up at him to say thank you and my breath is stolen from me at the strange unfathomable expression on his face. 'Why did you leave the club?' he asks.

'I went to the Ladies and met Nikki.' My voice is emotionless. Truly I don't feel any of the emotion I felt before. I just feel like a shell.

His face crumples. 'Oh, Snow. What do you want from me? I've never pretended with you. You knew what I was. I chased pussy. But, every one of those girls knew exactly where they stood with me from day one. I never cheated on anyone and certainly not her. Yes, I slept with her, but she was never anything to me and she knew that.'

'It was just a shock. I guess I am more jealous than what I thought.'

He looks at me curiously. 'What actually happened outside the club?'

'I'm really tired, Shane. Can we please talk about it in the morning?'

'OK, let's get you in bed.'

And the truth is, the trauma with Nikki and what happened outside the club has actually utterly exhausted me. I feel numb. The whole night is like a dream. My eye lids are so heavy they close even as my head touches the pillow. The last thing I remember before I fall into a deep sleep is his large, strong hand curling around mine.

He whispers something in my ear, but I don't catch it.

Twenty-two

SNOW

One year before ...

'Either the well was very deep, or she fell very slowly, for she had plenty of time as she went down to look about her and to wonder what was going to happen next.'

—Lewis Carroll, *Alice in Wonderland*

Kim, my new roommate in the YHA hostel, was not strictly beautiful, but she was attractive, with bright laughing eyes, dark shiny hair and, as I said before, had the biggest grin I'd ever seen in my life. And I warmed to her instantly.

'And I'm Snow,' I said.

'Cool name. So where're you from then?' she asked.

'India.'

She looked me up and down. 'No kidding. I thought Indians were brown.'

'Mostly. There are fair Indians up north, but in my case my mother is English and my father half-Portuguese.'

'So you ... like just arrived.'

'Today,' I said.

'And you've never been to this part of the world before?'

'First time,' I said with a huge smile.

'Excellent. I'm from Australia. I'll show you everything. I know all the happening, fun places. I presume you don't have much money.'

'Afraid so.'

'No problem. Part time work is so easy to get. You'll have to apply for a National Insurance number first, and that will take like six weeks to come through.'

My eyes widen. 'Six weeks!' I exclaim.

'But,' she grins, 'in the meantime you can just work illegally.'

'Really? Doing what?'

'Anything. Waitressing, bar tending, dancing in clubs, babysitting anything that gives you cash in hand. You're so gorgeous you could even make mega bucks as an escort.'

'An escort?'

'Yeah, all these lonely businessmen come to London to do business, and they pay hundreds of pounds for someone to sit with them and keep them company while they eat their dinner.'

'Don't they expect you to sleep with them after that?'

'No, you can say no, if you don't want to. It's up to you.'

I shake my head. 'No, that doesn't sound like me. I'm too shy to do something like that.'

'I've done it before. It's really, really good money.'

'You have?' I asked, shocked.

'Sure,' she said airily. 'I didn't sleep with a whole bunch of them. Finally, this really handsome American guy booked me and I'd have paid to sleep with him. So I did and he gave me $500.00. And you know the best part? When you go back to your own country nobody will ever know. Want to try? We can do it together.'

I frowned. 'Sounds like fun, but that's just not me.'

'Right. Let's cross that off the list. Can you do secretarial work?'

I bite my lip. 'No.'

'No sweat. You can wait tables, right?'

'I've never done it before, but I'm a fast learner.'

'That's the spirit. We'll register you with a catering employment agency tomorrow and see how that goes, ok?'

'OK,' I agreed happily. 'Besides, I'm not afraid of working hard in a restaurant kitchen, doing washing up or something like that.'

'Great, we'll do that tomorrow. Let's hit the town tonight.'

'Tonight? No, I just arrived. You go on ahead. I might just have an early night. And anyway, I'm afraid to waste the little money I have on a night on the town.'

'Oh, come on, don't be a spoilsport. We have to celebrate your arrival tonight because it's ladies' night. You won't have to spend a penny. The taxi and everything else will be my treat. I'll take you to this amazing place in Earls Court. It's jam-packed with Australian surfer-type blond boys. I promise, they'll love you.'

'Are you sure?'

'Absolutely.'

I looked at her gratefully. 'Thank you so much, Kim. I was a bit scared of how I was going to cope, but now you've made it all so easy and such fun.'

She grinned good-naturedly. 'Don't thank me. I'm using you as bait. In order to get to you they're going to have to buy me some free drinks too.'

'You don't need me to attract a man, Kim,' I said sincerely. 'You're really attractive.'

'Yeah, I'm not ugly, but I'm no beauty. I know that.'

'You are beautiful in my eyes. You have a beautiful soul,' I said, and she smiled back at me.

That night we got ready. I didn't have anything sexy enough so Kim lent me her pink mini-dress. It was made of Lycra and clung to every curve. I stood in front of the mirror uncertainly.

'You look amazing,' she said.

'You don't think I look too slutty?'

'You couldn't look slutty if you tried, babe,' she said. 'You have more class in your little finger than Kim Kardashian has in her whole body.'

She got into a backless orange dress, which set off her dark hair. I helped her put a fake tattoo on her back. Then we were both ready. She looked me up and down.

'You look great. Really great.'

'So do you.'

'Thanks, Snow.'

And so we went out. First we went to a pub. We had many offers, but Kim was very protective of me. Whenever it seemed someone was getting too familiar, she pulled me away. I had two glasses of white wine and I was already feeling a bit tipsy.

'I hate to be a killjoy, but I really have to get back,' I said.

'No, no, you'll sober up after we eat some food. The real fun hasn't even started yet. You have to come to this club. It's so awesome. Even celebrities go there.'

'Can't we go tomorrow?'

'No, we're out now. Remember, ladies' night. Come on. It'll be fun. I promise. Please, please?'

'All right,' I relented.

She started jumping on the spot. 'Thank you.'

So we left the pub and went down the road to a kebab shop. Kim had a burger and I got myself a chicken kebab. Kim insisted on paying for everything.

'My treat, remember?' she said.

We sat on high chairs facing the glass windows and ate our meals. And as men passed on the street, they looked in and gawked at us. We laughed back at them and I swear that at that moment I never had the slightest inkling of what awaited just a few hours away. Not a clue. All I felt was a sense of freedom. I was in England and I was doing what I wanted to do. I knew I had made the right decision to leave India. My new life in England stretched out full of excitement and promise.

After we ate, we took a taxi. From the outside, the club did not look glamorous at all. It was tucked away on one of the small streets off

Earl's Court road, but I couldn't find my way back there when I tried many months later.

There were two bouncers standing outside. As Kim had said, it was free for women that night so we sailed through. By then it was half past eleven. It was in the basement so we went down some stone steps into a small cramped area that was lit by red lights. A bored woman taking money off some guys barely glanced at us as we went through a black door into the club.

There was a dancing area and a few people were rubbing up each other, but mostly people were in dark corners making out.

'Come on,' Kim said, pulling me by the hand to the bar. As my eyes got used to the dark, I realized that the place was mostly full of men. There was no one our age. Both the men and women seemed to be decades older. And there were definitely no celebrities. The place could be described in one word. Seedy.

I looked at Kim, surprised. 'This is it?'

She tapped her nose. 'They come incognito. Wait until a bit later. For the meantime look at that guy checking you out.' A man with grey in his hair was staring at me. When he saw me looking back at him he smiled and nodded. And I don't know why I felt the hairs at the back of my neck rise in fear. I turned back quickly to Kim.

'Listen, Kim. I don't like it in here. I don't want to stay.'

'Just give it five minutes,' she pleaded. 'It's really good.'

'OK, five minutes,' I said.

At that moment she saw someone she knew. She waved at him and he started to come over. He was more our age and I relaxed a little.

'Hey, Andrew,' she greeted and threw herself at him. He kissed her on both cheeks and then looked at me. 'And who have you got here?'

'This is Snow. Are you going to buy us a drink?'

'Of course. What are you girls drinking?'

'A double gin and tonic,' Kim said.

'Orange juice,' I said reluctantly. I really wanted to leave, but I felt too frightened to find my own way back to the hostel so late at night. I knew I had too little money to take a taxi back. Back home I would have been driven to the club and the driver would be waiting outside to pick me up.

The drinks appeared on the bar next to Kim; she took them and passed mine to me. As I sipped my drink, Kim and Andrew carried on talking about people I didn't know. I was starting to feel really, really tired. In fact, I was getting so tired that I couldn't keep my eyes open.

'Can we go home, Kim?' I asked.

'What's the matter with you?' Kim queried, a frown on her forehead. 'Are you all right?'

'No, I feel dizzy. Maybe I'm jetlagged, and with the alcohol ...' I mumbled.

I felt as if I had no legs. Nothing to hold me up. As if my head was free-floating. In fact, my whole body seemed to be 'gone.'

I tried to widen my eyes and focus on Kim, but it felt as if I was detached from my body and physical surroundings. It was like being in a dream or a nightmare. Everything is fluid and strange. You move differently. I saw her grab my arm without really feeling anything. Neither fear or panic. There was no emotion at all. I felt Andrew and Kim grab my body and start helping me out of the club.

I couldn't walk.

'She just needs a bit of fresh air,' she told the bouncers. I could feel my legs hitting the concrete steps, but I felt no pain.

'You all right, love?' the bouncer asked.

I wanted to tell him that I had not drunk a lot, but the effort was too much. But even then I did not panic. If only I had made a real effort to tell him, everything would have been different. I was watching with great detachment as Andrew and Kim walked me down the sidewalk. We came to a car. Andrew opened it and together they put me inside. Both of them got into the front.

I remember dry heaving.

'Is she all right?' Andrew said.

Kim turned to me. 'Don't worry. We'll take care of you,' she said, but her voice was echoing.

When she turned and talked with Andrew, their voices felt like they were coming from very far away or from underwater. Then I blacked out. When I came to again, Andrew was pulling me out of the car and carrying me. The sidewalk was wet. I felt the drizzle fall on my face. I tried to talk. I wanted to know where Kim was, but I could not open my mouth. I had no control of any part of my body. I felt a shaft of fear then. It crawled into my head on all fours.

'Don't try to talk. It's OK. Everything is going to be OK,' he whispered.

But I remember thinking that he looked nervous.

Then I blacked out again.

When I came around, I still couldn't move a single muscle and I was in that dreadful hotel room.

Twenty-three

SHANE

I wake up suddenly with a jerk and freeze. Moonlight is filtering in through the curtains. Everything is still .... and wrong. Immediately I turn my head and look to the pillow beside me. It is empty. I jack-knife to a sitting position and listen. There is an intermittent scratching noise coming from the bathroom. I leap out of bed and rush towards the sound. There is no light coming from under the door. I rap on it. The scratching stops, but there is no answer.

'Snow,' I call. 'Are you in there?'

There is no answer. I can feel my heart hammering in my chest.

'If you don't open this door I'm fucking breaking it down,' I say. My voice has a thread of panic running through it.

Still she doesn't answer.

Dread is like an icy claw around my heart. I stand back and start kicking the door. After three kicks it smashes open. I switch on the light and find her naked and cowering in a corner. Her fists are covering her mouth. Above her fist, her eyes are large and wild. Her hair is messy and strands fall over her face. She stares at me without any recognition. As if she is not even looking at me.

What the fuck! It is an incredible shock to see her reduced to something so feral, but another part of my brain takes over. Calmly, it deduces where the sound has come from. She has been scratching the side of the bathtub with her fingernails.

I take a step forward and she presses her back into the tiles, a look of sheer terror on her face.

I lift my hand. 'It's just me, Snow. Shane.'

She stares at me without comprehension.

I very slowly get on my haunches, and when it looks like that that action does not spook her, I get on my hands and knees and start a half-shuffle, half-crawl towards her. 'It's me,' I urge softly. 'I'm not going to hurt you.' I stop a foot away from her.

'What are you doing here, Snow?' I ask in a conversational tone, as if I was asking her to pass the salt.

'I feel cold. So cold,' she says, and indeed her teeth are chattering.

'Here, let me warm you,' I say without making any move towards her.

'No,' she whispers. 'Nobody can warm me. I saw them again tonight.'

'Saw who?'

'The bastards who did this to me.'

'What did they do, Snow?' I ask, the blood in my veins turning to ice.

'This,' she says, and opens her thighs. She makes a fist with her small hand and is about to hit her own exposed sex when I grab it and stop her. I stare at her.

'No,' I say. 'You can't hurt that. That's mine.'

She doesn't fight.

'That's yours?' she asks in a small voice.

'That's mine, Snow. I don't care what happened before this, but that is now mine.'

'I was a virgin and they didn't even use a condom,' she sobs.

'Oh Snow,' I say, and feel tears start prickling my own eyes. The sensation is novel. I haven't cried since the day I found out they slit my father's throat. I blink the tears away quickly and gather her into my arms. At first she thrashes and hits out instinctively, but I hold her tight.

'I got you,' I tell her. I got you, babe. No one will ever hurt you again.'

'Something terrible happened to me in that hotel room, and I cannot tell you about it because it was too horrible.' Her body shakes with emotion.

I hold her tightly. 'It's not your fault this happened to you. Nothing you did made you responsible for your assault. Shhhh ... Shhh ... Shhhh' I whisper in her ear until her struggles cease and she is limp in my arms.

I slip one hand under her knees and the other around her back and carry her back to my bed. I lay her down, and when I try to disengage myself she clings desperately to me, so I sit on the bed and hold her. After a while she starts sobbing.

'Break open, Snow. Cry all you want. You deserve compassion from yourself. You are always being compassionate to others. Now be compassionate to yourself. You deserve this moment of grace. You're OK. You'll always be ok. You have nothing to be ashamed of. This world is a better place because you are in it.'

Then falteringly, with great shame in her beautiful eyes, she tells me what happened.

And my blood boils.

Twenty-four

SNOW

The first thing I saw when I came to that night was the ceiling. It was off-white and sort of fuzzy around the edges and I couldn't understand why. And then it came back to me that I had been very unwell. And Kim and Andrew must have brought me here because they couldn't take me to the YHA. My mouth felt numb, strange, and I was freezing cold. I realized almost immediately that I was so cold because I was completely naked.

That was when I heard voices. Men's voices.

I tried to move my head to find the owners of the voices, but I couldn't. My entire body was frozen. Not even my little finger could lift away from the bed. Desperately, I swung my eyes around. I was in a hotel room, not a good one, but not a grubby one either. It was one of those family rooms with a double bed and a single in it. I was lying on the double. The curtains were pulled shut, and I could see many bottles of alcohol on a desk in the corner of the room, and the men in different stages of undress were actually crowding around it and snorting lines from the table.

There were six of them. They had different accents. The only impression I had was that they were all excited. I could sense it in their voices and the air. It was like they were at a party. One, I could tell by his accent, was German. I'm not one hundred percent sure, but it was possible one of the men was Middle Eastern. Three were definitely European, but I was certain that none of them were English. There was an Indian man too.

When I first spotted him, I had the ridiculous idea that I could plead with him. Tell him I, too, was from India. Ask him for mercy.

Then they were on top of me until it felt as if they were thrusting hot metal rods. Burning. Burning. But I couldn't scream. I couldn't do a thing. Not one thing. They pinched my nipples. They were animals. Licking. Biting. Hurting. Their faces were alive with lust.

The whole time I could hear them talking to me; calling me a dirty little bitch. You like this don't you. You want more. Take that, slut. Give it to the bitch. Fill her up. I was like a life-size doll that they could bend, twist, flip, and pull according to their wishes.

Months later when more and more memories came back and I researched it on the net, I found other women with the same story to tell. I pieced their memories with mine and a picture emerged. Strangers went onto the dark net and paid to gang rape a woman in a hotel in London. I even remembered that one of them said he had flown into London for the express purpose of raping a drugged woman. The others had presumably included it as part of their holiday experience.

For hours they used my body. Every orifice. Even though I could not move a single muscle I felt it all. Tears continuously flowed out of my eyes, but they didn't care. They just carried on one at a time, two at a time, three at a time. For hours and hours. I was a human toilet.

I thought the night would never end.

But I won't carry on with any more gory details, you can use your imagination.

I don't know exactly when they left, but when I came back from the darkness I was alone. I wanted to get up and run away. I was afraid they would come back but I could not move. I didn't give up. I just kept on trying to move my finger. I knew Andrew or Kim had spiked my drink and it would wear away.

An hour or so later, I could move my fingers and my mouth. With all my strength I waved my fingers and, slowly, movement came back to me. I was so frightened and so filled with adrenaline that I did not feel any pain at all then. When I sat up, I saw that my entire body was blue-black with bruises and bite marks, and there was quite a lot of blood between my thighs.

When I tried to stand I fell over. My legs felt like they did not belong to me. They were like jelly. The whole time I was terrified the men would come back. I started to crawl and pull myself along the carpet. I dragged my body to the door, but my hands were almost useless. Crying with frustration, I finally managed to open the door and I was in the corridor. It was empty and silent. At the end of the corridor I could see a lift.

I had gone beyond fear. My mind was blank. All I had to do was reach the lift doors and someone would help me. The carpet burned my legs and elbows, but I felt no pain. Unable to see clearly, I pressed both the buttons on the consul. When the lift doors opened I saw a man standing inside it. He looked down at me with a frown. There were other people around him, but my vision was strangely blurred and I could only see his face.

For a brief moment I was afraid again. There was something about him that frightened me. I opened my mouth to scream, but no sound came out.

I fainted at his feet.

That man was Lenny.

Twenty-five

SHANE

For a seed to achieve its greatest expression, it must come completely undone. The shell cracks, its insides come out and everything changes. To someone who doesn't understand growth, it would look like complete destruction.

—Cynthia Occelli

'Lenny?' I repeat in disbelief. I am in such a rage that it is difficult to keep my voice from shaking.

'Yes, Lenny,' she says quietly. 'The hotel belonged to him. He was on his way up to the suite he keeps for himself on the top floor.'

I frown, but I don't share my thoughts about Lenny. 'So Lenny took you to the police?'

She shakes her head. 'No, he took me to his suite and when I woke up I didn't want to go to the police. I was in a state of shock.' She makes a small noise. 'To be honest I think I was a little mad. And I was so sick from the drugs they had given me.'

'Didn't he take you to the hospital?'

'No, he brought a doctor to the suite. The doctor cleaned me up and prescribed some pills.' She stops and says, 'I think I need one now. Could you please get it for me?'

I go out to the living room and look in her purse. The pills are in a transparent plastic tub with a white screw top. There is no label on the tub. I unscrew it, take one pill out, and slip it into my trouser pocket. Then I fill a glass with water and take it and the container of pills to her. I shake one out and hold it out to her.

'It doesn't have the label. What is it?'

She puts the pill on her tongue and swallows it down with water. 'I don't know what it is, but it helps me.'

I take the glass and put it on the bedside table.

'So,' I say. 'You never went to the police.'

'No. Lenny said it would have been too late anyway. They would all have left the country by then. Plus, I can't remember their faces clearly. They blur in my mind. Once, I hated them and I wanted them to be punished. I used to pray that something horrible would happen to them, but I don't think about them anymore.'

I look at her swollen face. 'They never used a condom. Have you had yourself tested for any diseases?'

She shakes her head. 'Lenny always uses a condom and that is why I am very careful with you too.'

I don't feel the kind of burning anger that I would have expected to feel. Inside, I am cold as ice. I want Snow, and I want revenge. And I will have both.

'Do you understand now why I am indebted to Lenny? I was so broken and he fixed me. I couldn't go home. I was too ashamed. And I couldn't hold down a job. He gave me money and protection. And all he asked for in return, when I was a little better, was ... a bit of comfort.'

'Fuck it. You don't owe him anything, Snow. He abused you.'

She shakes her head. 'No, no, you don't understand. There is an Old English word, *bereafian*. It means to deprive of, take away, seize, rob. That is what happened to me. I was seized and robbed. But not of my purse or money. I suffered shocking loss. Indescribable. It was so horrific that when I dragged myself out of that room I was like a dead person. I fell unconscious at his feet. He picked me up and took care of me, but I can't even remember that time properly anymore. It is a blur.'

She frowns trying to remember.

'It's as if there is opaque heavy glass between me and those images of me scrabbling around the floor like a spider, hissing, furious, ... helpless. I stopped eating. All I really remember is outside it rained and rained and my rage was like a dully burning metal inside me. The agony was so total, time stopped rushing forward. There was no future. For months I never went outside. If not for my pills and Lenny, I would not have survived. Can you believe I bathed only when Lenny marched me to the shower and turned on the tap?'

She looks at me beseechingly.

'He was patient with me for months. I was like a mad woman. I slept all day with the curtains drawn. Everything terrified me. I couldn't even walk down to the corner shop. He saw me through it all without ever giving up on me. The first time I felt human again was in spring when I was walking on the pavement and I saw an earthworm writhing on the concrete.'

She smiles mistily.

'I crouched down and Citra's face came into my mind. "When you see a worm on a pavement, remember that it is having a bad day. Pick it up and put it on some grass or soil." So I carefully picked it up and carried it in my cupped hands all the way to the park. I left it on the grass, and the simple act of how it had burrowed into the cool earth still made sense when the rest of the world did not. I felt then that there was order in the world. I was having a bad day, but I would find grass and earth again. One day.'

'He should have taken you to a proper doctor and had you examined and treated. Instead he caged you, manipulated you and used you.'

'It's not like that, Shane. It was not his decision. I didn't want to see anyone. Not even a doctor. I was too ashamed. I didn't want another person seeing or touching me. He brought me medicine.'

'I am almost certain that what he gave you is not proper medicine. The bottle doesn't even have a pharmacy label on it. Knowing him it's bound to be something that helped to make you even more dependant on him. And then he locked you away in an apartment and did not allow any other man to touch you, while he availed himself to any number of whores he wanted. How did you ever think he was helping you?'

Twenty-six

LENNY

Come on. The lift doors opened, and this exotic, raven-haired, green-eyed beauty literally crawled up to my feet and gave herself to me. I didn't ask for it. I didn't arrange for her to be kidnapped and raped and thrown to grovel at my feet.

I mean, what would you have done?

Taken her to the police and walked away?

No fucking way. I'm no Good Samaritan.

Besides, I didn't want the police crawling all over my hotel, minding my business for me. The way I saw it, she was like a gift from heaven. Yeah, of course she was covered in bruises. Jesus, the bastards sure worked her good. Six, she told me later. But even with her entire body covered in bruises she was a raving beauty.

So I took her back. I patched her up. You have to understand she was no walk in the park. She was bloody, fucking hard work. Those first few months were no joke. She wandered around mute and half-crazy. She used to try to scrub herself clean, scratching her skin like an animal until it was raw and bleeding. And then there were the nightmares, the waking up in the middle of the night screaming in agony as if she had a wound in her body and her soul was pouring out, the shaking, the crying, the catatonic trances.

But the funny thing is, I never thought to throw in the towel. She had been given to me. And in this shitty life it's not often that you are given anything that special. You have to fucking fight for every last inch, let alone a jewel like her.

My father used to say, you give a donkey a page from a fine book and it will eat it, you give a child the same page and it will scribble all over it, you give a learned man that page and he will read it. I always knew she was a page. The donkeys had tried to eat her. I knew I could never read her. But I could scribble on her for a while.

It took time before I could scribble on her. Months.

But the day came when I could part those white thighs and enter her. Fucking her was different than with any other woman. I can't explain it. When I fucked her it was like fucking a child or a dumb animal. Not that I have ever fucked either. Just what I imagine it could be like. She never responds because she doesn't enjoy sex. She never climaxes and I never try to make her enjoy it. You see, I kind of like that she gets no pleasure from it. It's kinda virginal and pure. Like in the olden days, when they grinned and bore it. That kind of woman doesn't exist anymore.

Now every fucking bitch is shoving a ten-inch vibrator up her wet cunt every chance she gets. No class at all. And I'm all about class. It's perverse, yet it excites me to think she doesn't want me in her body, but she allows me to because she's grateful. Because she belongs to me. The way your pet belongs to you. You can do anything because you're the master.

I enjoy being the owner of such an exquisitely beautiful human. I'd buy her a collar and take her out to town to show her off if I could. Maybe one day I will. I'll take her to one of those kinky places where the men come bringing their women on leashes. And the women have to crawl on their hands and knees like dogs. The problem with those clubs is that you have to share. And I don't think I could do that. Mine is the only dick that's going up that girl.

Everywhere we go I see men looking at her hungrily, but I don't see any interest in her eyes. Sometimes though, not often, maybe once or twice, I feel her wanting to fly away. She gets that look in her eyes, and those times I remind her again of that day I found her. I deliberately make her cry.

I make her realize that she's irreparably damaged and she needs me. I'm the one who took care of her. I'm the only one she can trust. In the beginning I used to tell her that no other man would have her once they knew she was so defiled. I mean six men in one session. No man wants that.

But don't ever make the mistake of thinking I don't care about her. When I don't see her for a few days I start to miss her. I miss her distant smile. I miss the taste of her skin. I miss her vacant eyes while I am pounding away into her dry little pussy. I miss the smell of her hair. I miss the way her tears roll down her cheeks.

Yeah, I'm missing my little pet right now.

Twenty-seven

SNOW

The sound of a woman's voice wakes me up. I sit up. There is a toweling robe laid on the bed for me and I slip it on and go to the door. I open it a crack and hear a peal of laughter. She comes into view and I realize that she must be a relative. She has exactly the same coloring as Shane, tall with long dark hair. She is visibly pregnant. Since she can't be much older than me, she must be his sister, Layla.

'Well, where is she then?' the woman demands. 'I'm dying to meet her.'

'Asleep, but she won't be for much longer if you carry on laughing like a demented hyena,' Shane says.

I open the door and step outside. 'Good morning,' I say awkwardly.

'You're up,' Shane says with a smile.

'Yeah,' I say. I feel embarrassed and strange. After last night I don't know how Shane feels about me anymore.

All I know is that I was awful. Enough to put the most ardent suitor off. I vaguely remember falling asleep in his arms after taking my pill.

'So you're, Snow. I'm Layla, Shane's sister.'

'Hi,' I say with a small wave.

'I hope he hasn't told you anything horrid about me, because I have far worse secrets about him,' she says and, coming up to me, envelops me in a huge hug. She is definitely not the typical reserved, stiff upper-lipped, English person. In fact, she is very much like an Indian, who has no real concept of personal space. I, of course, immediately warm towards her.

'I've brought you some clothes. They're not new, but they are clean. I brought all stretchy stuff so it'll be like free size. Of course, you'll have to fold up the jeans.'

'Thank you. I'll just change into them and join you,' I say, taking the bag she is holding out to me.

'I'll be in the kitchen having a bit of ice cream,' she says.

I look at Shane and he raises his eyebrows as if to say, are you OK?

I nod and, looking at Layla, say, 'Great I'll see you guys in the kitchen.' I go back to the room and close the door, but not all the way. I hear Layla say with a laugh, 'I thought you were never going out with any girl with white skin and black hair.'

'And I thought you were never going out with BJ,' he retorts.

I don't catch her answer as they disappear into the kitchen.

I dress in the T-shirt and skinny jeans that she brought. The jeans are too long so I fold them at the top. I quickly brush my teeth with the brand new toothbrush Shane has left by the sink. I comb my fingers through my hair and make for the kitchen.

Layla is sitting at the counter eating ice cream and talking animatedly about her son. She turns towards me. 'Would you like to have some ice cream?'

'Layla,' Shane says pointedly. 'Snow is not weird. She doesn't want ice cream for breakfast, besides, don't you have somewhere else to go?' he asks.

Layla slides off the seat with a sigh. 'I don't have anywhere to go to, but all right I'll go.' She grins at me. 'I'll grill you at my mum's house at Sunday lunch.'

'Oh, for God's sake, Layla,' Shane says exasperatedly.

'Byeeeee,' she says, and walks out of the kitchen. We hear the front door close behind her.

'How do you feel this morning?' Shane asks.

 233

'Yeah, fine,' I say uncomfortably.

'Good. What do you want to have for breakfast?'

'Shane?'

'Yes.' He appears solicitous. A stranger.

I dig my fingernails into my palm. Wow! It's been a long time since I did that. The pain of my fingernails dulls the other pain. The pain of thinking he regrets ever hooking up with me. Lenny accidentally revealed once that other men wouldn't want me after they knew about what had happened to me, and I grew up in India where the shame of being raped actually causes women to be killed. He always claimed he didn't care, but other men might not be able to take it. Some men are simply not strong enough to cope with such horror. Some marriages even break up after a rape.

'I'm ... sorry about last night. I haven't had a flashback in months. It must have been the shock of what happened outside the club that triggered it.'

'Don't apologize for last night,' he says harshly, striding towards me and stopping a foot away from me. 'You have nothing to apologize for.'

'Erm ... OK,' I say, taken aback by the sudden fury in his voice. 'Er ... Thanks for asking your sister to bring me these clothes. I'll just pop back to my apartment and get some of my clothes later this afternoon ... if you still want me to stay, that is,' I say uncertainly, my gaze searching his face for clues of reluctance or a change of mind.

His eyes are like frozen blue orbs and his words as sharp as razors. 'I've *not* changed my mind, and you're never going back there again. I've thrown away your red dress. From now on I pay for everything that goes on your back.'

'Oh,' I exclaim, stunned by the intensity of his words. The more I know him the more I realize that beneath the easygoing charm and humor lurks a much darker beast.

His expression warms suddenly, confusing me. 'Now, do you want blueberry pancakes, scrambled eggs and smoked salmon, a banana smoothie, waffles, warm brioche with butter and cherry-plum jam, or a full English for breakfast?'

'Oh!' I exclaim, overwhelmed by the choice. 'I usually just have toast or cereal.'

He smiles. 'Yeah, I've got that too.'

I pause. Why should I have the same old boring thing? 'Actually, the brioche with butter and cherry-plum jam sounds really good.'

His eyes twinkle. 'It's one of my favorites too. Sit and talk to me while I get it.'

'Can I help?'

'Nope,' he says immediately.

So I sit at the able while he moves about preparing our breakfast. Soon the entire kitchen fills with the lovely yeasty aroma of toasting brioche and hot coffee. He brings the food to the table and I realize just how hungry I am.

I watch Shane's large, capable hands tear apart the soft loaf and the steam rise from the middle of the bread. I watch him spread the jam on the pastry, not across the whole half, but just a corner. And on top of the jam a shaving of cold butter. Then I watch his strong white teeth bite into the piece and his sensual enjoyment of the complex tastes in his mouth, cold, warm, sweet, starchy, buttery, plummy.

As I watch him, I feel the thaw inside me. Ever since that horrible day I could not connect with anyone. I was frozen inside. I just felt utterly alone. Kim's betrayal made the whole world frightening. I knew I could trust no one. Everyone wanted something from me. Even Lenny.

For the first time today I feel something deep and real.

I feel love. Great love for the man sitting next to me.

After we eat, I look at him. Somehow I have to explain away last night. I can't just leave it like that.

'About last night.'

He lifts his head and looks at me expressionlessly.

'I know I was downright pathetic in the bathroom yesterday, but I guess I'm not a very strong person. I—'

'Not a very strong person? What the hell are you talking about? Fucking hell, Snow. You're one of the strongest women I know. You were strong even when your whole world was crumbling beneath your feet.'

He shakes his head.

'You came to England on your own in search of a dream. That's brave enough to start with. And then you endured an ordeal at *nineteen* that could have sent a grown woman mad. And the best part, you survived it all on your own, without any professional help, any proper medication or counseling to lessen the pain, and under the manipulative and insidious influence of a total psychopath.

'That, in my book, makes you an incredibly strong person. Strength doesn't always mean a woman never cries or has a breakdown, or a woman who never gives an inch to man because that could be interpreted as her being weak. But it definitely means a woman who quietly rebuilds her life after it is shattered through no fault of her own. You're a fucking warrior, Snow.'

Twenty-eight

SNOW

That day, Shane takes me shopping for some clothes. He seems very familiar with the art of taking a woman shopping. I quickly buy some cosmetics, a bottle of perfume, a pair of jeans, a couple of T-shirts, underwear, and tights.

'Right, you need something jazzy for tonight,' he says, and takes me to a boutique where the two assistants seem to know him very well.

He makes me try on three different dresses and buys them all.

'Have you got something for her to put her lipstick into?' he asks the girls.

They come back with three different evening bags and he nods approvingly. Afterwards, we have lunch in a cozy little café nearby, then drop by a shoe shop to get shoes for all three dresses.

'Tired?' he asks.

'A little.'

'Come on, I'll take you home and you can have a little nap. I've got errands to run.'

He drops me back to the apartment then goes out. I plan to clean the place, but someone has come in while we were out and cleaned the place thoroughly. I try to read a book, but I am too wound up. Despite everything Shane says about Lenny, I know I still owe him an explanation. No matter what anybody says, Lenny took care of me.

I sit down and write a letter to him. I tell him that I have fallen in love with someone else. I tell him that I will always care for him and be grateful for what he did for me. I tell him that one day we'll be friends. And then I tear the letter to shreds and throw it away. I know what is bothering me.

There is no happy ending to this story. Lenny is going to be furious with me. And he's going to want to know who has taken his possession away from him.

I sit on the couch and feel shivery, and frightened for Shane. What if Lenny hurts Shane? I know Shane can use his fists, I saw that in the car park, but this is different. Shane is too sweet to take on a ruthless gangster like Lenny. I see it in the eyes of all the people we meet, how wary they are of him. They wouldn't be afraid if there was nothing to fear.

By the time Shane comes back I am in a real state. I have convinced myself that Lenny is going to kill him. That I should never have started seeing Shane in the first place. Tears are pouring down my face. When he walks through the door he immediately comes to my side

'What's wrong?' he asks.

'He'll kill you, Shane. I know Lenny. He'll kill you,' I babble hysterically.

He sits back on his heels and looks at me. He reaches out a hand and strokes my wet cheeks. 'Do you really have so little faith in me?'

'You don't understand. I know him. I know what he is capable of.'

'Then rest easy that you don't know what I am capable of.' And something lurks in his eyes.

'Are you going to hurt him?'

'That's up to him.'

I cover my face with my hands. I can't help feeling so guilty. That all of this is my fault.

'I should have walked away from Lenny first. And then come to you. How stupid I've been,' I sob.

He pulls my hands away from my face. 'I couldn't have waited that long. This is not your fault. I chased you. You were minding your own business. I knew what I was getting into.'

'Nobody's going to get hurt?'

'Unless someone fucking asks for it,' he says.

'Promise?'

He smiles a little sadly. 'Promise. Now go put on one of your new dresses. I'm taking you out on the town.'

I slip on a knee-length black dress with diamante straps, a tight bodice and a flaring skirt and go out to meet him in the living room.

He smiles softly. 'Beautiful. Just beautiful,' he says with great satisfaction in his voice.

We go out to dinner at Layla's husband's restaurant. Again we are treated as if we are VIPs. Nothing is too much trouble. The food is excellent and Shane is courteous and attentive, but he seems distant and preoccupied. And I realize that since my meltdown last night we haven't had sex.

I start to wonder if Lenny was right. Knowing I have been gang raped would put even the most persistent man off. I start looking for little signs of change in his behavior. Is he looking at that woman? Why is he not reaching for my hand? Did he just avoid my eyes?

Then why is he helping me? Is it because he is just a nice guy and he doesn't want to hurt my feelings? The more I think about it, the clearer it becomes that ever since last night he is definitely more distant. He has hardly touched me all day and all throughout our meal.

A woman comes up to him.

'Shane,' she coos.

'Bella,' he replies coldly.

'You were going to call me,' she says, one beautifully plucked eyebrow raised.

I feel a burning in my gut. What a cheek? I am sitting here and she is hitting on my man. That brings me up short. Maybe he is not my man. And the thought brings tearing pain. For a year I felt no pain at all no matter what someone did or said, and now the ability to feel something more than just baffled sorrow at what happened to me that day in the hotel room is back. My body is responding to external stimulai again.

Shane shrugs his wide shoulders in a gesture of casual disdain. 'I figured that if I didn't call back you'd get the message.'

She turns to me. 'Don't gloat too much honey. He'll do the same to you one day.' Her voice is acid.

I feel the blood drain from my face.

'Sharpen your claws elsewhere, Bella,' he says menacingly, rising to his feet. A gesture meant to dominate by his sheer height and presence.

'Fuck you both,' she spits, and flounces away.

Shane resumes his seat. 'Sorry about that,' he says, his eyes seeking mine.

'It's OK,' I say lightly, but Bella's words are burned into my mind.

After dinner, Shane takes me to a club called Gibran.

'I've got to see someone quickly,' he tells me.

There is a long queue outside, but he leads me to the front and the bouncers come forward quickly.

'Good evening, Mr. Eden,' they greet politely, unhooking the red ropes, and standing back respectfully.

Inside we are whisked past the entrance ticket queue by a small middle-eastern man. 'This way, Mr. Eden,' he says, and leads us through the doors.

He looks up to Shane. 'How are your brothers doing?'

'Good, thank you. How's the family?' Shane replies.

'Very well, thank you.'

Hard rock music pulsates around us. Shane keeps a firm hand on the small of my back as we make our way through a sea of heaving, sweating bodies until we come to a VIP area. A group of people are sitting in a booth with low couches. There are brass lamps on the table.

My eyes are immediately drawn to a powerfully built man. He has shoulder length hair and eyes that are so light blue they look like chips of ice. He has a nasty scar that starts just under his eye and it zigzags down one side of his face. He is wearing a black vest that shows off an enormous tattoo of a fierce cobra with its hood and mouth open. It begins at the top of his muscular shoulder, its long body twisting around the length of his arm and hand, and its tail ending at the base of his wrist.

He looks menacing, very menacing.

He is leaning back on the low couches, but looking as relaxed as an animal about to strike. When he sees Shane, his mouth twists slightly. He makes a movement with his fingers and two half-naked girls entwined around him on either side stand and move away. His disregard for them as human beings is so blatantly callous it takes my breath away.

Shane pulls me forward and the man's eyes flick over to me quickly.

His eyes are both stunning and scary. I find myself instinctively moving close to Shane. Shane looks down on me, and smiles reassuringly. The man sits forward, the movement so quick, that again I am reminded of a striking cobra. When he stands he is as tall as Shane, but he vibrates with a kind of dangerous energy. They bump fists, only it looks nothing like any fist bump I have seen. This one bristles with their combined energies. If

Shane is white magic, this man is black magic. The difference is that stark.

'Will you have a drink?' he drawls. His voice is deep and his accent reminds me of Nikki, the nasty blonde I met in the ladies' toilet at Eden.

'Thanks, Zane, but I can't stay,' Shane says. 'Just checking to see that everything is going forward as planned.'

'Everything's good to go.'

'Good. Thanks, man. I owe you one.'

Zane smiles and nods slowly, and that slow nod makes me shiver. I can tell that the day will come when he will arrive to collect for whatever favor it is he is doing for Shane.

We walk away, my heart fluttering with tension.

As soon as we are out of earshot I tug Shane's sleeve. 'I don't like that man.'

Shane stops abruptly, leans down and takes my face in his hands. 'Listen to me, Snow. I trust Zane with my life, and so must you if anything happens to me. I brought you here so you could see him and he could see you. You will be financially well off and he will protect you from Lenny.'

My heart crashes with horror and I cannot stop the fear in my voice. 'Are you expecting something to happen to you?'

'No, this is a contingency plan.'

I frown. 'What about Jake? Why am I not going to him?'

'I don't want Dom or Jake to get involved. But especially Jake. He has been taking care of us for his whole life and that's enough. He has a family of his own now and it is time he put them first. No, Zane will sort it out. He is being well compensated for anything he does.'

'You're scaring me, Shane.'

'Don't be scared. I'm just writing my will. Not because I expect to die tomorrow, but because if I should, I want to go to my grave knowing that those I ... care about are protected.'

'Why did you choose Zane?'

'Because he is more, far more dangerous than Lenny.'

'And he's a friend of yours?'

'As friendly as you can get with the Russian mafia,' he says dryly.

'Shit, Shane. I thought you said you were not a gangster.'

'I'm not. But like I said, I know people.'

Thirty

SNOW

https://www.youtube.com/watch?v=k3Fa4lOQfbA

When we get back to Shane's apartment I am feeling tense and unsure of myself. Shane has showed no signs of wanting me sexually. As if all the passion has cooled since my meltdown.

'Nightcap?' he offers, walking into the sitting room.

'OK,' I say, following him in.

'What do you want?' he asks.

'Whatever you're having is fine.'

'I'm having Cognac.'

'Great.' I perch at the edge of the sofa and watch him pour our cognac.

He comes over and holds out my glass and then sits next to me, but not too close. There is a good three inches between my thigh and his knee. He leans back into the seat. I lick my lips and turn back to look at him.

'I don't have to stay here, you know. I feel strong enough to make it on my own now. I could get a room ...'

He frowns. 'What on earth are you talking about?'

I shrug. 'Well, ever since last night you are different. You're friendly and protective and kind, but it's as if you don't want me anymore, sexually, I mean.'

He stares at me incredulously. 'What?' he explodes. 'You think I don't want you?'

I bite my lip. 'It's not like what it was in France, is it?'

He sits forward and shakes his head in wonder. 'What a crazy thing to think?' It's not like France because I didn't want to rush you. Can't you tell I'm fucking fighting with myself to keep my hands off you because I don't know if you are ready after last night?'

'I'm ready now,' I whisper.

He smiles slowly, his eyes glinting. The old Shane is back. 'Prove it by doing a strip dance.'

'You own a strip club. I'd have thought you'd be bored with that by now,' I say with a smile. In truth I want to shout with joy. He still wants me.

'I want to see *you* dance.'

'Now?' I ask with my eyebrows daringly lifted.

'Can't think of a better time.'

'OK.'

He stands and walks to his music system and chooses something.

'What song have you chosen?'

'*Je T'aime ... Moi Non Plus* by Serge Gainsbourgh and Jane Birkin.'

'God, isn't that like a really old number? My mother used to listen to it,' I say, surprised.

He grins at me. 'My grandfather had a thing for Bridgette Bardot and Jane Birkin. I've got all kinds of boyhood fantasies around this song.'

I laugh. 'Do you know what the title actually means?'

'It translates as, 'I love you ... Me neither.''

'Interesting,' I say.

'That's what couples in the throes of lovemaking say to each other,' he says with a wink.

'Right. I'll be back in a minute,' I say crisply, and taking my glass of cognac with me and swaying my hips with attitude, walk to the bedroom. I close the door and go to his wardrobe. I pull out a white shirt. Quickly, I undress. I leave my panties on, but take off my bra. I put on his shirt and leave it unbuttoned to the waist. I don't do the last two end buttons either. Then I roll up the sleeves until my wrists show. Keeping my high heels on, I choose a blue striped tie and knot it loosely around the collar of Shane's shirt. I put on my new super shiny lip gloss. Then I look around the drawers and find a cap. I arrange it at an angle on my head and look in the mirror.

The look is just what I wanted. A little bit 'je ne sais quoi.'

I finish my glass of cognac, Dutch courage and all that, and walk out to the living room door and pop my head around the doorframe. He presses the remote on his hand and the music comes on. The old fashioned guitar cords of rhythm and bass guitars and snare drums fills the spaces between us.

'Je t'aime, Je, t'aime,' whispers in her breathy and ethereal voice, so high it is almost the unbroken voice of a little choirboy. But extremely erotic all the same.

I drape myself around the doorframe and, raising my leg slowly, caress the door with my foot. I step into the room and teasingly lift one edge of his shirt exposing the top of one thigh and a glimpse of my black lace panties. He doesn't know my sex is already wet. I catch his eyes and he is staring at me, mesmerized, and that gives me the confidence to go on.

I tug at the tie and it comes off. Holding it in my hand, I twirl it before flinging it at him. He catches it mid-air.

I face away from him and, swaying my hips, let the shirt drop off one shoulder, exposing bare flesh. I drop the other end and the shirt falls to my mid back. I turn my head back and look at him and smile.

The look on his face, the lust in his eyes, is priceless.

Very slowly and still gyrating, I let the shirt fall farther still, until it is skimming the top of my bottom. I play with the material seductively before dropping it lower still. Right on the fleshiest part, I rub the material in a sawing motion. Then slowly I drop it further until my entire ass is exposed. I quickly unbutton the shirt and slip it completely off. Holding it at arm's-length away, I allow it to dangle on one finger before letting it drop to the floor.

I gyrate the top half of my body in a large circle, like the belly dancers in France, so that all my hair falls forward and covers my breasts. Then I turn around and shimmy my hips as I walk towards him.

I put one leg on the sofa arm and immediately his eyes move to my pussy. He can see that the crotch of my panties is soaking wet. I put my hands around my neck and lift my hair so that my breasts are on display. The tips are hard and ready. Then I let my hair fall back into place again.

The heavy breathing noises of simulated sex start on the track.

I lick my glossed lips and he crooks a finger at me.

Instead of going to him, I make a pointing hand and slowly shake my finger at him while smiling regretfully.

He laughs, a deep sexy sound.

Lowering my hands, I begin caressing myself. Running them over my neck, circling my bare breasts, cupping the soft mounds of my bosom, and massaging them while my head is thrown back. I feel the ache in my nipples and rub my fingers lightly over the hardened swollen buds.

A sigh of pleasure escapes my mouth.

My hand roams lower and lower until it reaches the top of my panties. I linger tantalizingly before slowly letting my fingers slip behind the elastic. I look up to see his reaction. His gaze is transfixed on my fingers and he has a massive hard on. I move my finger in a circular motion. My breath hitches and becomes uneven.

'Aaaa ...' I gasp.

I move to the coffee table and sit perkily on it. I am only three feet away from him. I place both hands on my knees, and I draw them up and spread them so he can see just how wet the material of my panties are. Leaving my legs suspended open, I lean back on one hand while the other slips over the crotch of my panties.

'Oooo ...' I coo, my voice as breathy as Jane Birkin's.

Hooking a finger into the side, I push the material out of the way and expose the glistening pink folds beneath. I let my clit protrude for a whole three seconds, or at least until his gaze comes up to meet mine. His eyes are dark with lust. There never was anything for me to worry about. He really, really, really still wants me.

He pushes forward suddenly and, grabbing my arm, pulls me forward, and with hair flying and legs flailing, I tumble into his arms. My cap slides down and falls in my lap.

'Hey,' I protest. 'I'm not finished.'

'Sorry. Time's up. I can't wait anymore,' he says, his right hand ripping my panties.

He steps out of his pants and pulls his briefs off in a hurry. He lowers his head onto the couch and, holding me by the waist, lifts me up and over his face. He maneuvers my crotch over his mouth and slowly lowers my wet pussy over his extended waiting tongue. The hot, velvety tongue penetrates my flesh, and I cry out with pleasure and squirm. Holding me tight, he pumps in and out of me a few times.

'Oh, mon amour,' Jane Birkin whispers and sighs.

Ah, the pleasure. My head rolls back with how good a tongue fuck feels. I have never had one. His tongue probes every inch of my pussy. Then he moves me back a little and licks my clit. I place both my palms over his head and just close my eyes, enjoying the erotic sensation. I moan deliriously when he clamps his mouth around my clit and sucks it until my muscles start contracting.

I explode in a terrific rush. As I climax, he moves me again and fills my pussy with his tongue and I come hard on it.

'Oh my God,' I breathe, as he carries on slurping at my dripping pussy.

He wraps his hands around my ribcage and starts to move my body down his. I realize that he is about to lower me onto his cock.

'We need a condom,' I whisper urgently.

He stills, his expression unreadable, then nods and, putting me aside, goes to get one. When he comes back he rolls it onto his shaft and looks at me.

'Open your legs and show me again,' he says.

I obey and he inserts a finger into it. Instantly, my muscles clench around it. He takes his finger out and holds it in front of my mouth.

'Suck it,' he says.

I open my mouth and suck his fingers, tasting the musky sweetness of my own juices. He sits down and, putting his hands around my waist, lifts me onto his lap. He lets my body hover over

his cock. I hold it steady and he lowers me onto it. Slowly he travels deeper and deeper into my body.

'You belong to me now,' he says harshly. 'I'm going so deep into your body that you'll never even be able to think of another man inside you.'

And he does. He goes so deep I never thought anyone could go that far. My body breaks out in goose pimples and I move restlessly, lifting myself away from the relentless impaling, but he tightens his hold on my body and, keeping me tightly in place, carries on pushing me down onto his massive shaft.

'That's enough now,' I groan.

'No, you can take more,' he insists. 'Suck me in.'

So I let him go deeper and deeper into me until I can bear it no more and I cry out.

'You're mine,' he says, and pushes that last tiny bit deeper into me. And at that moment I feel him tense, his nostrils flaring as he climaxes hard, so hard he leaves fingerprints on my waist.

'I claim you as mine,' he growls gutturally in my ear.

Thirty-one

SHANE

I am jerked awake by the sound of the doorbell. I look at my watch. It's nearly two o'clock in the morning. Snow, too exhausted to fully awaken, stirs beside me and mumbles something.

'Go back to sleep,' I whisper, and vault out of bed.

I pull on my jeans and, with my heart hammering, I sprint to the door. I did not expect retaliation so soon. I'm not ready. I switch on the security video camera and see Jake standing there. For a second I blink. What the fuck is he doing here at this time? And then I know. I buzz him into the building and run my fingers through my hair. I really didn't want to deal with this now. I hear a soft rap on the door and I open it.

My brother comes in and he looks as fresh as a fucking daisy.

'Want a whiskey?' I offer.

'Yeah,' he says, and leads the way to the living room.

I pour us both large doubles. I down mine in one and move towards him with his.

'Is it true?' he asks.

'Is what true?'

'You're going with Lenny's girl.'

I sigh. 'Who told you?'

His mouth twists. 'Would you believe, one of your dancers?'

'Good old Nikki,' I say.

'Do you know I didn't believe it? You're going out with Lenny's girl.'

'Stop fucking calling her Lenny's girl. She's not his girl. She's mine.'

My brother stands and paces the floor. He seems barely able to keep his cool.

He turns suddenly to me. 'I never expected this from you. From a hothead like Dom, maybe. But you! You're too smart to pull a stunt like this. For God's sake, Shane. What are you thinking?'

'It's done now,' I say quietly.

'No, it's not. Walk away and I'll work something out with him.'

'No,' I say firmly. I have never said no to my brother. My respect, loyalty and love for him is so great I would truly lay down my life for him.

He frowns. 'Is she worth it?'

'Yes.'

He stares at me with disbelief 'Do you even realize what this means? You take his woman and you are declaring war. He's not going to ask you to put your hands up for a bare-knuckle fight. He's going to hire someone to knock you off when you least expect it.'

'I'm prepared to die for her,' I say seriously.

His eyes flash angrily. 'You're prepared to die for her?' he rages. 'What the hell, Shane? You're a fucking kid. You haven't even lived yet and you're prepared to die for her? No woman is worth that.'

'Would you die for Lily?' I ask quietly.

He starts and then he closes his eyes in defeat. 'How long have you known her?'

'A few days.'

'Right,' he says sarcastically.

'I know what I want, Jake.'

He sighs tiredly. 'All right, Shane. Leave it with me. I'll sort it out somehow.'

'I don't want you or Dom to get involved.'

He stares at me in surprise.

'This is my shit and I'll sort it out.'

I see a flash of temper in his eyes. 'Now you're really behaving like a kid. You can't handle Lenny on your own, Shane. He's a fucking snake. He'll clap you on the back and sincerely congratulate you for winning his girl and then bash your head in with a hammer two days later.'

'I have a plan.'

His eyes betray his disbelief that I could actually have a workable plan. I guess I'll be his snot-nosed kid brother forever.

'What's the plan?' he asks slowly.

'I've already said. I'm not involving you or Dom in this.'

He stands in frustration. 'Now you're being ridiculous. We're a family. When we fight as a family we're stronger.'

'Not this time. This time I go it alone.'

'Why? What are you trying to prove?' he asks with barely controlled impatience.

'Jake, ever since Dad died, you've been fighting all our battles for us. You put your own life on hold to keep this family together. Don't think I don't know how you used to come home and cut that cross into your own body. You did loathsome things so we could all eat. But now you have a family of your own. And for the first time you're happy. And I'd rather die than take that away from you.'

He sits down suddenly and gazes down at the floor. 'I can't let you deal with him on your own, Shane. You don't know what he's capable of. I do.' He looks up into my eyes. 'I used to work with him. And I know you can't take Lenny's girl and walk away unscathed.'

'He doesn't love her, Jake.'

'I know he doesn't love her, Shane. He's a psychopath. He doesn't love anyone but himself. But it's a pride thing. He'll take great pleasure in hunting you down and parading her on his arm in all the places where he's known.'

'Jake, you have to trust me when I say I know what I'm doing.'

'Oh, fuck,' he says, and runs both his hands through his hair. 'At least tell me what you're planning. I promise not to interfere.'

I look at him incredulously. 'You're not going to interfere? That's a laugh. You can as much stop yourself from getting involved as I can give her back to him.'

He gives a long sigh. 'Just remember I'm here for you. No matter what.' He sighs again. 'And whatever you are planning to do you better do it fast. Word gets around.'

No ... do not go around bragging, no ...
That you've stolen my heart
And I've nothing more to give...
-The loser, Enrique Iglesias

https://www.youtube.com/watch?v=tLcfAnN2Qg
Y&list=RDGMEMYvZjTda73N9EL0Qo2TnYngV
MtLcfAnN2QgY

Thirty-two

SNOW

After I hear Jake's words to Shane, I creep back to bed and, turning on my side, breathe deeply and evenly until I hear the front door close and Shane comes back into the room minutes later. He stands for a good few minutes looking down at me, but I just pretend to be sleeping. Finally, he goes to his side of the bed and quietly slips in.

For a long time he doesn't sleep. He just lays on his back staring at the wall. I can feel him thinking. Planning whatever it is that he is arranging. He never touches me. A last I hear his breath become even and he sleeps, but I never fall asleep again.

When morning comes, I carefully burrow under the cover and gently lick his sleeping cock. I am so gentle I do not startle him awake. I awaken him gently. His hand moves down and strokes my hair as his cock hardens with surprising rapidity. I take the beautiful, porcelain-smooth thing into my mouth, and let it slide along my tongue.

Oh! Shane.

It must have been delectable for him too, because he groans. A low, long sound of pure pleasure. He puts his hands around my head, gently forcing his cock to the back of my throat. His cock pulses and throbs in my mouth as if holding back from spilling its hot milk down my throat. I let him hold me there. If only he would hold me there forever. A few drops of pre-cum touch the back of my throat and I swallow them eagerly.

I drank my lover.

Let him be part of me. The action, the swallowing movement of my mouth excites him, and he begins to pull me up and down his shaft until his body clenches and he explodes. The force of his orgasm bursts inside my mouth, thick spurts of semen pouring into my throat. This I will take with me.

And I will remember this morning forever.

He pulls me up his naked, warm body and kisses me deeply. He rolls me onto my back and touches my naked pussy. He smiles slowly.

'You're wet,' he accuses.

'And what are you going to do about it then, big boy?' I ask.

'I'm going to eat you,' he says, and goes down on me.

My climax when it comes is bitter-sweet. Sweet because my whole body arches and strains with waves of pure bliss that feel as if they will go on forever. Bitter because they stop. And when they stop I lie drained and almost tearful.

Everything must come to an end.

But the pain of letting go is almost too much to bear. When you find something so beautiful you can't be expected not to cry when you are told you can't have it. Tears swim in my eyes. I blink them away.

He comes up my body and rests on his elbows. 'Hey, are you OK?' His eyes are concerned.

'Yeah, it was a really good orgasm,' I say, and I even manage to smile up at him.

He grins. 'How good was it?'

'Like a box of chocolates and a newborn German Sheppard puppy called Ghengis?'

'Really? As good as all that,' he teases.

'Yes, as good as that.'

He kisses the tip of my nose. 'Oh, Snow. There is just no one like you.'

'That's true,' I say, and kiss the tip of his nose. Against my thigh I feel his cock grow again.

'Really? You can't be wanting it again,' I say with a laugh.

'I'm fucking starving for you. But first, a trip to the toilet is in order. I don't want to be peeing inside you.'

'Ugh, you're disgusting.'

He gets off me laughing and disappears into the toilet. I watch his nude body walk away from me avidly. I will remember this.

When he comes back he sheathes his cock and pushes deep into me. I cry out. Not with pain or pleasure, but with gratitude. I will have this until the day I die. For the first time in my life I understood women who never remarried after they lost their love. Nobody else is good enough. Once you get that one person who is right for you, you will never again want anybody else.

Maybe I will marry. Actually, of course I will marry, my mother will make sure that I do, but I will never, never, never love like this again. Never.

And when we come we lock eyes with each other. It is beautiful.

'I'm yours,' I whisper, wrapping my legs around him tightly.

'Like you won't believe,' he whispers back.

Our bodies entwined, we lie there. It's hard to look into his eyes. They are so blue, so sincere, so awesome. I want to tell him. I want to tell him that I love him like I have never and will never love again, but I realize that my declaration would be neither here nor there.

So many women must have expressed that sentiment. So what if I do too. No, I won't. It will be my little secret. No one will ever know. Not him, not my mother or my father, or anyone. Maybe I will tell my grandchildren one day. If I have them. If I am not contaminated with HIV or even full-blown AIDS.

'Listen,' he says. 'I've got a full day today. Can you entertain yourself for a few hours?'

I smile. Can he see how much love I have for him? 'Sure, I'll clean the flat or something.'

'No, don't do that. I've got a woman coming in to do that. She'll come around about two this afternoon.'

'I'll read a book,' I say quietly.

'Good girl.' He pauses. 'Only thing, don't leave the apartment will you?' If you need anything just call me and I'll arrange for it to be brought to you.'

'I don't need anything, Shane.'

We get out of bed and use the bathroom together. It should have been mundane, a little domestic scene, but it is not. It is special. And it makes me think. How stupid we human beings are. We think that just because we do something all the time it is not special. It is. Just think that tomorrow is the last time you will ever brush your teeth with the one you love. See what I mean now?

So we brush our teeth and use the toilet. And he doesn't appreciate it, because for him it is just another boring task, and he thinks he will do it tomorrow with me too.

When he says, 'What do you want to have for breakfast?'

I know exactly what I want. 'I'll make breakfast,' I say.

He smiles. 'You don't cook.'

'You'll eat my burnt toast and like it,' I say with mock severity.

A strange look crosses his face, but I don't ask that thing that all lovers who are confident of their place in a relationship ask. 'What? What are you thinking of?

Instead, I go into the kitchen. I know exactly what I am recreating. I switch on the oven. 220 degree Fahrenheit. I take the cherry plum jam out of the fridge and put a few spoonfuls on two plates. I take the plates to the top of the oven and I put them there so they will be at room temperature when we have it.

I open the oven door and a blast of hot air hits me in the face. Perfect. I put the brioche rolls onto the metal tray and slide them in. I squeeze oranges and pour the juice into two glasses. I place the container of unsalted butter on the table and set it with knifes and spoons and forks. And the whole time Shane sits at the table and watches me with slightly raised eyebrows.

I take the brioches out of the oven, place them on the table, and sit next to him.

Shane looks at me. 'Thank you.'

'Bon appétit,' I say.

I watch him tear into the brioche. I watch the steam rise from the inside. I watch him cut a small bit of cold butter and lay it on the corner of the brioche that he has already spooned the cherry plum jam on. I greedily watch him put it into his mouth. I close my eyes because I know exactly how it feels and tastes in his mouth. Cold butter, hot pastry, warm jam.

I will remember this forever.

We eat and we drink and then it is time for him to leave. He doesn't kiss me deeply the way people who say goodbye do. He thinks he will be back in a few hours. He thinks I will be here when he comes home. He doesn't know I love him too much to allow him to ever risk his life for me.

I walk him to the door and kiss him goodbye as if I am kissing him before he goes to work. He walks out to the lift. I stand and watch him. The doors of the lift open. He goes in.

And my heart breaks.

I take a shuddering breath and suddenly he is coming out of the lift. He walks up to me, takes me in his arms and kisses me as if he will die without me, his tongue finding its way into my mouth. Entangling with mine. Pulling mine into his mouth. Sucking my tongue.

When he pulls away I am trembling.

'I'll finish that when I come back,' he says dragging his thumb along my lower lip.

I sigh and lay my head on his chest. I hear his heart beating. A steady fast rhythm. I will miss that.

'See you later,' I say.

'Alligator,' he says.

Then he walks into the lift and does not come out again.

I close the door and I go to sit at the kitchen table. I look at the breakfast things around me, the crumbs, the smeared jam, the knife slicked with butter, and my heart feels so heavy. I go into his study and I look around. Once I asked him why he lived in this apartment when he could afford something better. He said this was only a place to sleep in. He mostly lived in the country.

I sit at his desk and write him a letter. It is short. Goodbyes are best short. Besides, there is not much to say. Whatever it was, it's over now. Our time has run out. Soon the wind will blow me away. There is nothing else I can do. I touch my finger to my lips and lay it on the letter. There is a photo album on one of the shelves. I take it down and I turn the pages. His family are all there. I smile to look at their happy faces. How lucky they are.

I come upon one where he is alone. It is a recent one. He is on a boat looking like a film star. His hair wind-tossed, his beautiful body is tanned and relaxed and I wonder who took the picture. Carefully I take the photo out and, without bending it, I slip it into my purse.

Then I go into the bedroom. With my heart weeping, I stand there, memorizing the lingering smell of us, the sun falling on our tangled sheets. I'll dream of this little piece of heaven forever.

With a loud sob I run out of the apartment.

I take a taxi to my street and ask the driver to drop me off at the corner. Cautiously, I walk towards my apartment building. I look up at the windows and they are all shut, the curtains drawn close. Exactly how I left them. I cross the street and go into the building and up the stairs. The door opens behind me and I whirl around nervously, but it is only the woman from the floor above me. She nods and moves to the lift. I take the stairs.

The corridor is deserted.

I go to my door and listen. There is no sound inside. Very quietly I let myself in and stand for a moment. It is silent and still. Vellichor. Once I would have appreciated it. Now, I want nothing to do with it.

I walk into the middle of my apartment and look around at my scrupulously clean home. Everything in its place. Except for the smashed vase and the flowers scattered everywhere. So he has been here. And he is not happy.

I take a deep breath and steel myself.

Quickly, Snow.

Ignoring the mess, I hurry to the bedroom and unpick the mattress. I take out the money and stuff it into my bag. I don't take anything else. I am already at the door when I hear my phone ringing. I walk to it.

Lenny.

While it is still ringing, I take a piece of notepaper from a drawer and write on it. I thank him for everything he has done for me, but I tell him I have to return to India, back to my family. I say goodbye and I end it by saying.

Please don't ever try to contact me again.

I stand at the door and take one last look. The walls seem full of my grief. Other than that, there is nothing of me in here. Then I walk out of that place forever.

I take a taxi to Heathrow airport and buy the next trip to India, which is a noon Air India flight.

'You have a stop in New Delhi,' the woman tells me.

'That's fine,' I tell her.

At the check-in counter, the staff appears surprised and almost suspicious that I have no luggage. But I guess I don't look like a terrorist so they let me pass. I go through passport control and sit down on one of the seats. I feel numb.

On the flight I don't sleep. I close my eyes and think of Shane. I imagine him coming home and finding me gone. I imagine him calling one of his other women. I imagine, I imagine, I imagine. When the air stewardess comes around with the food trolley I have a raging headache. She gives me a couple of painkillers.

I take them and lie back in terrible pain.

Thirty-three

SHANE

We have a bitter north-westerly wind coming off the
sea today.
The cat is curled up and I'm about to do the same for
the afternoon.

I knew she was gone even before I got to the flat. I
guess I knew from the moment she did not answer
the phone. I open the door and the sound of
silence is deafening. A pressing sensation of
heaviness lodges itself in my chest. I walk to the
kitchen table and there is a letter there. I leave it
where it is and go out onto the balcony. I sit on a
chair and, lifting my legs up, rest my crossed
ankles on the railing.

I light a cigarette and take a long drag.
Warm smoke fills my lungs. I blow the smoke out
slowly. I don't think. I just smoke. When I'm
done, I kill the cigarette and go back into the
kitchen.

I pick up her letter and read it. Her writing is
delicate and neat. Just like her.

Hey Shane,

Before I go, I wanted to say it was fun while it lasted, and that I really enjoyed myself with you. You're the most beautiful man I've ever met.

I want to thank you for trying to help me, but more important than that, I want to thank you for bringing me back from the dead. If you had not come into my life ... I don't even want to think. You were like a lone star shining brightly on a dark night.

Anyway, I am returning to India today. In the end, that is my home. I will be safe there.

Take good care of yourself and thank you again, for everything. I'll never forget what you did for me.

Best,
Snow

p.s.
Nothing was a lie. I meant every word I said to you. Every breathless word.

I let the letter flutter down to the table surface, and go into my bedroom. I sit on the bed

 274

and, taking her pillow, bury my face in it. I inhale deeply and let the smell of her hair fill my brain. I should have known last night that she was not asleep. I was too caught up in my plan.

How can she go to India? She has no money.

And then a reluctant smile comes to my lips. She *had* money put away. Good girl. And though it cuts like a knife that she has gone, I am glad that she is out of harm's way. The best place for her at this moment is to be far away.

I put the pillow down and look at my watch. In three hours I have a meeting with Lenny. I'll get her back. This is just temporary.

Whatever it takes.

Beware...
Beware...
Of my hunger
And my anger
    - Mahmoud Darwish

Thirty-four

SHANE

He sits behind his desk, a cigarette between his lips, and squints at me. Cigarette smoke rises between us. His hand moves and the sickening gleam of white makes me think of him touching her body, and in a flash, before I can stop my thoughts, they have run on like stallions in heat. Him on top of her. Her on her hands and knees, and him pushing into her pussy. His ugly fingers digging into her little bottom as he slams into her. My gut twists with the kind of raw, tearing jealousy I have never experienced before. I want to fucking shatter the smug bastard's jaw.

He looks at me expressionlessly. 'What do you want, Eden?'

'You already know what I want,' I say coldly.

He laughs, a short bark of disbelief. 'You're one cocky cunt. You think you can come in here and ask for my woman and I'll just hand her over to you? What do you think she is? A cheap bottle of whiskey that I can pass on to you? Huh?'

'She's not your woman,' I say calmly.

'If she's not my woman, then what the fuck are you doing here asking for my blessing to keep on fucking her?'

'I'm here because you're a cunt, Lenny.'

His eyes flash, but his voice is polite. 'You're Jake's kin so I'll ignore that insult, but I suggest you stop right there. This is going to get ugly real soon and before you know it, it'll be outright war.'

I push my chest out. 'She doesn't love you.'

'My jacket doesn't love me. But it's mine and I use it whenever I please.'

His sneering tone and his choice of words are calculated to infuriate me. I unclench my hands. He will not get to me.

'Well, she is not a jacket. She's a woman, and she can decide who she wants to be with.'

'Let me tell you why she belongs to me,' he says conversationally, as if he is telling an amusing little anecdote. 'When she crawled up to me and begged me to help her, her entire body was covered in bruises and bite marks. There were grip marks on her cheeks where they held her face and fucked her mouth. They had filled her belly with their semen. When she vomited I saw it. Globs of it.'

My face whitens and he sees it.

'Awww ... I've upset the pretty boy. Well fuck you. Her anus was bleeding. She used to scream when she went to the toilet. Her cunt was so swollen she couldn't walk straight for days. She was like a mute child for weeks. I took care of her. I ran the bath and fucking bathed her, asshole.'

He stops and tilts his face upwards.

'She'd wake up in the middle of the night screaming and thrashing, reliving it all. Sometimes she didn't recognize me. She was half mad. One day she ran down the street in the middle of winter stark naked. I ran out after her, tackled her to the ground, and brought her back. I won't tell you the rest of the stuff I went through with her. She was a broken bird. Totally helpless. I could have done anything I wanted with her, but I never touched her for months. So don't come here with all your youth and arrogance and pretend you know how to take better care of her just because you fucked her a few times. Because you fucking don't. You don't know what we've gone through together.'

He laughs bitterly.

'For the first time in my life I felt pity for another creature. She moved something in me. They say that everyone, even the worst killer, has a divine spark in him. She touched that spark. She made me good.'

For some strange reason I actually believe he is telling the truth. That at some level he cares for her. 'If you truly care for her then give her your blessing. Let her be happy.'

'With you?'

'Yes, with me.'

He leers. 'Why? Because you like the taste of her pussy? Eh?'

My jaw clenches. 'Don't talk about her like that.'

'Look at you. You think you've got it all figured out. You think it's a fucking song taking care of her? Are you ready for the flashbacks? Are you ready to be sitting in the middle of a classy restaurant as she freezes up like a fucking statue, or worse for her to start screaming her head off for no goddamn reason? Are you ready to chase her naked body down the road in the dead winter? Are you ready for her to start sobbing while you're fucking her?'

The desire to sock him one hard, so hard he'll never be able to talk again, is so strong I have to clench my fists and force myself to stand still. I take a deep calming breath. I will not let him rile me. No matter what, I have one objective and I'm not going to let anything stand in the way.

'I'm not here for relationship advice, Lenny.'

'You're a young punk. What do you know about relationships? Do you think I don't know about you? Tell me, what's the longest a relationship has lasted with you?'

'She's different. In exactly the same way she touched that spark in you, she touched something in me too.'

He laughs with suppressed fury. 'Yeah, I'm sure you believe that too.'

'It doesn't matter what you think,' I say quietly. 'I'm not here to convince you of anything. I'm here for the videotapes.'

'What videotapes?' he asks, but I see the furtive gleam in his eyes that he is unable to hide fast enough.

'The videotapes that show every occupant in the lift getting off on the second floor of your hotel.'

'What makes you think such videotapes exists?' he asks slyly.

I look at him steadily. 'You forget we know the same people. Everybody knows you have surveillance in your lift.'

He looks at me calmly. 'The tapes are my property. As is Snow.'

'You should have handed those tapes over to the police. It's an obstruction of justice.'

His eyes turn mean. 'Are you threatening me, boy?'

'No, I have less incentive to give the tapes over to the police than you have. I want those men.'

His eyes glitter. 'Revenge. Yes, I thought about it. But it seemed like a wasted effort when I already had the bird in my hand. In a way I owed them thanks.'

'Just give me the fucking tapes. You got no use for them.'

He shakes his head. 'You have a lot of balls coming here asking for this, asking for that. Who the fuck do you think you are?'

I'm done playing with this fuck. There is only one way to deal with a psychopath. And it's not by expecting empathy or giving it. The only way is to yank their greed chain. 'You know the sweet deal you cut in Amsterdam?'

His eyes are suddenly sharp.

'That's my deal. You get any ideas about not playing along and I'll pull the rug from under you. The Russians will be down by two million euros and guess who they'll be coming after? How many breaths do you think you can take before they catch up?'

Lenny smiles tightly and nods. 'Well played, boy. And you did all this for her.'

'Yes.'

'And you want my blessing?'

'No, I don't need your blessing, Lenny. I know what you are. You saw a broken bird and you didn't take it to a vet so that it he could properly heal it, or even attempt to punish the sickos who hurt it. You just took it into your home and caged it, and hoped that it could never fly free again. And you made sure she had no friends so she had no support system outside of you. So don't give me your bullshit about how much you loved her. You did nothing for her that was not totally selfish.'

'She'll be so easy to break.'

I walk up to his desk and plant my palms on the edge. I bend my body menacingly over him. 'Try it,' I say softly. 'Just fucking try it and I'll fucking burn down everything you ever built and see you in hell.'

His color changes, but he looks at me scornfully. 'Do you imagine that I am afraid of you?'

'You should be. I'll tell you this just once: she's mine now. You get in my way and I'll break your damn neck with my own hands.'

He pushes his twisted face towards me. 'You're a fucking fool, Shane. You walk out of here and you're a dead man.'

I stare at him cold-eyed. 'From the moment I stop breathing, you become a walking time bomb. You want war, Lenny, I'll give you war. Or you could simply give me the tapes and I'll call us quits. You have your plum deal and I get my revenge.'

'And the woman?'

 283

'Is mine,' I state flatly.

'And if I say no?' His voice is calculating, probing.

'Then it's war and we both lose. I don't get the girl. You don't get your hands on those lovely millions and we both have some very pissed of Russians, but I figure they'll be more pissed off with you than me.'

'Get out of my office,' he shouts angrily. A vein has popped into existence on his forehead.

'I'm not leaving without the tapes.'

He flies up in temper and stomps over to his safe, opens it, and extracts two videotapes. They are held together with a rubber band. He deliberately chucks it on his desk in such a way that it slides on the surface and falls to the floor together with his pen. I bend down and pick both items up. Calmly, I return the pen to the surface of the table.

I meet his furious eyes. 'Obviously, my guys will be crosschecking with your staff about the records of all the occupants of that floor on that day, and they won't be expecting a frosty reception.'

'You got your tapes. Now fuck off,' he snarls.

'I'll see you around,' I say as I exit his office. Outside, his minders give me dirty looks.

Thirty-five

SNOW

Fifteen hours later, I arrive in Calcutta.

With a heavy heart, I change some money and walk out of the gleaming new Chandra Bose airport. Outside, I get into a taxi. The driver is a smiling, jolly man.

'No bags?' he asks in English.

'No,' I tell him. 'No bags.'

I give him my address and he starts the car. He tries to engage me in conversation with inquisitive questions, but I give him monosyllabic answers, and after a while he gets the message and begins to sing to himself.

I stare out of the window at the dusty billboards, the trees I have missed, the throngs of people, and the vehicles that honk for no good reason at all, and I remember my mother's unkind comment while I was growing up.

She said that Calcutta is like a giant mechanic's shop. A grimy and greasy place where there is no such thing as pure white. And maybe she is right. I can see that there is no building or anyone dressed in brilliant white, but perhaps white is overrated. The heart of this city beats as strongly, or even more strongly than London.

The taxi driver stops his noisy car outside the gates of my family home, and I pay him before getting out of the cab. He drives away and I walk up to the gates. They are locked.

I stand there, my fingers gripping the metal bars as I look into the compound. The year I have been away is like a fantasy I created in my head. Nothing has really changed. What happened in the hotel room was just a nightmare. Lenny is part of that nightmare. And Shane, he is just an impossible dream.

Of course, I could never have a man like him. I just conjured him up.

I look at the green, perfectly manicured lawn, the perfectly straight flowerbeds, and as I am standing there blankly, Kupu, the gardener, comes into the garden with a hose pipe. At first he doesn't see me. Then he looks up and does a double take. His jaw drops open in surprise and then he starts running towards me.

'Snow, Snow,' he shouts happily.

And for a moment my sad heart lifts. I love Kupu. This is my real family. Kupu, Chitra, and Vijaya, our cook. I have missed them. With shaking hands, he unlocks the padlock from a set of keys dangling from his tattered belt.

He opens the gate and I walk through.

He puts his palms together in a prayer gesture. His rheumy eyes are wet.

'How've you been?' I ask in Tamil.

'I'm so glad you've come home. It's not been the same without you,' he replies sadly.

'How is Papa and Mummy?'

'Your papa is lonely. He's lost a lot of weight, but he won't go to the doctor. He spends all his time in his room watching TV.' He drops his voice to a whisper. 'Your brother is home.'

I sigh. 'Thank you for the warning.' I touch his skinny, wrinkled arm. 'I'll see you later, OK?'

His hands come out to grasp my hand tightly. 'All right, child. Don't worry, God sees everything.'

And I just want to burst into tears. God didn't see anything. He let it all happen.

I turn away and walk up the short driveway to the portico of the house. My father's car is in the garage. I open the intricately carved, heavy Balinese doors, and I am standing in the cool interior of my family home. But for the emptiness inside me, it is like I have never left. I walk further into the room and my brother pops his head around the side of the couch, sees me, and raises himself onto his elbow.

'Well, well, the prodigal daughter returns,' he says sarcastically.

I walk closer. He is flipping through a sports magazine and eating monkey nuts. He puts the magazine down. 'Are you back for good?'

I nod.

'Why?'

I shrug. 'Just wanted to.'

His eyes glint with malice. 'The streets of London are not paved with gold after all, eh?'

'They are paved with the same gold as the streets of Kansas City,' I retort.

He looks at me with irritation. 'That was not my fault. Americans are just stupid.'

'Really, all Americans?'

'Yes, they are *all* as stupid as you are,' he says, cracking a nut and lifting the pod over his mouth, letting them fall in.

My brother will never change. He will always be peeing on other people's heads. I watch him chew. 'Where's Papa?'

'Where do you think?'

There is no point in talking to my brother. The longer I stay the more likely it is that we will end up in a huge argument. I turn away from him and start walking towards the stairs.

'Hey, you never said, what happened to your big dreams of becoming a teacher in England?'

'Who told you that?'

'Mother, obviously.'

'I see.'

'So you couldn't make it there then, not even as a pre-school teacher,' he notes gleefully.

'No, I could not make it there,' I say dully.

'You shouldn't have bothered to come back here. There's absolutely fuck all to do. And don't start making plans to set up here forever either. I'm in the process of persuading Mother to sell this house and buy a smaller one for the three of us. I want to use the remainder of the money to set me up in a business.'

I go up the stairs and knock on my father's door. Even from outside I can hear the TV turned up loud.

'Who is it?' my father growls impatiently.

I open the door and enter his room.

His bad tempered scowling face freezes for a second. Then he stands up and exclaims in shock, 'Snow?'

Kupu is right. My father has lost a lot of weight. His face is sunken in and his shirt is hanging off him. 'Yeah, it's me, Papa.'

He fumbles around the low table in front of him for the TV remote. He mutes it and turns towards me eagerly. 'When did you come?'

'I just arrived.'

'But why didn't you let us know? Who picked you up from the airport? Does your mother know?'

'I took a taxi from the airport, Dad, and no, Mum doesn't know. It was a spur of the moment decision to come home.'

'Are you all right?' he asks worriedly.

'Yes, I'm fine.'

'Are you sure?' he insists, frowning. 'I ... I mean, we ... have been so worried about you.'

'Yes, Papa. As you can see I am just fine.'

He nods a few times. 'Come in. Come in. Come and sit down with me. Are you tired? Do you want something to eat? Vijaya can make something for you.'

I go and sit down next to him. 'No, I'm not tired. I slept on the plane and I am not hungry. Are you all right?'

'Yes, I am all right.' He looks at me and sighs. 'You left a child and you have come back a woman. It is a man, isn't it?'

'Yes,' I whisper.

His eyes narrow. 'Are you pregnant?'

I shake my head.

'Are you sure?'

'Yes, I'm very sure.'

'Thank God. Oh, thank God for that,' he says with relief.

I find my eyes filling with tears.

 290

'Don't worry, Snow. *I* will find you a good husband. You are young and beautiful. Many boys from good families will come for you. Don't ever tell anyone about this man who cheated you. You know how it is. People will talk. The less they know the better.'

'Oh, Papa. No one cheated me. And I don't want you to find me a good husband. I promise I just need to stay here for a while and then I will get my own place and be out of your hair.'

'Your own place? Out of my hair? What is this Western nonsense? You are my daughter and you will stay with us for as long as you are unmarried.'

'Oh, Papa,' I sigh.

He grabs my hand. 'This is your home. As long as I am alive you have a home here. Nobody can kick you out.' My father exhales loudly.

'I've missed you, Papa.'

He nods slowly. 'I've made a mess of everything, Snow. A horrible mess. Do you know that you could recognize and follow my voice from the time you were born? You would turn your big, green eyes and stare at me. But I didn't have time for you. I was too busy. And for what? I lost it all anyway. Now I sit here in this little room and turn the TV up too loud and pretend to be bad-tempered so no one will come in. I'm an old fool.'

'You're not an old fool, Papa,' I say sadly.

291

'Yes, I am. No one will know my regrets, except me. Now go and see your mother. She will be very happy to see that you have come home.'

'I'll see you at dinner, OK?'

'Yes, yes,' he says softly.

I stand up and kiss him.

I leave my father's room and as I am closing the door I see my mother coming down the corridor. She is dressed in a housecoat. She stops mid-step. Her eyes widen.

'Hello, Mum.'

She recovers herself and walks up to me. A year has made no difference to her. She is as beautiful and as distant as ever.

'You look different,' she tells me. She stares at me. 'Something happened to you ...'

I drop my eyes.

'Something bad,' she says.

I inhale a quick breath and meet her inquisitive gaze. 'Yes, but I'm fine now.'

'Tell me what happened to you,' she says sternly.

I shake my head. 'Oh, Mum. You know what happened to me.' In spite of myself my voice breaks.

'I warned you, but you've always been too wild, too rebellious, too clever for your own good.' Her tone is cold and unforgiving.

And then I see it in her face. She is not sorry for me. She is glad that I have been punished. I have acted impulsively and I have been punished.

'Is it OK for me to live here for a while?' I ask softly.

'Of course. Where else would you go?'

'Thanks, Mum.'

'I'll go and tell Vijaya to lay an extra place for you for dinner. Why don't you go and have a shower and freshen up? You can fill me in later. It's been so long since I've been in London.'

And then she walks away. I turn to watch her go. *What have I ever done to you to make you hate me so?*

I know my time here will be short. I have a little money still and I must find a way to go to the city and find a job there. I *will* make it on my own. I *can* make it on my own. I *will* become a pre-school teacher.

I think of Shane. He seems to belong to a different world. I wonder what he is doing now, and immediately I feel a tearing pain in my chest. I take his photo out and look at it. *Are you well? Are you safe, my darling?* I trace his jaw line with my finger. I stroke his body and the tears come hard.

Oh, Shane, Shane, Shane.

Thirty-six

JAKE

I enter the smoky back room of the Chili Club, and Lenny is sitting behind his desk. I close the door and he rises and comes forward.

'How are ya?' he asks, pumps my hand and gestures to a chair. His friendliness doesn't disarm me or take me off my guard. Lenny and I go back many years. I know him well. He is nicest before he sticks a knife in your back.

'Good. You?'

He turns the corners of his mouth downwards. 'Can't complain.'

I sit, lean back, and watch him take his seat behind the desk. He opens a silver cigarette box and holds it out to me. Technically, I've stopped smoking. But I still indulge once in a while. I reach out and take one. He flips open a black lighter. I lean forward and wait for the tip of my cigarette to burn cherry bright.

'Thanks,' I say and leaning back, inhale deeply.

He lights his own cigarette and sits back, making his chair tip back. I watch him inhale and exhale. His eyes find mine through the haze of smoke.

'Like old times, eh?' he says.

'Like old times,' I repeat. My voice is easy.

'What do you want, Jake?' he asks slyly.

'My brother came to see you?'

'Yeah,' he says. 'We came to an agreement.'

I don't show it, but deep inside I feel a flare of pride and joy. I came here thinking I'd have to bargain, threaten, and even murder if necessary, but Shane's got it all covered. My baby brother's grown up. He fought his own battle and won. How the fuck did he do it though?

I take a lungful of hot smoke. 'Right. So we're good.'

He jerks his head backwards as if even the thought of war between my family and him would never occur to him. 'You know me. I don't keep grudges.'

And I know why too. Because Lenny always settles the score until he's satisfied that he has had his pound of flesh. 'Yeah, you're a straight guy, Lenny.'

'I'd never harm your family, Jake.'

I fix him with a stare. 'No, you're too clever for that.'

He flicks ash into the ashtray. 'War between us is good for no one. The Mafia learned that the hard way, eh?'

'He's young, I hope he didn't give too much away,' I say.

He barks out a laugh, short and sharp. 'Too much? Shane? You don't give him enough credit.'

I say nothing. I drag another lungful of smoke and exhale it slowly. Suddenly I feel worried. What has Shane got himself into? What could he possibly have done that Lenny is so pleased with himself. I expected to find him spitting blood.

I frown. 'What exactly did you agree to with him?'

'Relax, Jake. He's a chip off the old block. He didn't have to give too much away. It was no big deal. I was happy to give her up. She's damaged goods. I was keeping her as an act of charity.' He looks at me craftily. 'He helped set me up with a juicy deal.'

He glances at his cigarette tip. 'And the little punk introduced me to two of the best whores I've ever had. I'm flying them both over for this weekend. One of the fucking bitches is double-jointed. She can suck her own pussy.'

He stops to catch my gaze, and there is something chilling about his eyes. 'They put up a good show. I could give you their phone numbers if you want?'

There is a sour taste in my mouth. Amazing to think this was my life for so long. It wasn't me then, and it's certainly not me now. I grind the cigarette butt in the ashtray on the table. 'Thanks, but I'll pass.'

Lenny watches me with his empty eyes. I know he is hiding something. That bullshit about keeping Snow as an act of charity, my four-year old daughter could see through that one. Shane has something on him, but I don't need to know how far Shane has gone. Shane did what he had to do. All I need to know is that Lenny has not been left with a grudge. And I am satisfied that no retaliation is due. I stand up.

'See you around, Lenny.'

'Give my regards to Snow,' he says.

I turn around and stare at him.

He smiles slowly. 'Bad joke,' he says.

I open the door and walk out of his property never to return.

Thirty-seven

SHANE

I stand outside the gates to her parents' house.

There is a bell, but before I can ring it, a skeletal man in an old shirt and stained baggy trousers starts crossing the garden and comes towards me. His face is full of wrinkles and he has only a few yellowing sticks for teeth. He stands a foot away from the gate and peers worriedly at me.

'Snow. Is Snow home?' I ask with a friendly smile.

And suddenly his face splits into two with a happy greeting. Nodding vigorously, he unlocks the gate and lets me in. I wait while he relocks the gate, and when he makes a beckoning gesture with his right hand, I follow him. He opens the front door, kicks off his rubber slippers and looks pointedly at my shoes.

'Of course,' I say, and take off my shoes.

He points to a sofa. I sit and he quickly disappears. I look around me. It reminds me of a Balinese interior with beautiful hardwood furniture and two fans tuning lazily on the ceiling. I walk to the window and look out … and I immediately see her.

She is in the garden sitting on a covered swing reading a book. I turn away to go to her and find a blonde woman in her early to mid forties standing at the entrance of the room. She is beautiful in a hard sort of way, and even though no two women could be less alike, I know immediately that this is Snow's mother. She has the chilly, stern air of a school mistress. Her eyes sweep over me disparagingly. Oh fuck! T-shirt and jeans. *Not a good look, Shane, my boy*. She would have warmed better to a sharp suit and a Rolex watch.

She comes forward. 'You are looking for my daughter, I believe,' she says in such a strong British accent that she must take great pride in it to keep it so strong after all these years of living in a foreign country.

'Hello, Mrs. Dilshaw.'

She inclines her head to acknowledge my guess. 'I'm afraid I have no idea who you are.'

'I'm Shane Eden.'

'Have a seat, Mr. Eden.'

I walk to the settee I just vacated. She perches daintily on the one opposite mine. 'May I ask what you want of my daughter?'

I smile. 'I guess you could say that I've come to ask your daughter out.'

Her eyes become hostile. 'Didn't my daughter run away from you?'

'No. She misunderstood the situation. I've come to explain.'

'I'm afraid that won't be possible, Mr. Eden.'

I frown. 'Why not?'

'This is not London, Mr. Eden. We have different customs here. Certain ... niceties have to be observed. Reputations are so easily ruined. Snow's father is in the process of negotiating a marriage for her. I'm sure you'll appreciate how confusing it will be for her to have your presence here now. I'm sorry you have had a fruitless journey, but I'm afraid you won't be able to see my daughter.'

'I totally understand. Thank you for being so frank with me,' I say and stand.

She stands too, but with surprise etched in her eyes. I don't think she expected such an easy victory.

I start walking to the front door and she follows.

The thin man is sitting on the front steps. When he sees me he stands up and runs towards the gate. I slip on my shoes.

'Goodbye, Mrs. Dilshaw,' I call over my shoulder and start walking towards the gate. The old man lets me out. I step outside and he immediately padlocks the gate. The mother is still waiting at the front door. I wave at her. She does not wave back. I thank the old man and I start walking down the road.

I walk on until I reach the edge of wall to their property. Then, praying for an absence of guard dogs, I climb over their neighbor's wall and drop into their garden. I run along the wall that separates the two properties until I am about halfway down, where I estimate Snow's back garden to be on the other side.

I put my hands on the top of the wall, pull myself up and over, and drop into the springy, perfectly manicured grass of Mrs. Dilshaw's garden. Twenty feet away I can see Snow gently rocking on the covered swing. There is an open book in her lap, but she is staring at a far away spot on the horizon. She is wearing some kind of breezy Indian costume with a long soft-green top and trousers in the same material. Her hair is down her back in a one long plait.

She looks vulnerable and lost.

I stand watching her with an ache in my chest, and I remember a National Geographic documentary of two elephants reuniting after a separation of twenty years. Since they did not know how the elephants would react, they let them meet in a barn with a thick metal gate between them. The younger strong elephant put its trunk through the gaps in the bar and stroked and hugged the other elephant, but such was their desire to get closer that they bent solid metal.

That is what I felt like at that moment.

I could bend metal to get to her. To hug and press her body to mine and never let go. I want to carry her off to my hotel room and claim her all over again, but I don't do that. Her mother's words are still fresh in my mind. For her sake I must be mindful that the culture here is different. I am a foreigner. A white man. I don't want to embarrass her. I don't know what she has told them about me. I take a few more steps towards her, but she doesn't see me. She is totally lost in her own world.

'Hello stranger,' I call out.

She nearly jumps out of her skin, the book falling to the grass, her hands rushing up to clutch her chest. Our eyes meet. Hers are as round and shining as a startled cat's. Then a look of such wild joy rushes into them that the desire to throw her on the grass and take her is almost unbearable.

Her mouth opens. 'What ... Why ...Why are you here?' she stammers.

I take a step towards her. 'Guess.'

She shakes her head as if in disbelief. 'How did you find me?'

I shrug and go closer still. 'I saw your passport while we were in France remember? Besides, Elizabeth Dilshaw is not a hard name to find in India.'

'But how did you get in here?'

'I scaled your neighbor's wall and jumped into your compound.'

'You did what?'

'What's so surprising about that?' I grin. 'Technically speaking, I've climbed mountains and crossed seas to get to you.'

She doesn't smile. 'You can't fight Lenny. I don't want you to, Shane.'

'I'm not starting a war with Lenny.'

'But he will hurt you if he finds out.'

'Lenny's taken care of,' I say shortly.

Her eyes narrow suspiciously. 'What do you mean?'

I shrug casually. 'He's given us his blessing.'

She stares at me. 'That can't be. Lenny would never give his blessing to us.'

'You have my word that it is true.'

She frowns. 'How can that be? I know him. I've seen him in action. Even Jake warned you how vindictive he can be.'

'Tsk, tsk, you been listening at doors again,' I say lightly.

'Did you do something to him?' she asks urgently.

I walk up to her and get down on my haunches in front of her. I take her soft small hands in mine. 'I didn't hurt him if that is what you are asking. Let's just say that he and I have an understanding.'

She frowns. 'You make it sound so easy. It couldn't have been. The Lenny I know is very vindictive. He enjoys hurting people.'

'Lenny is a psychopath. Like a reptile he's motivated by self-interest at all times. He had something I wanted, but then I had something he wanted more than the thing he had that I wanted. So we made our exchange. Besides, he knows a war with the Edens would have left blood on the floor, most probably his.'

'So what do we do now?' Her voice is so soft I almost do not hear. I see her body tremble through the thin material of her outfit, and I remember again how she trembled with trepidation every time she wanted me in Saumur. I smile inwardly.

'You had a dream. You have to follow it. Come back to England with me.'

'Just leave. Just like that?'

I grin. 'We can kiss first.'

She looks around nervously. There is no one around, but she shakes her head. 'That would be a bad idea.'

'I met your mother by the way.'

'What? When?'

I grin. 'Before I dropped over the wall. I tried the gate/front door route, but your mother gave me my marching orders.' I change my voice to a falsetto. 'This is not London, Mr. Eden. Certain niceties have to be observed.'

She giggles.

'She also informed me that your father is in the process of arranging a suitable wedding for you. Obviously, no one had informed her that you are mine.'

'What? My father is doing no such thing,' she says crisply.

'Mr. Eden,' a stern voice calls from the French windows.

I wink at Snow. 'I have to go, but will you come see me later at the Oberoi Grand?'

'Yeah, I'll come to see you,' she says with a sultry look in her eyes.

And my fucking randy cock dances excitedly.

'You're not going to jump over the wall again, are you?' she asks.

'I think I'll brave your mother one more time. See you later,' I say, grinning at her.

'Alligator,' she says.

I turn. 'Coming, Mrs. Dilshaw,' I say, and start walking. As I get closer I can see how furious she is.

'How dare you?' she rasps.

305

'Sorry, but you'd have done the same if you had travelled thousands of miles to see someone.'

'Get out of my house.'

I smile widely. I'm in a good mood. So I'll be generous. 'I have a funny feeling, Mrs. Dilshaw, we're going to be seeing a bit more of each other than you're expecting, so it might be a good idea to keep it civil. Good day, Ma'am,' I say, and walk out through the front door again.

My heart is soaring.

Thirty-eight

SNOW

I've been to The Oberoi grand a few times. It is one of the oldest heritage luxury hotels in Calcutta. As soon as you walk in from the crowded street, you enter a different world. Back to a time when the Indian Maharajas did 'posh' far better than the English. There are framed prints of birds and bejeweled, turbaned men on the walls. The reception floors are gleaming black marble with little diagonal white marble squares, and the dark wood paneling in the lobby is carried right through to the elevators and all the way to the toilet seat covers.

The door is held open for me by a uniformed doorlady. She is genuinely courteous and friendly. I walk up to the lobby and they call Shane's suite for me. They probably think I am a prostitute, but I don't care. With an impeccably polite smile, the receptionist passes the phone to me.

'Hi,' I say into the receiver.

'Stay there. I'll come down,' he says.

'No, I'll come up. I know my way to the deluxe suite.'

I get into the lift and go up to his floor. I knock on the door and it opens after the first rap.

Before I can say anything he pulls me in and, fisting his hand in my hair, swoops down on my lips. I gasp with shock and his tongue enters my mouth. His other hand comes around my waist and slams me into his hard body. He sweeps his tongue through my mouth. The raw animal desire radiating out of him makes the blood pound in my veins. From the first day I have been helpless in its wake.

Never taking his mouth away from mine, he walks me backwards towards the bed and we fall in a tangle. Our clothes come off haphazardly. The sound of zips, something tearing, something else whispering, and our hearts booming, fill my starving senses. Then we are naked. I hear the sound of the foil. And then he fills the aching, empty hole inside me with his beautiful, big cock.

'Ahhhh ...'

The orgasm when it comes lasts and lasts. With white dots before my closed eyelids. I slump against the headboard, exhausted.

'I was so hungry for your flesh I couldn't wait to fuck you again,' he growls.

'The insides of my thighs ... they are trembling ... for more,' I whisper.

'Tell the insides of your thighs I haven't even begun.'

Hours we are in that bed. I am aware of all the places his hands have been, my ankles, the soles of my feet ... the insides of my wrist ... the delicate skin at the nape of my neck.

And then his phone rings. 'Aren't you going to answer that?'

'No,' he says, and carries on kissing all the small bones of my spine.

But his mobile rings again. And again. He stops with a frown and answers it.

He sits up. 'Yeah.'

He turns slightly away from me. 'I'll be there in a couple of days. Why?' He listens again and sighs, his shoulders sagging. 'Fuck. Right. Yeah. Tell Ma I'll be there.'

He ends his call and turns to me. 'Look, I wanted to meet your parents properly and all, but we have to go back tonight. My mother's father is on his deathbed and he wants to see the whole family before he passes on. My mother wants me there.'

I sit up and touch his throat. He is so perfect I could weep. 'You go ahead. I'll join you in a couple of days. There's something I must do first.'

He looks at me. 'No, Snow. I don't want to leave without you.'

'I promise I will leave the day after tomorrow. I have to go and see Chitra.'

He looks at me curiously. 'Why?'

'I don't know why. I just know I have to go and see her before I leave.'

'Where is she?'

'Kupu knows where she lives. He will take me.'

'Is it far away or dangerous?'

'No.'

'Regardless, I'll arrange for someone to go with you and Kupu. You're not travelling around on your own.'

'OK, but you don't know anyone here,' I say with a grimace.

'Listen. You know me.'

'Yeah. I know all about you.' I smile gratefully.

'When was the last time you saw her?' he asks curiously.

'I haven't seen her since I was ten. Something happened and one day she was no longer there.'

'All right, go and see her. I'll arrange a ticket back for you for the day after tomorrow. Don't let me down.'

'I'll never let you down.'

'Chitra's poor, isn't she?'

'Very,' I say sadly.

'Would you like to give her some money?'

Immediately my eyes fill with tears. 'Yes,' I say, swallowing hard, unable to believe that he would be so generous to someone he had never met.

'Oh, sweet Snow. What a soft-hearted thing you are.'

'Thank you, Shane. You have no idea what this means to me.'

'Here's what I want you to do. I want you to go see her and give her enough to change her life. Buy her a little house or something. You decide what is best for her, OK?'

I stare at him in astonishment. 'You'd do that for a total stranger?'

'You're my baby and you love her. So she becomes part of my family.'

OMG! He called me his baby! I feel so happy I think my head is going to burst. And I almost blurt it out that I love him then, but I don't. I just don't have the guts.

'You're leaving tonight?'

'Yeah. My brother's secretary has already booked me a flight.'

I nod. 'Go and meet the old devil.'

'I really wanted you to come.'

'I know, but I'll be there the day after tomorrow.'

'I will arrange for you to be picked up at Heathrow and brought to my grandfather's place. Have you got a mobile phone?'

'I haven't got around to getting a new one yet.'

'I'm going to transfer some money into your account tomorrow. Get a mobile phone immediately so you can call me, and more importantly I can call you anytime I want,' he says with a grin.

'OK, I will.'

We make love one more time. My body tingles, and then it is time for me to go. It feels strange to let him go again. At the door, I lay my cheek against his chest. I can hear his heart pounding, and wish I could stay there forever just listening to its steady beat.

'Hey,' he says softly. 'It's only two days. Nothing can keep us apart again.'

Thirty-nine

SNOW

To my horror, Kupu takes me to the slums in the outskirts of the city.

'Chitra lives here?' I ask in disbelief.

'Yes, Snow,' he says as if living in this rubbish heap is normal. 'She lives here now.'

I am almost speechless with shock when we go down a dusty mud path filled on either side with corrugated iron roofed huts. Kupu stops outside one of the shanty huts and calls out for Chitra.

She shuffles out wearing an old sari and is holding a dirty, folded-up cloth pressed to her mouth. Her gaze falls on Kupu and then flutters over to me. For a few seconds her eyes squint and her head cranes forward with disbelief. Then her eyes widen and she stares at me as if she is seeing a ghost.

We look at each other. Then she screams with joy from behind the cloth pressed to her and

almost trips over the doorway in her rush to hug me. Tears pour down her face.

I hug her tightly and join her in her tears. She is happy to see me, but I am horribly saddened and frightened to see the state of her. She is a shadow of her former self. Her eyes are deeply sunken and her body is a bag of bones. That she is very ill is clear. I can hardly believe this is *my* Chitra. Wiping her tears with the ends of her sari she bade us to enter her tiny hut.

I look around at the bare, pitiful surroundings. There is only one plastic chair, a little stove, some cooking utensils, and some cardboard boxes with her belongings in one corner. It is like an oven in this small space and I actually feel claustrophobic and oppressed. To think that Chitra spends her whole life here is unthinkable to me.

'What's wrong with you, Chitra?' I ask.

'I have tuberculosis,' she says, suddenly breaking in a hacking cough that causes her to double over with its intensity.

'But tuberculosis is curable. Why are you like this?' I ask when the coughing fit is over.

'I've been treated for lung problems for more than a year now, but because the doctors have been making wrong diagnoses and prescription errors, they have made the disease stronger rather than curing it. Now my doctors keep changing the drugs, but nothing seems to work. The only thing they have not yet attempted to do is surgery to remove the infected parts of the lungs, but I can't afford it and anyway I am so weak now I don't think I can even survive it. Because of all the wrong diagnoses I have hearing loss, terrible joint pain, you cannot imagine how they ache at night.'

That afternoon I call Shane on my new mobile and tell him exactly how I want his money for Chitra to be spent. I want her to have the best doctors in India to perform her surgery, and when she is better I want her to come and stay with us for a while. He says he will get someone to immediately start making the arrangements for her surgery and treatment. In less than an hour he calls back to give me the address of a private hospital to take Chitra to recuperate.

We admit her there and I breathe a sigh of relief. It is air-conditioned and clean and modern. The nurses there immediately take over. I stand at reception and cry from pure release of the fear and tension I had been holding ever since I saw the state Chitra was in.

I tell Chitra that I have to go to London, but I will be back for her.

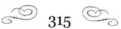

She hangs on to my arm pitifully. 'Go, my beloved daughter. I will always love you,' she says, and both of us burst into tears.

When I tell my mother my plan to join Shane in London, a massive argument errupts. For the first time ever in my life my father takes my side.

'Just let her go,' he says.

'Did you actually see the man she's going to?' my mother snaps.

'No, but I trust Snow,' my father says quietly.

'Well, I saw him and he looks like the worst kind of player.' She turns to me and demands. 'What is he? Irish?'

'He's a gypsy.'

She clasps her hands and shakes her head in disbelief. 'Oh my God! I can't believe it. He's a gypsy! They're the worst. They're just a bunch of thieves. What does he do?'

'He's in business.'

'Business? What business? Stealing manhole covers during the night and selling them for scrap?'

'Mum, please leave it. Even if he is poor, and he is not, I'm going to him.'

'He'll get you pregnant, break your heart, and he'll leave, and then you'll come running here with his bastard baby in tow.' She turns angrily to my father. 'Is that what you want for her?'

'I want Snow to be happy,' my father says stoically.

I look at my father and he quickly winks at me. My eyes widen with surprise. I swiftly look at my mother and thank God she missed the wink.

'I'm talking to two brick walls here,' she bursts out. 'He *won't* make her happy. She's infatuated with his looks and superficial charm. It won't last.'

'I don't believe that it won't last.' He turns to look at me. 'Snow is special. It's hard to leave her.'

I smile at my father. And he smiles back.

'Well, don't turn around and say I didn't warn you,' she huffs.

My mother is so furious with me she refuses to come with me to the airport.

Shane had led me to believe that someone holding a placard would be picking me up at Heathrow airport. So it is a great shock to see him standing there with a massive bunch of flowers and an even bigger pink teddy bear. I don't run into his arms. I stop so suddenly the person behind bangs into me, and I stare at the sight he makes. All at once he is cute, ridiculously edible, and heart-stoppingly gorgeous.

He crooks his finger at me so I rush to him and hug him while he holds the big bear and flowers at the sides of his body.

'A teddy bear?' I ask.

'It's Layla's idea,' he confesses sheepishly.

I laugh. 'Your sister thought you should buy me a teddy bear?'

'Yup, I get it.' He spots a little girl standing nearby and he holds the bear out to her. 'Want this?' he asks.

The girl nods big-eyed and immediately takes it.

Her mother says, 'Oh, that's so kind of you. Thank you.'

'No problem,' he says and turns to me. 'God, I've missed you. I actually can't wait to get inside you.'

And that is what he does. We get into the car and, halfway to his grandfather's home, we stop on a small country lane where he rips my panties off and gets inside me ... perfection!

His grandfather's home is a small bungalow with tarmac outside, and chintz curtains, lace covered armchairs, and a patterned carpet inside. His grandmother is a grey woman who has the cowed, beaten eyes of someone who has spent some of her teenage life and her entire adult life with a bully. A woman who lives like a silent ghost, terrified of provoking her husband's rage, just for the crime of existing.

She is in the kitchen making a famous Romany dish that Shane tells me is called Jimmy Grey. Beefsteak, liver, chicken and pork, onions and swede, shallow fried in animal fat.

As a race, the Romany gypsies are proud people. They eat, sleep, grieve, and celebrate only with their own kind. Jealously guarding themselves from infiltration by non-gypsies, they neither trust nor like the ways of others. Perhaps their mistrust of other races comes from centuries of persecution and hatred they have suffered no matter where they go. As soon as I am brought into her presence, I feel that instant wariness and mistrust.

I am a gorger, a non gypsy.

So I hold back too, and just watch the large personalities around me set about preparing for the death of one of theirs. After introducing me around to a whole bunch of uncles, aunties and cousins, Shane takes me into the bedroom.

Death is already in the room, in the smell and the odd stillness. There are fresh wild flowers in a vase by the bedside, and candles have been lit even though it is in the middle of the afternoon The old man must have been large in his day, for even after more than a year of cancer eating through him he is still a big, strongly built man.

Under his bushy grey eyebrows he has fierce black eyes that alight on me. Shane brings me closer and he stares at me with his black eyes. I want to say something, but I am almost hypnotized by his strange stare. Silently, without having uttered a single word, he turns his face away after about a minute.

'Come on,' Shane whispers in my ear and we exit the room.

I exhale the breath I was holding. 'That was weird,' I say.

'Yeah, who knows what is going through his head? Come on. I want you to meet my mother.'

Shane's mother is outside drying clothes on a washing line.

'Ma,' Shane calls, and she turns and looks at us. There are clothes pegs in her mouth. She takes them out and holds them in her hand as we walk up to her.

'Hello, Snow,' she says, her eyes sliding over me. She is not overly friendly, but she is different from her mother and father. She has kindness in her eyes, and a deep love for her family.

'Hello, Mrs. Eden. I'm sorry about your father,' I say.

'Don't be sorry, my dear. It'll be good for my mother. She'll finally be free.'

'If he was such a horrible man in life, why did your mother rush her whole family here?' I ask Shane curiously.

'Gypsies are superstitious people. The belief is that people can come back from the dead to wreak revenge on the living. So when someone is dying, their families, friends, acquaintances and even enemies come to them to ask for forgiveness and settle any strife, for fear of the mulo, a type of undead.

That afternoon Mickey passes away. The funeral is a massive affair. More than a thousand people travel from all over Britain to come to the old

man's funeral. He was a great boxer in his time and was highly regarded.

The dead man is dressed in his best attire, his gold watch, and his favorite pipe are put into the coffin with him.

Part of the tradition is to have the body at home, and have mourners and relatives pay their respects by coming to the house, so a marquee is erected. A skip is hired and left outside the house to light a bonfire in. People come and go all hours of the night. There is a lot of cooking, drinking, toasting to the dead man, and singing. The entire affair is characterized by abundance, public mourning, and solemn ritual.

It all ends with a massive procession of hundreds of people walking the five mile walk to the cemetery. The convoy includes the horse drawn carriage that carries Mickey, eight cars, lorries carrying wreaths and floral tributes. They celebrate the life of Mickey. Children, even Lilliana and Tommy, ride up front in a horse drawn cart alongside the hearse.

After the funeral, all of Mickey's possessions are brought out and burned. It is a form of destroying all material tied to the dead.

That night in the hotel, we are both lying on the bed, tired. Shane turns to me and says, 'I don't want to use condoms anymore. I want us both to take our tests.'

I don't look at him. 'OK,' I say quietly.

Forty

SNOW

Three days later, after Chitra has been successfully operated on, the letters drop through the letter flap. I pick them up and take them to Shane. He is working on his laptop, but he looks up when I come into the room holding the envelopes in my hand. For a second I imagine I see dread in his face, but then it is gone in a flash. He closes his laptop and grins. 'Do you want to go first or shall I?'

'You,' I say, a knot in my stomach.

He walks over to me and takes the envelope I am holding. He tears it open and glances at it. He looks up at me. 'I'm clear.'

'Oh, good,' I choke. 'Right,' I say and, taking a deep breath, I tear my envelope. My hands are shaking so much I can't even take the letter out. His hand covers mine. 'It doesn't matter either way. Whatever it is we'll deal with it, OK?'

'OK,' I whisper.

I pull the letter out of the envelope and unfold it. I let my eyes skim it. My eyes start to tear up. I'm in the clear. I look up and his face is a picture. He is pretending as if he doesn't care either way. And suddenly I am so full of joy and happiness I want to play. I want to say, 'No, all is not well,' but I find I can't even do that to him. It's too much. So I just shake my head.

His eyes widen. 'What?' he gasps.

I stare at his reaction. My God! He has been terrified about the results. Probably even more than me. My mouth opens to tell him it is just a little joke, but the penny drops for him and he snatches the paper out of my hand and reads it. He looks up, his eyes totally blank.

I start walking backwards. 'It was just a joke. I just wanted to see your expression. Come on. It's funny,' I say cajolingly.

He lunges forward, grabs me by my thighs and, hauling me up, throws me over his shoulder like I am a sack of something unprecious.

'I'm sorry, I'm sorry,' I say, but by now I am laughing so much. *I'm clear. I'm clear.*

He takes me to the bedroom and throws me on the bed.

'Hey,' I protest.

He reaches forward and unbuttons my jeans and pulls the zip down. Then he grabs the material at the heels and yanks so hard my jeans come off in one swift movement.

'I don't know what you're so angry about. It was just a joke,' I giggle.

He throws my jeans behind him and hooks his fingers into the tops of my panties. They come off real easy.

'Come on, Shane,' I coax.

Silently he pulls my T-shirt over my head and, while I am slightly raised off the bed, unhooks my bra and flings that away too.

'Awww ... baby, don't be so evil,' I whisper.

With a totally granite face he undresses, his cock stiff enough to be a coat stand, and crawls on the bed. The violet specks in his eyes are glowing as he grazes his thumb across my lower lip. Delicious.

'Now why would I be evil? This is a fucking celebration. We're both in the clear, my darling.'

'Exactly,' I whisper.

He curls his hands around my ribs. His lips brush my ear. 'Flip over, Princess.'

Something about his voice makes me look again at him, but he smiles innocently. I get on my stomach and he presses his long body against mine and slides his cock in. My body arches with pleasure.

It is the first time. It is our first time.

His arm comes around my body and I thrust my breast eagerly into it. He rams into me hard. Really hard. It's what he's wanted to do for a long time. Come inside my body. And he's going for it.

It is raw, uncivilized, brutal and beautiful.

And when, finally, he gets to spurt his seed deep inside me, it is with a kind of sigh. A sound of deep satisfaction. As if something long desired had been achieved. For some seconds he remains inside me, throbbing. Then he withdraws and I feel his fingers enter me. Not to arouse me, but to smear his seed all around my sex even between my ass cheeks. He takes great pleasure in it. He even bites my ass. Then he turns me around.

'Your turn,' he says.

And I smile, because my turn means the world is about to turn upside down. And upside down it goes. He massages my wet flesh. I moan. He sucks my clit. It doesn't take long before I jerk violently and climax. Does he stop? No. Of course not. His fingers milk me. Again and again. Until I shriek and spasm uncontrollably.

Does he stop then?

Noooooo ...

Emotion wells up inside me, a humbling, breaking typhoon. I'm free. I'm actually disease free. I don't have to worry about infecting him ever again. Tears slide down my cheeks. He licks them. The way a dog would. I like dogs. They are loyal creatures.

'You're mine,' he says and kisses, licks, sucks and strokes every inch of me. Every crevice has its day. We do everything. He tastes my skin as if tasting it for the first time. He holds my thighs and drinks from my pussy. And then he comes inside me. Again. We go at it for hours.

It is afternoon when I cry. 'No more, Shane. No more. I can't take anymore.'

'Yes, you can,' he says.

And he is right. I can.

Trembling and breathless I climax again. I flop on my back, exhausted and limp. Shane lies beside me, our fingers entwined. For a while neither of us speak. I look up at the ceiling. 'What if I get pregnant, Shane?'

'Don't worry. We'll just get an abortion,' he says.

My head whips around. 'What?'

He turns his head to face me. 'What's wrong?'

For a moment I can't believe what I am hearing and then I start punching his arm. 'You bastard,' I accuse, laughing.

He grabs both my hands and pulls me on top of him. We are both sweaty and our bodies slip.

He doesn't laugh. 'Do you know how sad and destroyed I was when you shook your head earlier? I felt as if you had stabbed me in the heart with a knife.'

Immediately I am contrite. 'I'm sorry. I shouldn't have done that. It was no joking matter. I think I was so relieved I kind of lost of my senses. I thought it would be funny. I see now how wrong I was. Will you forgive me?'

'There's nothing to forgive. Remember what the most famous person in your land of birth said, Love does not measure. It just gives.'

'Mother Theresa,' I whisper.

'I love you, Snow. You'll never know how happy I am that your tests came back negative.'

My head swings around. 'What?'

'Yeah, I'm in love with you. Can you fucking believe that?'

I stare at him. 'It's not another retaliation joke, is it?'

'No, it's not a joke. But I was kinda hoping you might return the sentiment. A bit.'

I start laughing with joy. 'I love you, Shane Eden. I love you so much, I thought I'd die when we parted. I used to dream about you telling me you loved me, but I never believed that it would happen,' I reply.

'You know what you make me feel like? You make me want to dance in the kitchen with you. And go out with you to used bookshops and rescue the oldest, saddest books in them. Or go to the market and buy up all the lobsters in it and set them free in the ocean.'

My eyes start filling with tears of happiness.

'Do you know that poem by Pablo Neruda, If You Forget Me?'

I shake my head.

'It reads, if little by little you stop loving me, I shall stop loving you little by little.' He traces my cheekbone with his finger. 'Not for me. Nothing you do or say can ever make me forget you and nothing can extinguish my love for you. My love is a guest of eternity. I'm never ever letting go.'

Dizzy with happiness, I get on one elbow and, resting my head on my palm, I circle his nipple with a finger. 'So when did you realize that you loved me then?'

'I always felt really possessive of you. From the first moment I saw that slime ball touch your thigh in my club, I felt something, a burning anger, deep inside as if he was stepping into my territory. I think it made me a bit schizophrenic. Sometimes I worried about hurting you and sometimes I was rougher than I should have been. And when I dropped you off after the holiday I was like a bear with a sore head. I drove straight to my mum's house and I was in such a fowl mood my mother actually chased me out of her house.'

I giggle.

'You can laugh, but you don't know how I burned with jealousy. Fuck, even thinking about it now makes me feel uneasy. I didn't sleep that night. Short of going up to him and bashing his head in, I did everything in my power to make sure he would be kept up so late, he wouldn't get it into his head to take an early flight and turn up at your place that night. But I couldn't sleep. I realized that I didn't feel good when you were out of my sight. I wanted to protect you. In my head you were already mine, you just didn't know it yet.'

'Really?'

'Yeah,' he says with his trademark mischievous grin.

'But when did you realize you *loved* me?' I probe.

'I think it was when I saw you surrounded by those idiots outside the club. Oh, my God. I have never felt such a mad rage in my entire life. I knew I could have killed them. And then when I looked into your face. I was so frightened that somehow I was too late, they had hurt you. You couldn't speak. You couldn't move. Jesus, I've got goose bumps now just thinking about it.'

He touches my face. 'You just looked so broken and I didn't know what to do. That was when I knew I loved you, and I would have done anything for you. Anything to wipe that look from your face.'

I frown thinking of that night. 'I don't know what happened to me that day. I just froze. I couldn't move a single muscle.'

'Fuck don't tell me that, Snow. I won't be able to let you go anywhere without me. It terrifies me to think that you are that defenseless.'

'I'm not defenseless. I think I was already in a state because of the shock Nikki gave me, and then them ... Anyway, it doesn't matter. Nothing happened.'

'Yeah, and nothing fucking will. I'm getting you a bodyguard.'

I jump up in horror. 'What? No way. I'll feel silly.'

'Hmmm ...' he says absently, and I can hear all the wheels in his head turning away.

'I'm serious, Shane. I'm not having a man following me around as if I'm some celebrity. It's just ridiculous.'

'Then you won't fucking go anywhere without me then,' he says flatly.

'Oh, darling. I'm not going to let them ruin my life any more. I'm not afraid. Not anymore. Every day, ever since you came into my life, I have become stronger and stronger. My greatest regret is that I never went to the police and at least attempted to punish them. It's not revenge although that would be sweet. It's just that I know all of them will do it again to other young girls like me. They enjoyed it too much not to. My memories are all jumbled. Who knows, my evidence could have saved someone from what I suffered?'

Forty-one

SNOW

The day of our wedding dawns bright and cold.

It is such a mad rush, the process of getting ready, but finally I am. Nobody allows me to see the mirror until my ensemble is complete, down to my satin covered shoes and my bridal bouquet.

'Oh, Snow,' Layla says in an awed voice. 'You look like a fairy tale princess.'

I look at myself in the mirror and my mouth drops open in astonishment. I *do* look like a fairy tale princess!

The dress is everything I ever dreamed of. It has an illusion sweetheart neckline, a ball gown silhouette, and lace sleeves that are longer than my fingers, giving it the impression of a medieval costume. There are delicate lace details on the edges of the sleeves and a stunning appliqué on the bodice. On my head sits a glittering tiara made of stars.

I have to blink to stop myself from crying with happiness. I can't believe I am getting married to Shane. It's like a dream. It's just too perfect.

'No, no, no,' cries Lily. 'Don't you dare cry and ruin all the make-up artist's work.'

That makes me laugh.

There is a knock on the door. Layla runs to open it and my father comes into the bedroom. His eyes are filled with pride. At that moment I am suddenly painfully aware that my father, who is twenty-five years older than my mother, won't be on this earth much longer. He kisses me gently on the cheek.

'I haven't been a good father to you, but I'm so proud of you,' he says gruffly. There is regret etched on his face.

'No, Papa. You've been wonderful. I wouldn't exchange you for all the world.' And it's true, no matter how distant we have remained through the years, I have loved him. I truly, truly love him. As I look into his shining eyes I suddenly remember being a small girl sitting in his lap and him whispering in my ear. 'You're my princess,' and then my mother coming into the room, and my father putting me away as unobstructively as possible.

As the image recedes, there is a commotion at the door and my mother comes in. Automatically my father takes a step back, almost guiltily. And I see what I have never seen before.

The unconscious pattern of our relationships. All of us afraid to show affection to anyone but my mother.

My mother takes a deep breath. 'You look wonderful, Snow,' she says.

And I smile at her. As if she really means it. As if she really loves me. I know she thinks the dress is too big and not elegant enough, but I don't care. It doesn't matter. I love her, anyway. I just have to remember what Shane said, 'Love does not measure. It only gives.'

'You look beautiful too, Mum.' And she does, in a cream suit with her trademark pearl necklace around her throat.

'Thank you, my dear,' she says politely.

'Well, I guess we better get going,' my father chips in.

I turn to him, beaming. 'Yes, we should.'

In the car, with the fragrance of my bridal bouquet enveloping us, my father turns to me. 'She does love you in her own way, you know?' he says.

'I know, Papa. I know,' I say and squeeze his hand.

'You have a heart of gold, Snow. A heart of gold,' he mutters. 'To everyone else you may look like a grown woman, but to me you will always be in pigtails and asking me what God eats, or why mice are not striped like tigers?'

We arrive at the castle and an assortment of people are waiting outside; the planner, photographer, and some other organizers. Little Liliana is one of the flower girls. Dressed in a black and white printed dress with a flower crown and carrying a miniature green wreath, she looks utterly adorable. She grins and waves at me. And Tommy, the ring bearer, is all dressed like a mini man, and trying very hard to look up someone's skirt.

As we walk to the entrance, we pass lovely moss-covered animal topiaries. Pigs, bears and rabbits. We enter the impressive doorway and walk down a dark stone corridor.

My father turns to me. 'Are you ready?'

I nod silently, speechless. They open the great doors and the little girls go ahead, strewing rose petals.

Everyone turns to look at me, but I walk down the aisle in a daze, my eyes searching for Shane. I see his dark head almost straight away. He has turned and is looking at me. Through my veil our eyes meet. And my breath is snatched away.

He is so incredibly handsome.

My feet stumble and I cling automatically to my father's arm. He glances at me anxiously, and Shane makes a slight movement as if he is about to leave his position and come to me, but I recover, and we carry on down the aisle under Shane's watchful gaze.

My father lifts my veil and kisses me on my forehead. Shane breaks tradition and hugs my father as if they are old friends. My father nods, overcome with emotion and turns again to me. He hugs me tightly and then pulls away. As he is turning away, I call him as if I am a little girl again, 'Daddy?'

He twists around, tears in his eyes, and I hug him again. 'I love you,' I whisper in his ear.

And he says, 'I hope you know I've always loved you the best.'

And I whisper back, 'Yes, I know that.'

Then I am given to Shane. He holds out his hand and grins irrepressibly at me, as if he too can't believe his luck.

The words of the service sound like they are coming from the bottom of the sea. I repeat them carefully. It is truly like a dream. I just cannot believe that I am marrying Shane. As if in slow motion, I am holding out my hand and Shane's strong fingers are slipping the ring onto my finger. I look up at him.

'You may kiss the bride,' the priest says.

 338

Shane bends his mouth and, as his lips touch mine, all the hundreds of guests fire their cap guns at the same time. The reverberating sound startles me. I gasp and a laughing Shane gathers me in his arms and takes my mouth in a long, deep kiss.

'God, I love you, Snow,' he says, looking into my eyes.

The organ music reaches a crescendo triumphantly.

'Let's go,' Layla says to me after we have posed for photos in the castle and on the lawns, 'Time to change.'

'Change? Into what?'

'It's a surprise,' she says with wink.

We go into one of the smaller rooms next to the great hall where the reception will be held, and there is a deep red and gold traditional Indian bridal costume hanging on a hanger. I turn around and look at Layla. 'I'm wearing an Indian costume?'

She laughs gaily. 'We all are. It was Shane's idea.'

I laugh in disbelief. 'Really?'

'Yes,' she says excitedly.

'OK,' I say, getting into the groove of an Indian wedding. I think of Chitra sitting out there in the crowd. She'll be so tickled.

Layla and Lily quickly help me out of my wedding gown and into the Indian costume. The hairdresser gets to work next, taking down the tiara, and putting gold pins in my hair, and stringing a forehead decoration into the mix.

Red and gold bangles are slid up my arms. An Indian make-up artist from Hounslow uses eyeliner to enhance my eyes, making them appear dramatic. Gold antique jewelry is loaded onto my body: necklaces, forearm decorations, rings, chains. I am surprised by my reflection. I have never seen myself look so flushed and excited before. I am so happy I want to weep with joy.

Layla appears beside me. She looks gorgeous in a lovely blue lehenga. She smiles. 'You look absolutely lovely. I wish I had done an Indian version for my wedding too.'

I just laugh.

'One last hug,' Layla says and we do a quick A line hug, since her pregnancy is showing even more now.

We leave the little changing room, and outside I am surprised to see that the others have changed into Indian costumes too. They look beautiful in their bright lehengas, saris, and salwar keemezes.

Feeling suddenly shy, I follow Layla through the crowded hall. People keep stopping us to congratulate and compliment me. Just outside the room where the reception will be held, Shane is waiting for me in a Sherwani. He looks so dashing it takes my breath away. Jake and Dom are also wearing Kurtas, and they stand beside Shane and smile at me. I smile back and feel so touched that they have all made such an effort to embrace me into their family. Shane comes up to me. He takes my hand and exhales slowly.

'I always had a fantasy of bedding an Indian princess,' he tells me with a grin.

I glance at the main table and see my mother. She looks stiff and uncomfortable. My father catches my eye and waves. I release my fingers from Shane's. He looks down at me.

'I'll only be a minute,' I say.

'Hurry back,' he says.

I walk over to my mother. She alone has refused to wear Indian attire.

My father stands. 'You look absolutely beautiful, my darling.'

'Thank you, Papa,' I say and kiss his cheek.

He squeezes my hand and, leaning forward, whispers, 'I'm so proud of you.'

I turn to my mother. She knows she is being watched so she stands and smiles at me. 'Yes, you look very ... nice,' she says.

I know she is surprised by the wealth she has witnessed today. When Shane came in his T-shirt and jeans she assumed he was a poor gypsy boy. Now she can see how wrong she was.

'You've done very well,' she says stiffly.

'I married Shane because I love him, Mother. I would have married him even if he had nothing.'

'It's good then that Shane has a bit of money, isn't it? I was thinking of sending your brother to England. Give him a fresh start. Maybe your husband can help him find a job or set him up in a business.'

I feel a twinge of sadness then. Even now, on my big day, my mother cannot just be happy for me, but uses the occasion to try and help my brother. And then I think of Shane saying, 'Love does not measure. It just gives.' I love my mother, and if there is anything I can do to make her happy, I will.

'I'll ask Shane,' I say softly.

And she beams happily.

The food was prepared by one of Dom's chefs and it is fabulous. There are speeches from Jake, my

father, Dom, and Layla's husband, BJ. Then Shane stands up to make his.

He thanks the ushers, the bridesmaids, and all the people who have attended. 'If I forgot anybody, what can I say?' he says.

Then he turns to me. 'There is no Romeo or Juliet that ever was, is, or ever will be, that could ever compare to what is you and me. There is no sonnet or song that has been written that comes close to describing my level of fucking smitten. You are not just the love of my life, but the fabric, the reason, and the basis for my life. And when time has passed and everyone else sees you as old and gray, I will still see you as you are this day. So I'll finish by saying that we'll be moving to a new home soon, so do not come around because we'll be banging and screwing at every opportunity we get. Thank you all for coming.'

The crowd loves him. I look for Shane's mother and she is smiling. I swivel my gaze towards my mother and she is grimacing. I meet her eyes and suddenly I don't care that she disapproves of me, or that I would never be good enough for her. I look towards Shane and guess what? He is gazing at me with stars in his eyes. *You can't spoil my day, Mum. Never again.*

'Are you ready for your first dance, Mrs. Elizabeth Snow Eden?'

I am just about to say yes, when Layla hits the stem of her glass to indicate that she wants the floor.

And Shane groans. 'Oh shit.'

Layla stands and raises her hand. 'Well, normally, the sister of the groom never speaks, but I just have to repay the favor my brother paid during my wedding when he stood up and gave some friendly advice to my husband.'

She looks sideways at her brother and then proceeds to tell everybody two of Shane's most embarrassing alcohol-soaked stories.

One involves him getting so drunk when he was sixteen, he ended up losing his keys, climbing up the drainpipes and jumping in through his upstairs bedroom window, only to find that he was in the next door neighbor's bedroom.

'The widow was glowing the next day,' she says to whistles, catcalls, and a thunderous applause of approval.

Layla then suggests that I sew our front door keys to his clothes.

The other story also involves a younger Shane getting so drunk that he falls into a patch of rosebushes and gets scratched to bits. He goes home and carefully applies plasters all over his face and falls into bed. In the morning, their mother finds about ten plasters in the shape of his face on the mirror. The crowd roars with laughter and Layla advises me to plant thornless roses in my garden.

And with that, she ends with the words, 'Jokes aside, you're both so incredibly lucky. At the end of this ceremony, Shane, you get to go home with a wife who is warm, caring, beguiling, and who radiates beauty and grace from every pore. And, Snow, you will go home tonight having gained a lovely dress and a gorgeous ring.'

That brings a smile even to Shane's sour lips.

Afterwards, Robbie Williams' *She's The One* comes on, and Shane takes me by the hand and leads me to the dance floor.

'Do you know what I love most of you?' he whispers.

I shake my head.

'Your lips.'

'So soft and delicious. I once dreamed of licking them.'

As we whirl and dip, I feel as if I am floating on air. There'll never be another day like this. Never.

And then suddenly the disco lights come on and bangra music starts, professional dancers fill the floor, and Shane lifts his hands and starts doing the bangra! I cover my cheeks with my hands and laugh. My goodness! He really doesn't do things by half. And then I join in as well. Layla, BJ, Jake, Lily, Liliana, Dom and Ella all hit the floor. And all of them have some 'moves' they have learnt.

My heart feels as if it will burst with joy at this beautiful, beautiful family I have fallen into. All those years when I yearned to be in a happy family are suddenly here. Shane catches me in a totally non-bangra move and, laughing, I realize there'll be many days like this. Many more.

Forty-two

SNOW

Christmas Eve

I hear the key in the door and I run to it. Standing on tiptoes, 'I,' I say, and kiss his forehead, 'love' I say, and kiss his nose, 'you,' I say, and I kiss his right eye, 'Shane,' I say, and kiss his left eye, 'Eden,' I say and kiss his lips. It was meant to be a peck, but he deepens it and kisses me passionately. I pull away and look at him in surprise.

'Is that the I-want-to-take-you-to-bed kiss?' I ask with a smile.

'It wasn't a bedroom kiss. I have something for you,' he says very seriously.

My eyebrows rise. 'What is it?'

He takes my hand and leads me to his study. He sits me down at his desk and opens his laptop screen. He turns the machine towards him and taps a few keys, then rotates it back to face me.

'What is it?' I ask curiously.

'Your Christmas present,' he says quietly, and walks out.

There is an arrow pointing to the left in the middle of the screen. I click on it and my eyes widen and my hands fly up to cover my open mouth.

In a panic I hit the arrow, the video stops playing, and I close my eyes. My heart is pounding and my breath is coming out sharp and fast. For a few seconds I do nothing, just stare at the frozen screen.

The frame shows a man, his eyes horrified and his mouth open wide in a scream of white hot pain. He has been tied up to some kind of wooden contraption, and behind him a black man with the biggest penis I have ever seen in my life is sodomizing him. To their right there is another man standing by and watching impassively. My eyes return to the man screaming. *I recognize you.* He was not screaming then. He was laughing, taunting ... lusty. 'Give it to her, give the bitch some cock.'

To my surprise a smile comes to my lips. *Give the bitch some cock.*

My hand moves seemingly of its own accord and my finger presses the arrow.

The images start moving. My smile stays, then widens cruelly. *Now you know what it feels like to be totally helpless.*

I watch the coward slobber and scream and beg. Snot runs down into his mouth.

Tsk, tsk, even I didn't cry like that.

When the black man is finished, the other man takes over. He doesn't use his cock though. He uses a frighteningly big dildo. I peer closer. The dildo is studded. A mad giggle escapes my lips.

The man shakes his head and begs for mercy. *Well, well.*

They untie him and make him sign a letter. I cannot see what he is putting his scribble to, but he signs it with a shaking hand.

Then they beat him so mercilessly I hear the sound of bone crunching.

Ah well, Karma. It's a bitch.

I sit through another five little clips. Two of the faces I cannot remember, and that bothers me. Just imagine if I had been in a shop or some other public place and they had come in, I would have had no idea they were rapists. I would have spoken to the bastards normally. Why, they even looked like decent blokes.

At the end there is a template copy of the letters all the men have signed.

Dear Friends and Family,

Last summer, five other sickening perverts and I met in London to gang rape a drugged, innocent nineteen-year old girl in a hotel room.

I am sending you this letter so you know the real me.

Yours sincerely,

Then the video cuts to the impassive man saying that the letter and a copy of the recording have been hand-delivered to the men's families, and an email sent to every single person, even takeaway addresses on their phones and email list.

I close the screen and feel a strange sense of lightness. In this unfair, cruel world where the poor and the helpless always get trodden on, Shane found my justice for me. With a sigh of contentment I get up and go into the kitchen.

Shane is standing by the kitchen sink looking out of the window. When he hears me, he turns and looks at me. For a moment I do not recognize him. It is shocking that someone as beautiful as he is could ever be so cruel. I feel the same way I felt when I saw a lion killing a poor impala. How could such a beautiful beast do that?

And then he smiles at me and I recognize him. He is *my* beautiful beast.

'Are you OK?' he asks.

I nod. 'Thank you for the black roses,' I say quietly.

'It was a pleasure.'

I walk up to him. We are accomplices. We are now bonded by revenge and blood. 'How did you find them?'

'Lenny had the surveillance tapes the whole time.'

I gasp with the stab of pain. 'I trusted him,' I whisper.

'I know, but you were so traumatized you would have believed anything.'

'I'm a fucking bad judge of character, aren't I? Again and again I trust scum,' I say bitterly.

'No, you're not. You're beautiful. If only the whole world would be as innocent and trusting as you, then it would be an unrecognizable, beautiful place.'

I look up at him. Sometimes I still can't believe he is really mine. 'Oh, Shane. You did all that for me. Have I ever told you you're my hero?'

He grins. 'A gypsy hero? Does such a beast even exist?'

'Yes, it does. I caught one.'

He laughs. 'Let's have a drink. Let's drink to those men's poor wives and children.'

So we drink ourselves silly and then I say in a slurred, slutty voice, 'I have a present for you too.'

And he grins. 'Oh yeah?'

'It's in the bedroom. I'll just go and get it.'

'I'll be waiting right here,' he says, plumping the cushions behind him and settling down.

I go into the bedroom and quickly undress. Naked, I get into high heels and wrap a big red ribbon around myself and tie a huge bow at my waist. Then I walk out to the living room.

'Here's your present,' I say.

And I swear I see forever in his eyes.

SHANE

Christmas Day

Liliana is sitting on my lap and telling me tales tall enough to make any full-blooded gypsy proud.

'Santa came to my house, you know,' she says importantly, 'because I've been a very, very, very good girl.' She drops her voice to a hoarse whisper. 'I saw him.'

I keep my face straight. 'You saw him?'

'Yup.' Her eyes are huge.

'When?'

She fingers a bow on her dress. 'Last night. I saw him eat two cookies and drink half of the milk that I put out for him.'

'Wow,' I say in an impressed voice. 'Did he say anything to you?'

'No,' she says shaking her head vigorously. 'I was hiding behind the door.'

'Why didn't you show yourself?'

'I didn't want to frighten him, Uncle Shane,' she says as if that is the most obvious thing in the world.

'Anyway,' she carries on, 'he left three presents. Two for me because I've been so good, and one for Laura because she's just a little baby and babies just need milk.'

'Right.'

She cups her hand over my ear and whispers, 'Don't tell anyone, Uncle Shane, but I woke up early and sneaked downstairs when everybody was still sleeping, and opened all my presents.' She claps her hands. 'And then I closed them all back.'

'So you know exactly what you've got for Christmas?' I ask, amazed that she actually did that. Even I never did something like that at her age.

She nods happily.

'So what will you do when you open your presents later and everybody looks at you?'

'Pretend to be surprised and happy,' she says coolly.

I have to laugh. 'Show me your surprised and happy face,' I ask.

She opens up her eyes, drops her jaw, and smacks her cheeks with her palms while managing to look like she is grinning. 'Yeah, that'll work.'

She makes her face normal again. 'Did Santa leave you presents?'

'He gave me mine early this year.'

She crosses her little arms over her chest. 'What did he give you?'

'He gave me a wife.'

She frowns and looks at me as if I am stupid. 'Auntie Snow is not a present. A present is like a real thing. Like a toy or a doll.'

'That's true. Maybe he's left one under the tree for me.'

She slips off my lap. 'I'll go and look for you, OK?'

'OK, but don't peek.'

She shakes her head solemnly. 'No, I only peek at my own presents.'

At the front door, I hear Layla, BJ's and Tommy's voices wishing my mother a merry Christmas. Liliana forgets about looking for a present for me, and rushes off to the front door. Jake returns from the garage where my mother keeps her fridge, carrying two bottles of whiskey. It has started snowing and there are snowflakes on his hair and shoulders. He sets the bottles on the table.

'What time will Dom be here?' he asks.

I look at my watch. 'Anytime now.'

At that moment BJ and Layla come through the door. BJ is holding a baby carrier. The room fills with the sound of us wishing each other a merry Christmas. A pink-nosed Layla kisses both Jake and I and then disappears off to the kitchen to see what the women are up to.

BJ leaves the baby carrier on the floor by the chair next to me and collapses into the chair. 'Where's the fucking alcohol?' he asks.

I laugh and Jake pours out whiskey for us all. Before we can take a sip, Dom and Ella arrive. Ella is carrying their little boy, Noah. Jake pours another glass. Again the room fills with sounds of Christmas greetings.

'You guys started without me,' Dom complains, as Ella goes out with Noah.

'Nope,' Jake says and pushes a glass into his hand.

We raise our glasses. 'May it always be this good,' Jake says.

And we drink. Life is good.

Just before lunch, Snow comes up to me. 'I've got a surprise present for you,' she says, her eyes shining.

'I thought I got mine last night?' I tease.

'This is better.'

I raise my eyebrows. 'Better than the one I got last night?'

'Much,' she says, her eyes sparkling.

She puts her hand out, I take it, and let her lead me. She pulls me upstairs to my mother's guest bedroom.

'Are you ready?'

I guide her hand to my crotch. 'Is that ready enough for you?'

She gasps and says sternly, 'It's not that kind of present.'

'Well, then it can't be better than last night's.'

'Shane?' she whispers.

'Yes'

'Don't spoil it.'

I put my hands up in surrender.

She opens the door and we enter ... and a male German shepherd puppy is sitting inside a large metal cage.'

'Merry Christmas,' she shouts.

I turn my head to look at her. 'This is my present?'

'Yes, isn't he wonderful?' she enthuses ignoring my unenthusiastic tone.

'So my present is a dog from your favorite breed?' I ask.

'Yes,' she says blithely, and goes to open the cage door. The dog immediately jumps all over her excitedly. And I can see that she is dying to pick him up, but she doesn't.

'Have you any suggestions for a name for him?' she asks instead.

I shrug.

'You could call him Ghengis ... if you want to,' she suggests.

I turn away from her and say, 'Ghengis.'

The dog immediately looks at me with its bright, intelligent eyes.

I turn to her. 'How strange. He seems to answer to that name.'

She bites her lip. 'I might have called him by that name once or twice,' she admits.

'So, how long have you had him?'

'I've been keeping him here secretly for the last two weeks. I wanted to house train him before I gave him to you. I know the apartment is too small for him, but we'll be moving to our new house in two months, right? And Chitra will be coming to stay with us so she can help take care of him too.'

'Right.'

'See how perfect it is?'

I smile. 'How old is he?'

'They're not sure because he was abandoned, but he's about four months. Look what he can do, though,' she says scooping the bundle of excited fur up in her arms. She takes a treat out of her pants pocket and holds it in front of his nose.

'Off,' she says and the puppy stills.

'Look in my eyes,' she says firmly, and the puppy immediately ignores the treat and looks into her eyes.

'Take,' she orders, and the puppy immediately gobbles down the treat.

'Good boy,' she approves. She brushes her chin against his head and looks at me. 'You can teach him so many other things.'

I grin. God I love this woman so much I could eat her. She just solved my biggest problem. Here is the bodyguard that I was looking for. I will train him myself. This dog will go everywhere she goes and be her protector when I am not around.

SHANE

Christmas Night

I get back from the toilet and there is a dark shadow on my side of the bed. I go closer and it raises its head and gives a low growl.

'What the fuck?' I swear.

I hear a giggle from Snow's side of the bed.

I switch on the light and Snow has her head buried under the cover, trying to stop herself from laughing, but her shoulders are shaking silently. On my side of the bed, Genghis has his teeth bared and his eyes are downright frosty. It looks quite comical. Then Snow pops her head out of the blanket and she is laughing behind her hands.

Suddenly I freeze with the realization of how precious this moment is. I wish that I could hold it for a hundred years. My four-month-old, usurper puppy trying to claim my woman for himself, and my woman giggling like the most beautiful, carefree child.

But I know the puppy will become a loyal dog, the giggling beauty will become a woman who will have my children, the dog will die, and the woman will become old, wrinkled and frail.

And then we'll all become a fistful of dust.

But today ... my cock is throbbing with hot blood and I am king of my empire of dirt.

I chase the dog away, rip open my dressing gown, and claim the woman. A big cock wrapped up in a ribbon and a bow is extremely difficult to resist.

The dog is too young to know: the second mouse always gets the cheese.

The End.

Dear Reader,

Thank you for purchasing this book. It is an honor that I very much appreciate. The Edens, BJ Pilkingon, and Zane wish you a very Merry Christmas and a Happy New Year.

If you are interested in reading Zane's story, it will be coming after Gold Digger.

Merry Christmas Everybody. :-)

xx*Georgia*

Coming Next...

GOLD DIGGER

Georgia Le Carre

CHAPTER 1

'**W**hatever you do, don't *ever* trust them. Not one of them,' he whispered. His voice was so feeble I had to strain to catch it.

'I won't,' I said, softly.

'They are dangerous in a way you will never understand. Never let your guard down,' he insisted.

'I understand,' I said, but all I wanted was for him to stop talking about them. These last precious minutes I didn't want to waste on them.

He shook his head unhappily. 'No, no, you don't understand. You can never let your guard down for even an instant. Never.'

'All right, I won't.'

'I will be a very sad spirit if you do.'

'I won't,' I promised vehemently, and reached for his hand. The contrast between my hand and his couldn't have been greater. Mine was smooth and soft and his was gnarled and full of green veins, the skin waxy and liver-spotted. The nails were the color of polished ivory. The hand of a seventy-year-old man. His fingers grasped fiercely at my hand. I lifted them to my lips and kissed them one by one, tenderly.

His eyes glowed briefly in his wasted, sunken face. 'How I love you, my darling Tawny,' he murmured.

'I love you. I love you. I love you,' I said.

'Do your part and they cannot touch you.'

He sighed. 'It's nearly time.'

'Don't say that,' I cried, even though I knew in my heart that he was right.

His eyes swung to the window. 'Ah,' he sighed softly. 'You've come.'

My gaze chased his. The window he was looking at was closed, the heavy drapes pulled shut. Goose pimples crawled up my arms. 'Don't go yet. Please,' I begged.

He dragged his gaze reluctantly from the window. His thin, pale lips rose at the edges as he drew in a rattling breath. 'I've got to go, my darling. I've got to pay my dues. I haven't been a good man.'

'Just wait a while.'

'You have your whole life ahead of you.'

He turned his unnaturally bright eyes away from me, looked straight ahead, and with a violent shudder, departed.

For a few seconds I simply stared at him. Appropriately, outside the October wind howled and dashed itself into the shutters. I knew the servants were waiting downstairs. Everyone was waiting for me to go down and tell them the news.

Then I leaned forward and put my cheek on his still, bony chest. He smelled strongly of medicine. I closed my eyes tightly. Why did you have to go and die and leave me to the wolves?

In that moment I felt so close to him I wished that this time would not end. I wished I could lie on his chest, safe and closeted away from the cruel world. I heard the clock ticking. The flames in the fireplace crackled and spat. Somewhere a pipe creaked. I placed my chin on his chest and turned to look at him one last time. He appeared to be sleeping. Peaceful at any rate. I stroked the thin strands of white hair lying across his pinkish white scalp, and let my finger run down his prominent nose. It shocked me how quickly the tip of his nose had lost warmth. Soon all of him would be stone cold.

I wondered whom he had seen at the window. Who had come to take him to his reckoning. My sorrow was complete. I could put my fingertips into it and feel the edges. Smooth. Without corners. Without sharpness. It had no tears. I knew he was dying two hours before. Strange because it had seemed as if he had taken a turn for the better. He seemed stronger, his cheeks pink, his eyes brilliantly bright and when he smiled it appeared as if he was lit from within. He even looked so much stronger. I asked him what he wanted to eat.

'Milk. I'll have a glass of milk,' he said decisively.

But after I called for milk and it was brought to him he smiled and refused it. 'Isn't this wonderful?' he asked. 'I feel so good.'

And at that moment I knew. Even so it was incomprehensible to me that he was really gone. I never wanted to believe it.

'In the end you wanted to go, didn't you?'

There was no answer.

'It's OK. I know you were tired. It was only me holding you back. You go on ahead. Find a place for me.'

He lay as still as a corpse. Oh God! I already missed him so much.

'I understand you can't talk. But you can hear me. When it is my turn I want you to come and get me. I'll be expecting you to come in through the window. Go in peace now, my love. All will be well. They will never know the truth. I will never tell them. To the day you come back to collect me.'

And then I began to cry, not loud, ugly sobs, but a quiet weeping. I didn't want the servants to hear. To come rushing in. Call the doctor waiting downstairs to come in and pronounce him dead. I knew what waited for me outside this room.

Another hour...or two wouldn't make a difference. This was my time. My final hours with my husband.

The time before I became the hated gold digger.